GHOST SQUADRON
1

ERIC THOMSON

We Dare

Copyright 2019 Eric Thomson
First paperback printing December 2019

Published in Canada
By Sanddiver Books Inc.
ISBN: 978-1-989314-22-7

Sanddiver
Books

— One —

Aleksa Kine always knew her luck would eventually run out. Undercover police officers rarely retired with an unbroken string of successful missions. But surely not today of all days, after she'd spent months infiltrating the Saqqa Cartel, a major player in the horrific business of interstellar human trafficking.

Her work as a hired gun protecting the cartel's legal and quasi-legal business interests and her obvious intelligence compared to the rest of the mercenaries had finally caught the attention of her cartel superiors. They'd sent her to New Oberon, the frontier colony where she believed the cartel operated its main slave transshipment base. There, she would join the inner cadre, people who worked on the most heinous and profitable business lines, under a boss by the name Rabmag Rafalko.

And what Kine discovered after entering the vast, isolated compound hidden away in a wooded valley far from New Oberon's capital, Titania, chilled her to the core. She was able to send one last report through the subspace net when

Rafalko allowed her twenty-four hours of liberty in Titania alongside half a dozen other inner cadre prospects, sociopaths with whom she'd spent two weeks under the boss' scrutiny. One last outing before they took up new duties. Or so she thought.

When the cartel first hired her, or rather a mercenary by the name Goldie Neves, a woman with a long and verifiable record, including a supposed stint in a military prison for almost beating another soldier to death, she faced a few weeks of probation, nothing more. Time enough for a background check and to watch her performance. Here on New Oberon, Kine expected the same — a week or two under evaluation by Rafalko so he could decide whether she and the others were a good fit.

After all, she was a known quantity, a loyal foot soldier whose professionalism had been noticed. And she'd impressed them without having to compromise her oath as a Commonwealth Constabulary officer. The cartel's outer layer of security kept strictly to the letter of the law, if not always the spirit, so it might avoid undue scrutiny by the authorities. In that sense, her colleagues weren't much different from the mercenary rent-a-cops prevalent on human colonies, especially those in frontier star systems.

Yet on the morning after their outing in Titania, Rafalko, a tall, whipcord-thin, olive-skinned man with a prominent nose and a hairless skull, assembled the prospects in the antechamber of a building that had been out of bounds until now. He informed them they would undergo a rite of initiation to become full-fledged members of the Saqqa Cartel.

Initially, Kine felt more excitement at the prospect of peering into the cartel's dark corners than apprehension at what the initiation might entail. Many of the oldest organized crime groups in existence practiced rituals, and they were almost always symbolic. However, Rafalko didn't describe what they would undergo. He merely explained how they would go through the door behind him one by one.

Yet, as he spoke, a gleam of anticipation lit up his sunken eyes, and for the first time, a shiver of unease ran up Kine's spine. She already knew Rafalko and his inner cadre were murderous scum who deserved exile for life and slow death on Parth's Desolation Island or better yet, execution. But at that moment, an aura of depravity worse than any she'd ever sensed before seemed to surround him.

Rafalko pointed at the first man.

"You. Follow me."

Both vanished through the door, leaving them with one of the senior inner cadre, a stout, brutish woman called Adra. Contrary to her boss, she didn't seem possessed by a deeper evil or own much in terms of a soul and observed the prospects with a dead stare. At an unheard and unseen signal, Adra gestured at the next man in line then pointed toward the door.

"Go."

After a while, only Kine remained. None of the others came back, and her apprehension grew, but she knew better than to show even a shred of emotion in front of the silent, stone-faced Adra. Finally, it was her turn.

"Go."

Kine found herself in an empty passageway pierced by metal doors every few meters. Its walls were made of extruded concrete and painted a painfully institutional white that almost glowed under the harsh lighting. If Kine didn't know any better, she might think herself magically transported into a prison facility. Which made sense, considering she'd seen enough evidence of human trafficking over the previous two weeks.

Shuttles landing and lifting at strange hours; the feeling that the sprawling compound, especially those parts forbidden to the prospects, teemed with life; muffled screams in the distance; the occasional glimpse of bodies being taken out into the woods for disposal and large food shipments arriving from Titania in unmarked stasis containers.

The only thing Kine needed was a glimpse into where she suspected the cartel held its victims before shipping them off to their final destinations. Proof for the Shield Sector's Organized Crime Division to swoop in and shut Saqqa down. Or at least this part of their sprawling criminal empire.

Absent such proof, the Commonwealth Secretary for Public Safety on Earth, or rather his minions, wouldn't allow the Constabulary to act. As Kine knew from bitter experience, cartels such as Saqqa enjoyed the protection of powerful interests because they made those interests obscenely wealthy.

If, in an alternate reality, the Chief Constable were to send his Professional Compliance Bureau investigators after the Commonwealth Senate and the senior bureaucracy, the population of exiles on Desolation Island would double. But in this reality, law enforcement needed irrefutable proof to overcome the political protection keeping cartels in business.

One of the metal doors slid aside at her approach, and Rafalko's raspy voice reached her ears.

"In here, Goldie."

Her apprehension grew by leaps and bounds as she entered a room that suggested a pathology lab or abattoir rather than a prison cell. Plasticized walls shone under artificial sunlight, as did closed cabinets lining one wall. A metal table with raised sides occupied the center.

On it lay an unclothed man, bound and gagged. His terrified eyes met Kine's, and her heart missed a beat. Rafalko stood on one side of the table, near a tray of surgical instruments, watching Kine with sick fascination. As her brain processed the scene, she fought back a surge of nausea.

"From time to time," Rafalko said, "we receive cattle that are too dangerous or useless for onward processing. They stay here and serve as training dummies or to cement a prospect's entry into the cartel family."

A detached part of Kine's mind roared in outrage at his use of the word cattle to describe the human being lying on the table, trussed up and waiting for death while her thoughts raced in desperate circles seeking a way out.

"We can absorb the loss, in case you're worried." He gestured at the tray. "Prove your commitment to the Saqqa Cartel by disposing of this worthless specimen. Use whatever method you wish, but you must spill blood because only through blood will I accept your oath on the cartel's behalf."

"What if I don't want to kill that poor SOB?" Kine was grateful her words came out in a normal tone instead of a strangled croak.

She couldn't murder the prisoner, not even to keep her cover intact. Nor could she incapacitate or kill Rafalko. The prospects were unarmed, and Rafalko was a deadly hand-to-hand fighter, as Kine knew from sparring sessions. And even if she incapacitated or killed him, there was no escape from the building, let alone the compound.

"Well now, that would be a problem." Rafalko tilted his head to one side as his eyes narrowed. "But surely you aren't squeamish. Your military record shows you possess a propensity for deadly violence and a noted lack of empathy."

"I'll kill if I'm threatened, but slitting that poor bastard's throat for a promotion? Not my style." Kine's heart pounded in her ears while sweat broke out on her forehead.

"That's how it works here. If you want to join my inner cadre, I need to see you take a life. Besides, you'll be doing this one a favor. If he doesn't die here and now, we'll ship him where his fate will be worse than death. Ours is a hard business, but the rewards for our inner cadre are limitless, as are the cattle we round up and sell to the highest bidder. No one cares about them. No one will notice they're gone. You could almost say we're cleansing the gene pool by disposing of the useless ones."

"Let's forget the promotion, and I go back to my old job." Kine already knew what he would answer but needed to say the words anyway.

Rafalko studied her in silence for a few moments.

"I'm afraid that won't be possible. Once you entered this room, your existence changed irrevocably. There can be no going back. I'm sure you understand why."

"So, either I kill him, or you kill me."

A bark of mirthless laughter escaped Rafalko's throat.

"Kill you? No. I will kill him myself because I find it enjoyable. You will take his place in the next shipment and vanish forever like everyone who passes through here." He gestured at the tray again. "One swipe across his throat with a scalpel and we're done."

Kine shook her head, not trusting herself to speak as she realized her life was over.

Suspicion suddenly creased his forehead.

"Damn." The word came out as a soft hiss. "You're a cop, aren't you? A fucking Constabulary infiltrator. I should have known a mercenary with your combination of background and wits was too good to be true. What are you? Shield Sector Undercover and Surveillance Division?"

"I'm nothing of the sort," she finally replied through clenched teeth. "But I won't murder a man in cold blood to join your club. Give me another job, somewhere I can be useful, and you can make sure I don't speak out of turn."

Rafalko shook his head regretfully.

"Sorry. Either he dies at your hand, or you both die. Only you will suffer unspeakable agonies before giving up the ghost."

When she did not reply, contenting herself with a murderous stare, or at least what Kine hoped was a murderous stare, Rafalko clapped his hands once. The sound echoed off the bare walls like a gunshot.

"Then we're done here. A shame. You showed great potential, but I cannot trust someone who won't kill on command. Especially now that I think you're a cop. Oh, don't worry, I won't try to interrogate you. There's no point, and if you're conditioned, then I'll lose a healthy specimen who might amuse one of our best customers."

He glanced over her shoulder.

"Ah, Frayne, there you are. Goldie decided she loved her scruples more than her ambitions. She's no longer one of us. Put her with the cattle headed out in the next shipment."

Frayne, who could pass for Adra's male twin, wrapped a meaty hand around her upper arm and squeezed. Hard.

"Dumb fuck. And I was beginning to enjoy working with you," he growled in Kine's ear. "Now, you're just another walking slab of meat."

"Goodbye, Goldie," Rafalko said. "We will not meet again."

Less than thirty minutes later, Frayne shoved her into a cage filled with despondent men and women clad in the same orange one-piece garment she now wore. None of them paid her the slightest bit of attention, and she realized the cartel kept them in a drug-induced haze. Probably via the food they ate. And that meant she would join them in their vacuous state before the day was out.

Kine's only hope was that her Constabulary colleagues would eventually come looking and pick up her implanted tracker's signal. If they figured out where the Saqqa Cartel intended to ship her.

But since New Oberon was within a few hyperspace jumps of the worst techno-barbarian worlds in the known galaxy, that could well be somewhere beyond the remit of both the Constabulary and the Armed Services. A place from which there was no rescue.

— TWO —

"Atten-SHUN." Major Joshua Bayliss' deep voice cut through the buzz of conversation filling the 1ˢᵗ Special Forces Regiment's main lecture hall. The officers, warrant officers, and command sergeants of 'A' Squadron snapped to attention.

A tall, slender, middle-aged woman in naval uniform wearing a captain's stripes and executive curl on the shoulder boards of her waist-length blue garrison tunic walked in. She was trailed by 'A' Squadron's commanding officer, Lieutenant Colonel Zachary Thomas Decker, Commonwealth Marine Corps. The latter wore a black version of the garrison uniform, complete with a lieutenant colonel's silver oak leaf wreath and twin four-pointed stars.

A senior officer such as the chief of staff of Naval Intelligence's Special Operations Division traveling to Fort Arnhem from Fleet HQ in Sanctum, Caledonia colony's capital, and briefing the Marines of what most now called Ghost Squadron wasn't unusual. Its primary mission was acting as the Division's direct-action arm. But Captain Hera Talyn, well known by most of the troopers assigned to the Special Forces' home station, held a rare distinction for a naval officer.

She'd earned the expert Pathfinder wings adorned with combat jump stars on her left breast, and many in the Special Forces community considered her one of Naval Intelligence's deadliest and most effective agents. Or at least Talyn had been when she and Lieutenant Colonel Decker, working as an undercover team, sought out the Commonwealth's domestic enemies and terminated them with extreme prejudice.

Stuck behind a desk for good since she would become the next head of the Special Operations Division when the incumbent, Rear Admiral Kos Ulrich received his third star, Talyn no longer found occasion to display her deadly skills as an assassin. But no one with half a mind was about to check if they'd become rusty.

One look into her expressionless eyes sufficed. They were the only notable feature in a face trained over decades to appear bland and unremarkable, a must for a field agent. Her shiny brown hair, longer now than it was back in the day, did little to soften a gaze that civilians might find disquieting.

"At ease." Talyn looked around the room, smiling. She knew each of them by name, knew their strengths and weaknesses, and what they could do if given a chance. "Nice to see you again."

"Likewise, sir," Bayliss, Ghost Squadron's deputy commanding officer, another career Pathfinder commissioned from the ranks, replied on behalf of the assembled officers and noncoms. "This must be a good one if you're here in person."

He glanced at his commanding officer, knowing that whenever Talyn visited Fort Arnhem, she normally stayed overnight and didn't use the guest bedroom in Zack Decker's quarters. And that Decker spent many weekends in Sanctum, where he also didn't use the guest bedroom in Talyn's apartment. They had been more than just work partners for years.

Lieutenant Colonel Decker, a big, muscular man rapidly approaching middle age, with short sandy hair and intensely blue eyes in a square face hewn from granite, gestured at the tiers of seats.

"Park your butts, people, and let's get this show on the road. You can hoist a drink with the captain in the Pegasus Club at happy hour after we're done here."

Bayliss, who was almost Decker's size, though darker complexioned and with silver-shot black hair, nodded to himself. An overnighter. He and Squadron Sergeant Major Teppo Paavola, another solidly built, albeit leaner Marine in his early forties, exchanged a knowing look.

"Are you planning on re-qualification jumps this visit, sir?" Bayliss asked while Decker and Talyn made their way to the rostrum on the low stage. "The School is running an advanced Pathfinder course right now, and

I'm sure I can reserve a slot in one of the sticks tomorrow morning."

"I'm sure you can, Josh," Talyn replied, amusement dancing on her thin lips.

Bayliss had been the Pathfinder School's regimental sergeant major before taking his commission. And as one of Decker's oldest friends, he had taken it upon himself to keep their jump statuses current whenever Decker and Talyn were on Caledonia between undercover missions.

"But since I'll never need to step off a perfectly good shuttle in low orbit again, I plan on allowing the qualification to lapse. Consider my wings honorably retired."

"If you say so, sir." Bayliss made a dubious face.

"Navy captains don't jump, let alone make the extreme high-altitude sort. Union rules." Talyn stepped behind the rostrum, Decker at her side. "Good afternoon, Ghost Squadron. I'm sure you're recovered from the last mission by now and are ready to rip through the galaxy again."

"Darn right," one of the troop leaders said. Talyn inclined her head toward Command Sergeant Q.D. Vinn, who led H Troop and had worked with Talyn and Decker on two separate occasions when they were running black ops for intelligence.

"Good to hear. This mission will, however, be a tad unusual."

She touched the rostrum's surface, and a large display behind her came to life with a woman's face. Lean, almost hungry looking, with short black hair, hazel eyes, and prominent cheekbones framing an aquiline nose, she appeared to be in her late thirties or early forties.

"Warrant Officer Aleksa Kine." Talyn pronounced the last name *Kee-neh*. "Commonwealth Constabulary. She's a twenty-year veteran of the service and has spent the last ten in the Shield Sector Group's Undercover and Surveillance Division. From what the Constabulary told me, she's the best undercover officer in her unit. Dozens of successful missions, hundreds of arrests, and a lot of bad guys spending what remains of their lives in maximum security on Parth or other penal colonies. Those who weren't executed that is. Her latest mission was infiltrating a suspected human trafficking organization. Everything was good for the first few months.

"She sent regular reports to Shield Sector HQ until two weeks ago. By then, she was on New Oberon, which, as you might remember, is on the wild frontier between the Commonwealth and our beloved techno-barbarian friends in the badlands. Shortly after making her first report from New Oberon, she vanished without a trace. The New Oberon Constabulary detachment tried but couldn't pick up her tracker implant when Sector HQ put out a quiet call to its commanding officer. At that point, Kine's superiors asked Naval Intelligence for help, fearing she stumbled into a situation she couldn't handle. Based on her last report, the human trafficking operation could be larger than anything the cops have seen in living memory."

Major Bayliss' hand shot up.

"Why contact your lot, sir? This is a missing person investigation, a police job."

"Thank you for being my straight man and asking, Josh. At first glance, it seems to be a police problem, not one for intelligence, let alone Special Forces. What frightened — and I use the term with great care — our Constabulary cousins is the extent of the human trafficking operation Warrant Officer Kine hinted at in her final report before vanishing. Our analysts agree. This may be a Commonwealth security issue rather than a simple police matter. Hence my being here with you."

"Glad the gray-legs are showing a spirit of inter-service cooperation," Bayliss replied, using the nickname for the Commonwealth's federal police, on account of the color of their uniforms.

"Times are changing, Major. We recognize the same enemies and share the same interests nowadays."

Bayliss nodded, remembering his first encounter with the sort of black ops Decker and Talyn used to handle.

"True, Captain."

"We, meaning my division, sent a pair of operatives to New Oberon. They'll look for Warrant Officer Kine. But if she's right, those agents can't do anything beyond recon work. I already briefed Colonel Decker on the matter, and he agrees. This is a mission for Ghost Squadron."

"With unlimited, albeit unofficial authority to pursue, in a way that would piss off Earth, the Senate and the SecGen," Decker said in a low growl. "But fuck 'em. As the captain will tell you, we won't be facing nice sophonts. Human trafficking has been a thing since before our species bothered wearing loincloths, but someone figured out a way to take this beyond anything seen before if Warrant Officer Kine's findings can be trusted."

The image of a planet replaced Kine's face on the main display. A red dot pulsed inland from the largest continent's eastern coast. Talyn touched the rostrum's controls, and the image dropped from high orbit to low altitude in a breathtaking zoom.

"This blurry spot, north of Titania, the planet's main settlement, is where the Constabulary's surveillance satellites last picked up Kine's tracking implant. As you can see, the satellite feed has been tampered with to obscure any details. But beneath is a sprawling country estate belonging to one Allard Hogue, a big man on New Oberon. He comes from the Hogues who've been providing one of Arcadia's two Commonwealth Senators for the last three decades."

"Which makes sense. New Oberon started as a colony of Arcadia before coming under direct Commonwealth rule after a rather contentious Senate vote a few years ago," Command Sergeant Kaori Nomura, Ghost Squadron's intelligence noncom said, nodding. "Leave a

Hogue there to protect the family's interests and make sure the colonial government does as the Hogues want."

Talyn inclined her head.

"Precisely. And that's another reason this is a Ghost Squadron op. Neither the local police nor the Constabulary would make progress investigating Kine's disappearance. If the Hogue compound is a staging area for human trafficking along the frontier and into the badlands, it will be one of the most protected sites in the entire star system, both physically and politically. The New Oberon authorities will not dare listen to accusations against Hogue or set foot on his property unbidden, even if a federal judge issues a warrant. Assuming the Constabulary can find a judge in the entire Shield Sector willing to sign off on one."

"What's the degree of confidence that bad shit is happening on Hogue's property?" Bayliss asked.

"Warrant Officer Kine's last report. A known psycho called Rabmag Rafalko was evaluating her along with six other mercenaries as prospects for the Saqqa Cartel's inner security cadre."

When she saw eyebrows go up at the mention of the cartel's name, she nodded.

"That's right. The Saqqa Cartel. Which means our confidence is high. Those would be the not nice sophonts Colonel Decker mentioned. It's a well-organized, tightly run operation that uses legal or gray zone business ventures as a cover for their nefarious activities. Law enforcement can't indict Saqqa's members for their crimes, mainly because they enjoy political protection. Like most of the large criminal cartels, Saqqa generates a lot of tax-free wealth and can pay its sponsors handsomely. If they're indeed trafficking humans into the badlands, the amount of money they can make is almost limitless. The techno-barbs will gladly exchange massive amounts of precious metals and gems for trained engineers, scientists, or anyone who can help them bootstrap their preindustrial societies into the modern age. As Colonel Decker can attest."

The latter grunted once.

"If it were up to me, I'd wipe the barbarian bastards out. But since that's not an option, we'll see about taking Saqqa off the board. Permanently."

"Kine reported that the other six mercenaries were some of the worst characters she'd ever met. Soulless creatures who would torture or kill anyone without feeling a shred of empathy. In other words, the same sort as this Rafalko, who is well known to the Constabulary as an extremely violent individual, one who has so far eluded arrest. Although Kine didn't directly witness any activities proving human trafficking or see people held against their will, she picked up enough signs that a large-scale operation was using the Hogue property.

"My agents will check the place out and tell you what's what by the time Ghost Squadron reaches New Oberon. The final go-no-go decision will rest with Colonel Decker. If illegal activities are occurring, then you will end them with extreme prejudice. If those activities include human trafficking, you will rescue the victims, destroy the compound, and terminate every Saqqa Cartel member. Then, you will find Warrant Officer Kine and bring her home."

"This will be a sterile operation," Decker said. "Should we rescue any victims, they will be told we're mercenaries hired by anonymous benefactors interested in fighting slavery."

Most in the auditorium nodded. Sterile meant making sure they left no evidence that could point at the Commonwealth Armed Services. They would not wear Marine uniforms or insignia, nor identify themselves as Marines. Their equipment would be unmarked, and they would travel on a Navy starship disguised as a freighter.

"*Mikado* is inbound as we speak," Talyn continued, naming one of the Q-ships belonging to the Fleet's Special Operations Command. "You leave in thirty-six hours."

"And that means no one gets shit-faced at the Pegasus tonight," Sergeant Major Paavola said. "The boss and I will inspect the squadron in sterile gear no later than fifteen hundred hours tomorrow."

— Three —

"Do you regret you're not coming with us, Captain?" Major Bayliss handed Talyn a glass of gin and tonic and raised his beer mug. "Sláinte."

"Your heath, Josh." She took an appreciative sip. "Well mixed as always. To answer the question, part of me misses being at the sharp end, using my stiletto as it was meant to be used. But even if I want to join you on this operation, I can't."

Talyn tapped the side of her head. "I carry too much in there that would interest our enemies."

"Don't I recall hearing you're conditioned against interrogation?"

A thin smile tugged at her lips.

"You of all people should remember a true artist can break conditioning. I'm not the only one with that skill. There are others and some work for the opposition. Besides, what I'm doing now is just as important. Perhaps even more so. And it is interesting. I see the Chief of Naval Intelligence at least weekly and brief Grand Admiral Larsson once a month. Admiral Ulrich wasn't kidding when he said he'd prepare me to take over the division once his third star comes through."

"And what are we talking about?"

Zack Decker, ale in hand, joined his deputy commanding officer and their guest at the far end of the Pegasus Club's polished, brass-adorned, wooden bar. The club, named after the mythical flying horse which had long been a symbol of airborne troops, was an all-ranks facility serving the units, Pathfinder and Special Forces, who called Fort Arnhem home.

They were in the main lounge, a space larger than most outdoor sports fields yet with a strangely intimate feel, thanks to easy chair groupings scattered under soft lights and a carved beam ceiling designed to absorb the noise of several hundred separate conversations. An equally well-designed dining hall matched it on the sprawling structure's far side. In between, smaller rooms allowed for more intimate gatherings, private dinners, or simply places where Fort Arnhem's various lodger units could gather away from the rest.

"Josh is trying to convince me I should come with you."

"But apparently, the captain is having too much fun prowling the Puzzle Palace's corridors of power," Bayliss said, using the less than respectful nickname for the Armed Services Headquarters complex on the outskirts of Sanctum.

"We who scheme in the palace's darker corners also serve the greater good, Josh." She winked at him. "Without me, you'd be on your own looking for missions to keep the troops sharp."

"True. I suppose you are our procurer, so to speak."

Decker, who was about to take a sip, snorted into the silver mug inscribed with his name.

"Careful, Josh. She may no longer kill with a blade but annoying someone capable of dismembering your career is never wise. You're fortunate our Hera has a sense of humor. It's a bit strange yet fitting for a staff officer who lurks in the shadows ready to pounce on unsuspecting Marines."

Talyn cocked an eyebrow at her partner.

"Remember, I always carry a stiletto somewhere on my person."

Decker glanced at Bayliss with a leer.

"I love staff assistance visits from HQ, especially when I sense a scavenger hunt in my immediate future."

Bayliss raised his hand in a restraining gesture. "Let's back away from this particular topic, shall we?"

"Yes, lets." Talyn jabbed Decker in the midriff with her elbow. "What's your sense of the mood, Josh?"

"There's nothing Marines hate more than slavers, which means they're looking forward to taking out the trash. That we might execute a few of the bastards along the way won't bother anyone."

"Good. We can't afford prisoners on this mission. The opposition will suspect the Fleet's involvement, but without proof, such as Saqqa Cartel members moving through the legal system, we keep plausible deniability."

Bayliss nodded.

"Roger that, Captain. And since we're on the subject, there's a question I didn't want to ask in front of the command team. What if we face the need to violate the Senate's edict forbidding military operations beyond the Commonwealth sphere?"

Talyn pointed at Decker.

"That'll be Zack's call as the mission commander. Since this operation will never be acknowledged or recorded, *Mikado*'s log won't show her sailing into the badlands without permission from Earth."

"I assume Sandor Piech still has *Mikado*. Is he good with that possibility?"

"Yes, and yes," Decker said. "Sandor won't argue. If nothing else, the mission to Pacifica we ran just before I took command of the squadron gave him a taste of true black ops."

"Good." Bayliss noticed movement out of the corner of his eyes. "Curtis and Emery are coming to make their manners, so I'll shove off and discuss the loading plan with Jory and Hovan."

Captain Jory Virk and Warrant Officer Hovan Kondou were respectively, Ghost Squadron's operations officer and adjutant.

"Sir, welcome back to the holy of holies," Captain Curtis Delgado, the officer commanding Erinye Company, said, smiling at Talyn.

"Glad to be back, Curtis," Talyn replied. "And how are you, First Sergeant?"

"Just grand, sir." Emery Hak dipped his head in greeting.

A dark-haired, olive-skinned man in his late thirties, Hak seemed carved from the same granite as Decker and Bayliss, though his was a more taciturn disposition. Delgado was First Sergeant Hak's exact opposite.

A few years younger than his company top kick, Delgado was lean, almost rangy, with sharp features and a pale face beneath copper tinged hair. He possessed an easy, open personality and was quick with a grin.

"That's an interesting mission you laid on us, Captain. Putting a bunch of traffickers out of business will be a balm for my soul's salvation, and guys such as me need every bit of positive karma they can get."

Decker gave Delgado a knowing look.

"What Curtis means is that he's still the love 'em and leave 'em type. How many are pining for you down in Carrick these days?" He asked, referring to the provincial town a few kilometers outside the Fort Arnhem military reservation.

Delgado put on an air of exaggerated innocence. "I'm sure I don't know what you're referring to, Colonel."

"Like hell you don't." Decker glanced at First Sergeant Hak only to see the ghost of a smile on his lips. "Even Emery knows what I'm talking about."

"It will take Captain Delgado a lot of rescue missions to make up for the tears," Hak said in a somber tone.

"Well, it seems I'm outnumbered here, and if I learned anything in this outfit, it's the ability to spot a losing proposition. Again, nice to see you, sir. Come on, First Sergeant. Let's go while the going is good."

Decker and Talyn watched them head for the cluster of 'A' Squadron officers and command noncoms on the other side of the club's main room.

"Curtis will go far in this outfit, mark my words. He's well ahead of the other company commanders when it comes to figuring out the deeper intricacies of black ops. Besides, any man who earns Emery Hak's trust and loyalty is worth watching. Shall we join our flock or stay here and pretend to be aloof?"

Talyn arched an eyebrow at Decker. "Oh, definitely join them. Your aloofness is no match for mine, and I'd rather you didn't look inferior compared to a naval officer in this sacred Pathfinder shrine."

**

"How is 'A' Squadron?" Rear Admiral Kos Ulrich, head of Naval Intelligence's Special Operations Division, asked when Talyn poked her head into his office at Armed Services HQ the following afternoon. A bald man in his sixties with a boxer's square features, he had recruited Talyn into Naval Intelligence as a field operative several decades earlier. Ulrich waved at the chair in front of his desk. "Sit. There's nothing that can't wait a little longer for your undivided attention."

"Decker's Ghosts are ready, willing, and able, as usual." She dropped into the chair. "They should lift off in about twelve hours. If *Mikado* hasn't arrived yet, it won't be long before she's in orbit."

"Good."

"Is the boss aware this mission may see Fleet units operate beyond the Commonwealth sphere?" Talyn asked, referring to Admiral Kruczek, the Chief of Naval Intelligence.

"I told him this morning. He said he'd mention the possibility to Grand Admiral Larsson the next time they met. No one will bat an eyelid if that happens. Provided everyone involved makes sure they leave no evidence our esteemed senators from the Centralist Coalition can use to further push for Larsson's dismissal. They aren't happy with his plan of reducing military garrisons in the Core Worlds so he can strengthen the frontier sectors."

"Between handing the Senate's Out World caucus a victory and being forced to beef up their planetary defense forces in the core, I'm not surprised they might want his head on a platter. But I'm pleased politics on Earth aren't forcing us to put a leash on Zack and his folks."

"Yet."

"They won't leave any evidence, Admiral. Suspicions, sure. The opposition will know we did it, especially if Zack brings back victims eager to talk about mysterious private security troops on an errand of mercy. Do you think there's a chance they might make us scale back our activities to avoid the risk of a scandal that might cost the grand admiral his job?"

An expression of vague uncertainty creased Ulrich's face. "Since I won't take counsel from my fears, I doubt it'll come to that. Any potential successor would carry through with Larsson's plans."

"Unless the SecGen appoints Admiral Bavadra. She's in favor of the current dispositions, which make her 1st Fleet the largest in the Navy."

Ulrich shrugged. "Command of the 1st Fleet is a political appointment controlled by the Centralists, though they think we don't know, which is why Larsson is reducing it. No one here would accept Bavadra as commander-in-chief, and the SecGen knows it. He's also smart enough to understand alienating the Out Worlders in the Senate would cause no end of problems for his administration."

"Once a few more colonies achieve the status of sovereign star systems, the next SecGen's nomination won't be decided by the Centralists." A cold smile briefly lit up Talyn's features. "Where would we look for entertainment without politics?"

"We wouldn't exist. Politics permeate every facet of human existence, even though we may not wish it were so. The only thing we can strive for is keeping the worst aspects under tight control, so we don't experience a third civil war."

Talyn grimaced.

"And that's heading in the wrong direction these days, isn't it, if we're continually forced to intervene in violation of Commonwealth law."

"We are the lesser of two evils, Hera. Until the situation changes, we can either let matters deteriorate or act to keep the ship of state on an even keel just that much longer. But a reckoning is coming."

"You think?"

"It's been coming since Grand Admiral Kowalski's day, but I get a feeling in my bones the process is accelerating. The bad blood between the core and outer star systems is getting worse by the day."

"In that case, we'd better be the ones shaping the outcome, not the Centralist Coalition and their minions in the federal government."

Ulrich cocked a bushy eyebrow at his chief of staff.

"What do you think we're doing in this division if not shaping an outcome? Just because we work on the micro level doesn't mean we're not affecting the macro level."

"I understand that, sir."

"The last operation you and Zack pulled on Pacifica before coming in from the field is still causing ripples in political circles, largely because it warned our Centralist friends we wouldn't let them decide the Commonwealth's future anymore. That's about as macro as it gets short of a shooting war."

"Yet, you think the shooting war might still come."

Ulrich nodded.

"I'm afraid it's becoming increasingly unavoidable."

"Hence Grand Admiral Larsson reducing the size of the Fleet formations in the core star systems, in case their commanders decide they would rather take their orders from Geneva than Sanctum."

"Now you're getting it, Hera. We'll make a strategist out of you yet. And yes, Sabine Bavadra would obey Geneva in a heartbeat, as would the generals commanding the 1st and 2nd Marine Divisions as well as those commanding the 1st and 2nd Army Corps. That's why the grand admiral is drafting orders to reduce those formations in size by shipping the best of their troops to new duty stations in frontier sectors."

"Good thing the Commandant of the Marine Corps and the Army Chief of Staff are not only on Larsson's side but sit in office suites next to his."

"That was the genius of Grand Admiral Kowalski's reforms. She might not have anticipated the current situation, but she was savvy enough to know the Commonwealth would need a full-scale political reset sometime this century."

—Four—

Decker squinted at the night sky as his eyes spotted several moving lights among the stars. *Mikado*'s shuttles. Twelve of them. Enough to lift the three hundred and fifty Marines of 'A' Squadron, 1st Special Forces Regiment, and their gear in one go. He, along with those Marines, stood at the edge of Fort Arnhem's vast parade ground, which would become a landing zone for the occasion.

Since it was easier to transport body armor by wearing it, Ghost Squadron's troopers, armed and in full fighting order, including backpacks, looked as if they were ready for combat and not a trip across interstellar space. Each company also had several containers of collective gear and other supplies sitting on anti-grav pallets, waiting to be loaded. Marker lights at regular intervals outlined the rectangular area while a two-person ground control team from regimental headquarters sat in a command post van.

Soon, a distant whine of thrusters reached his ears, telling him they were on final approach, and he fancied he could make out their shapes as they occluded the background stars. Single yellow markers in orderly rows and columns lit up on the parade ground, giving each craft its assigned spot, so they landed per Josh Bayliss' plan. The troopers knew their shuttle assignments, and when Decker gave the signal, they would embark in a matter of minutes and be off before anyone in the nearby barracks could complain about noise at three in the morning.

His helmet radio came to life with the voice of the senior ground controller.

"Two minutes, Colonel."

"Roger." He changed his frequency to the squadron net. "Ghosts, this is Niner. Stand by. They're two minutes out."

Seconds later, those who'd left their helmet visors up sealed off their suits. Decker waited until the last moment to close his before a miniature storm created by twelve shuttles descending with their thrusters at full power roiled the air above the parade ground.

He watched as they dropped vertically, slowed until they were only a meter above the ground, then settled in unison, light as feathers, precisely on the twelve markers. It was nicely done, and the Navy pilots' way of letting their Special Forces passengers know they were just as professional and capable. Twelve aft ramps dropped as one, and a new voice sounded on the traffic control net.

"Ghost Niner, this is your flight commander. You are free to board."

"Thank you." Decker turned to Josh Bayliss and pumped his gauntleted fist above his head, the signal to move. "Mount up."

He remained in place and watched his Marines file into the waiting shuttles by team and troop, taking the anti-grav pallets with them until only he, the company commanders, Bayliss, and Sergeant Major Paavola remained. The three company commanders raised a hand above their head to signal their companies were loaded, then headed for their assigned craft.

Decker, with Paavola on his heels, boarded the one piloted by the flight commander, while Bayliss, the last to leave, took another of the three squadron HQ shuttles. Once aboard, they shoved their packs behind the netting strung across the compartment's center for that purpose. Then, Decker headed for the cockpit while Paavola took a seat on one of the two inward-facing benches running along the outboard bulkheads.

"We're good?" Decker asked, slipping into a jump seat behind the pilot who glanced over his shoulder.

"We are, Colonel. Traffic control just gave us the go-ahead, and everyone is buttoned up. Welcome aboard. I'm Lieutenant Rhada Adjeng, *Mikado*'s assistant combat systems officer, and for my sins, the senior shuttle pilot."

"That was nice precision work, landing in perfect unison, Lieutenant."

"Thank you for noticing, sir. We rarely fly twelve craft at once."

"I'm sure you'll get the chance a few times on this mission."

"Excellent." Adjeng turned back to his console. "Ko-Ko Flight, liftoff in twenty seconds."

"Ko-Ko Flight?"

"You know where the name *Mikado* comes from, right?"

"Sure." Decker felt the vibration of thrusters spooling up through the soles of his armored boots. "The Fleet names its Q-ships after pre-diaspora stage productions, the sort where nothing is ever as it seems."

"Right. It goes back to the Shrehari War last century when they built the biggest Q-ship ever, *Iolanthe*. Anyway, one of the roles in the comic opera called 'The Mikado' is Ko-Ko, the Lord High Executioner of Titipu. Using character names to designate shuttle flights is a Q-ship tradition that started after the war. If you've ever looked at the list of names in 'The Mikado,' you'll understand Ko-Ko is among the least strange of them."

Decker felt the shuttle rise, and a glance through the starboard porthole showed the lights of Fort Arnhem dropping away.

"Who chooses those designators?"

"The captain. If ever he's annoyed with me and I'm stuck leading a flight, he might assign the name Yum-Yum or Pooh-Bah, which makes talking with traffic control a bit of a pain in the ass. So, I try to stay on his good side."

"No doubt." The Marine chuckled. "Perhaps I should find myself a good comic opera and use its character names as company call signs when we're operating incognito.

Ghost Squadron is, in many ways, the ground pounder version of a Q-ship. Heck, maybe I'll even start a new tradition."

"You should find plenty of time to sift through our database during the trip, Colonel."

Decker sat back and smiled to himself. An amusing idea, though perhaps not for the company commander who annoyed him in some fashion. Although knowing his people, they would probably take a perverse pleasure in the most outlandish call sign.

**

Mikado wasn't a small starship, but she still wasn't big enough for Ko-Ko flight's spacecraft to land in unison, as they'd done at Fort Arnhem. The shuttles filed through the two space doors one at a time before landing on their assigned spots.

Once the space doors were closed again, the inner airlock opened, and a stocky, silver-haired man wearing a merchant captain's uniform entered the hangar deck, followed by spacers in unmarked civilian garb. Simultaneously, the shuttle pilots dropped their aft ramps, allowing the Marines to disembark with their gear and form in three ranks. Decker emerged from Ko-Ko flight's lead shuttle, flipped up his helmet visor, and headed toward *Mikado*'s skipper.

He didn't offer his hand as he greeted Piech. The armored gauntlet could crush bare knuckles.

"How's business, Sandor?"

"Judging by the orders I received, it must be booming. But then, things are never quiet around you, are they?"

"Story of my life."

Piech gestured at the spacers behind him.

"My bosun's mates will guide your lot to the barracks. When you've taken off that tin suit, join me in my day cabin for a cup of coffee."

"It's the middle of the night for us, so you know."

"Then coffee is definitely called for so you can shift to shipboard time, which is almost nine in the morning, by landlubber reckoning."

Decker grinned at Piech.

"You mean two bells in the forenoon watch. We Marines understand the Navy's hoary customs. Let me find my bunk. If the wardroom has a few spare sticky buns, I wouldn't say no."

Mikado's barracks, aft of the central hangar deck, weren't the height of luxury, but then neither were the crew quarters. Still, as mission commander, Decker rated a private cabin almost large enough to contain his bulk and gear. The remaining officers and command noncoms berthed in pairs, while those below command sergeant settled into cabins with ten bunks each.

Decker neatly stowed his armor beneath his cot, secured his carbine and sidearm in the cabin's sole locker, and slipped his Pathfinder dagger into his right boot. In keeping with the rest of Ghost Squadron, he wore a black tactical uniform of the sort preferred by private military contractors and adorned with nothing more than mercenary-style rank insignia.

After a quick tour of the barracks to see where everyone was bunking, he headed for the Q-ship's heavily armored heart where he would find the bridge and the combat information center. Sandor Piech's day cabin lay halfway between them. Its door opened at his approach, and *Mikado*'s captain waved him in.

"Happy with the accommodations?" He pointed at the coffee urn sitting on a sideboard. "Help yourself."

"We're in the lap of luxury," Decker replied, grabbing a mug with *Mikado*'s crest, a stylized torii surrounded by chrysanthemums, on it. "Your Lieutenant Adjeng runs a good shuttle flight, by the way. They made a neat, synchronized landing. Very impressive."

"Glad to hear it. Rhada's a good officer. He should be on the next lieutenant commander's promotion list along with Monique Dulay, my senior combat systems officer. I'll be sad to lose both."

"So, no Yum-Yums or Pooh-bahs in his future?"

Piech burst into laughter.

"I gather he told you the story of how Q-ships name their shuttle flights."

"And gave me an idea about company call signs when we're operating undercover."

"Should I worry that he's unleashed a monster?"

"Nah." Decker dropped into a chair facing Piech's desk. "But I'll comb through your database for ideas. When are we getting underway?"

"We broke out of orbit shortly after the shuttles landed and are accelerating toward the hyperlimit. Now, tell me about our mission. SOCOM said it was a hush-hush, undercover raid on New Oberon involving 'A' Squadron, 1st Special Forces Regiment with Lieutenant Colonel Zachary Decker as mission commander and nothing more. Considering what you pulled the last time I took you aboard, this has to be a doozy if you're bringing three hundred and fifty of your closest friends."

A lazy grin spread across Decker's face.

"You'll love this one, Sandor. What do you know about human trafficking in the frontier sectors, especially the Shield?"

Piech shrugged.

"Nasty shit. It's run by human cartels who are worse than the old-time, pre-diaspora slavers on Earth. The Constabulary's been trying to wipe them out, but the money involved buys a lot of crooked politicians. Are you saying we'll take out a cartel on New Oberon?"

"In a nutshell."

Decker explained about Warrant Officer Aleksa Kine's infiltration, her findings, and her subsequent disappearance.

"Meaning this is as much of a punitive raid as it is a missing person case?" Piech asked when Decker fell silent. "I'm good with that."

"Kine could be in the techno-barb badlands by now. Are you good with violating the Senate directive against military operations beyond our sphere?"

"Fuck the Senate."

Decker's grin broadened. "That's the spirit."

"Look, I abetted an unauthorized punitive operation on a sovereign Commonwealth planet because it was the right thing to do. So what if we enter the badlands?" Another shrug. "What will HQ do this time? We got away with the Pacifica business."

"Hand out promotions and medals for everyone involved if we eliminate the Saqqa Cartel and retrieve its victims. Or at least those we can."

"Meh." Piech made a dismissive gesture. "We're not in this business for fame and glory. I'll take sending bad guys into the netherworld over another trinket on my dress uniform any day."

"And send them to hell, we will. If our advance party confirms the Hogue compound is a way station on the slaver trail."

Piech raised his cup in salute. "From your lips to the Almighty's ear."

— Five —

Chief Warrant Officer Hazel Charlam, Commonwealth Marine Corps, and Lieutenant Commander Gerold Savarese, Commonwealth Navy, both assigned to Naval Intelligence's Special Operations Division, emerged from the Titania Spaceport's main terminal amid a throng of new arrivals. Veteran undercover field agents able to blend with any crowd effortlessly, their eyes were in constant motion as they scanned their surroundings, searching for potential threats.

Neither resembled the pictures in their personnel files nor would any observer figure they were active-duty military personnel. Charlam, a dark-haired woman of middle height, middling weight, and middle age, could pass for anything — accountant, merchant starship navigator, or colorless bureaucrat. She wore the sort of pale face one forgot after a few seconds. Savarese, stocky, with thinning brown hair, and dark, hooded eyes, was equally bland, though darker complexioned.

Their credentials identified them as commercial representatives for an obscure hardware brand based out of Scandia in the Rim Sector. Anyone taking a glance at the pair wouldn't doubt their cover identities.

When a municipal ground transport pulled up, Charlam and Savarese climbed aboard along with other passengers from the ship they'd taken to New Oberon. They left the vehicle in downtown Titania and walked via a circuitous route to the address HQ gave them for the safe house bought by Naval Intelligence for just such an occasion, one of many on colonized worlds across the frontier sectors.

Though a Commonwealth Marine Corps battle group garrisoned New Oberon, the agents would steer clear of its base unless beset by a problem that might blow their covers and, therefore, the mission. In an ideal world, they would do their jobs, hand the situation over to Ghost Squadron, then take the next ship out. No one would ever know they'd been in the star system.

As expected, the safe house was in a bland middle-class part of the city where people ignored each other while they carried on with their lives. New faces arriving wouldn't arouse much curiosity. If they vanished after a few weeks, no one would notice their departure. The house itself, a small, rectangular bungalow identical to every other bungalow in the residential complex, was guarded by an AI program. It accepted their credentials without a hiccup and admitted them.

Again, as expected, the agents found a carefully hidden lockbox containing weapons, ammunition, interrogation drugs, useful gadgets, and everything they needed to alter their identities and appearance. The Special Operations Division playfully called these the 'Perfect Little Spy Kits,' and they were in every safe house, the location known only by the agents and the contents only accessible if they carried the right credentials. Anyone trying to force a spy kit open would trigger a small incendiary charge, which would destroy the contents. The safe houses and kits were innovations implemented by Captain Talyn when she became the division's chief of staff.

"Change faces now, then look for food?" Charlam asked. "Or keep these faces for the day?"

"Keep the faces," Savarese replied after a moment of thought. "Until we case the Hogue compound, there's no point in shuffling the deck."

"Agreed."

After a quiet evening meal in a local eatery, they returned to the bungalow and, using naval grade seekers, began tunneling into the New Oberon net, looking for data about the Hogue compound without triggering alarms.

"Major perimeter security," Charlam said after an hour of probing. "The sort normal planetary governments don't allow for private citizens, let alone suspected cartel nodes. Allard Hogue enjoys serious top cover."

"Concur." Savarese looked up from his device. "If the local news sources are believable, he's a good friend of the governor, breaks bread regularly with the speaker of the colonial council and pretty much every notable on New

Oberon, including the police commissioner. That means we'll do this the old-fashioned way and hike into the hills."

"A shame we can't tap into the satellite constellation." When Savarese opened his mouth to reply, she said, "I know. Too risky. *Mikado* can hammer the target area with her sensors when she gets here. Should we buy hiking gear with our current faces and go walkabout with new ones?"

"Yes, and we bring the arsenal with us. I won't run a field recon unless I can shoot my way out. Not if a cartel is involved."

"Agreed."

Savarese touched a control surface, and a three-dimensional topographic map of Titania's immediate surroundings, including the Hogue property, materialized in the middle of the bungalow's living room. The compound itself, however, seemed blurry, as if someone was deliberately obscuring the finer details.

"This feed comes from the New Oberon Geomatics Office, right?" Charlam asked.

Savarese nodded once.

"Yep. Hogue has heavy-duty top cover all right. That level of blurring is reserved for military or other sensitive governmental installations only — by law. Whoever is doing him a favor took risks."

"Only if there's a complaint. How much do you want to bet no one here would dare, and even if a brave soul tried, I doubt it would go anywhere other than the nearest garbage bin."

They studied the projection in silence for almost fifteen minutes.

"It will be a challenge to get close," Charlam finally said. "If they're smart, they've seeded the outer security perimeter with sensors and put a few on the hills overlooking the compound. It's what I would do, and cartels don't stay unindicted by being careless."

"Did you see a floater or a drone in the spy kit?"

"I think I spotted a mini-floater, though we can probably buy and modify a recreational RPV. But we can't risk a direct overflight, in case they run an air defense setup sensitive enough to pick up even a small eye in the sky. One hint someone's snooping, and we could blow the whole mission before Ghost Squadron even gets here. We should find a spot beyond their probable surveillance perimeter high enough for a direct line of sight, so we need not deploy the floater much above the treetops. Even the little suckers are detectable if they're riding where there's no background to foil sensors."

Savarese crouched at the edge of the projection and fiddled with its controls.

"There." He pointed at a hill south of the compound. "The top of that thing has a direct line of sight into the target, but it's also a good five clicks from the blurry zone. And there's a logging road running nearby. Here's what I propose. We rent a ground car, take the mini-floater, and head for that hill tomorrow. If we can't get enough visual data from its sensors, we'll regroup and figure out a new plan."

"Concur. I suggest we find ourselves a rental place and buy hiking gear in the morning." Charlam climbed to her feet. "And I'm off to bed after making sure the AI's perimeter security routine is on."

**

The next morning, wearing new faces and gear that identified them as outdoor enthusiasts, Savarese and Charlam left their rental ground car by the side of the logging road near the hill chosen as the observation post. Careful to leave as few traces as possible of their passage, they slipped through the dense undergrowth, boots sinking a few centimeters into a spongy layer of decaying vegetation with each stride. But the dense mat rebounded within seconds, filling the indentations and erasing their footsteps.

As the ground rose, the vegetation became sparser, making it easier to forge a path, guided unerringly by the positioning system Savarese carried. When the slope petered out, he stopped and studied their surroundings.

"This is the summit."

"Right."

Charlam wandered around in an ever-widening circle, looking for a gap between the treetops large enough to accommodate the tethered floater. When she found one to her satisfaction, she knelt and dropped her backpack. From it, the agent retrieved an ovoid object not much bigger than a football. Propelled by a miniature anti-grav pack at its heart, the floater was covered in a chameleon coating allowing it to blend with the surroundings. Charlam attached a sensor package to the floater's underside and joined both with a quasi-transparent tether to the control station she pulled out next.

After testing the assemblage, she glanced at Savarese.

"Ready."

"Let her rip."

Charlam guided the floater through the branches, her attention on the control station's screen, which displayed what the sensor pack saw. When it emerged into the morning sunshine, she stopped its ascent. Then, millimeter by millimeter, she let the floater creep up again until its electronic eyes locked onto the Hogue compound, five kilometers away.

"We are in visual contact with the target. Starting to scan."

**

One of the newly initiated inner cadre security guards by the name Logan Kars poked his head into Rabmag Rafalko's office.

"Hey boss, the sensors picked up a ground car taking the old Aivas logging road forty minutes ago with two people inside. We finally ran the tags, and it's a rental from Titan Cars. Ghamuret figured I should tell you since rental means non-locals. He's trying to find out who rented it, but Titan isn't talking."

Rafalko looked up with a thoughtful expression. Ghamuret Deyman ran the compound's control center and was an old hand who knew the area better than anyone. Ever since the regrettable incident with Goldie Neves and the possibility she might have been working undercover for the Feds, he felt a little twitchier than usual.

But hikers from Titania often used the old logging trails as their way into this patch of New Oberon forest. Besides, the Aivas Road was a good five clicks from the edge of the Hogue property, with a few hills in between, and it ran parallel to the property line.

He tapped his communicator. "Rafalko to Deyman."

"Yes, boss."

"Send a team down the Aivas Road and check out the people in that rental, but take pictures only, nothing more. We're probably dealing with legit hikers, and I don't want to spook anyone who might blab back in town. Savvy?"

"Understood, boss."

Rafalko cut the link and waved Kars away. His gut instinct told him this was nothing. But it wasn't infallible.

**

A frown creased Charlam's forehead. "I'm not sure if it's anything to worry about, but a skimmer is leaving the compound, a four-seater, possibly armored. The thing puts me in mind of a military scout car. Unmarked, no visible weapons."

"Perhaps it's a regular patrol, but let's not take chances. Did you record long enough to obtain worthwhile data?"

"As much as we'll get short of leaving it up for the day."

"Can we? Leave it up a whole day, I mean."

She nodded.

"Sure, but the longer it floats, the greater the risk of someone spotting it. The chameleon coating fools visuals, but there's not enough shielding to prevent a good sensor from pickup up stray anti-grav emissions, even at five clicks."

"Bring it down. We'll head back to the car but make a wide loop, so it seems that we're coming from somewhere other than this hilltop."

With floater, sensors, and tether back in Charlam's pack, she pulled two data chips from the control station before stowing it, pocketed one, and held the other out to Savarese.

"Here. The recordings. They're encrypted, of course. Without the right codes, it's nothing more than white noise. Just in case I end up ditching my backpack."

**

Rafalko's communicator chimed unexpectedly. "Yes?"

"The guys found that rental parked on the side of the road behind Tolo Hill. You know where I mean?"

He thought for a moment, then nodded to himself.

"Yep. Tallest in the area, but covered by forest, right?"

"That's the one. Can't see a damn thing from the top, so it's not known for having a kick-ass vista that'll bring in hikers. No one around, and they can't figure out exactly where the car's riders went. What should they do?"

"Do the guys have a tracking module with them?"

"Negative. But I'll make sure there's one in every skimmer from now on."

That's why Rafalko trusted Deyman. He was always ready to fess up and always with a solution, so fuck ups didn't happen again.

"Send the guys back to the main road and see that they hide the skimmer. When that rental comes out of the trail, follow it until they can see where the hikers are staying. From there, we'll find out who they are."

"Will do, boss."

— Six —

"We may have picked up a tail. Does that resemble the skimmer you saw leaving the compound?" Savarese asked shortly after they turned onto the main road toward Titania.

Charlam glanced at the rear-view display.

"Same make and model. If it's the same vehicle, they were waiting for us."

"What are the chances?"

She grimaced.

"Good, under the circumstances. We probably triggered an outlying sensor on the way in."

"Crap. Well, we can't play spy games and try to shake them, nor can we go back to the safe house while they're on us."

"How about we make for downtown Titania, the waterfront district, where we can send the car to its rental lot on automatic while we play tourist for a few hours."

"Sounds like a plan," Savarese replied. "They'll either tire of following us, or we'll be able to shake them without being obvious. But we must assume they'll record our current faces for posterity, which means they're compromised."

The skimmer stayed with them through the suburbs and into the city center. Its passengers weren't even trying to be unobtrusive, meaning whoever was aboard didn't know much about running surveillance operations. Once on the main plaza separating the colonial administration buildings from the Lysander River, Savarese stopped the car in one of the curbside unloading bays. He and Charlam climbed out, grabbed their gear and walked away while the vehicle, now under AI control, merged back into the sparse traffic and headed home.

Oberon Plaza, like its counterparts on every world settled by humans, commemorated the colony's founders with monuments to their glory. Benches lined granite walkways wending around planters filled with native flora, inviting passers-by to sit and admire the Lysander's dark waters as they flowed past.

Small native avian life forms flitted around, emitting high-pitched chirps. Some landed on the bronze and granite statues for a few seconds, then zoomed away. Though Titania was well upriver from the ocean's planet-girding expanse, the agents could still feel a slightly salty tang in the late morning air.

"Three o'clock," Savarese muttered, telling Charlam the cartel skimmer was entering the plaza immediately to their right. "It's pulling over. I don't know if they saw us leave the rental or not."

When the skimmer didn't follow their now-empty car along one of the avenues leading away from the water's edge, he added, "They're wise to us."

He nodded at a nearby wood and metal bench.

"Let's sit and see what happens. They won't do anything stupid within sight of the government complex."

Both agents settled on the bench, imitating out-of-town visitors intent on drinking in the peaceful ambiance of a public square snoozing under the midday sun.

**

"Those hikers, a man and a woman, ditched the car. They're sitting smack dab in the middle of Oberon Plaza. Just two dumb, happy tourists, watching the universe go by," Deyman reported when Rafalko picked up his communicator. "Our guys are still inside the skimmer, parked in one of the curbside bays, which means they can't stay there forever. The plaza is usually overrun by bored cops looking for an easy infraction. What next, boss?"

Rafalko rubbed his chin with the back of his hand, lost in thought. Either they were harmless, in which case there would be no point in tailing them. Or they spotted the tail and planned on losing his men by moving through downtown on foot. Or they were not harmless, didn't make the skimmer, and were staying somewhere in the center of town. Or… A pained expression crossed Rafalko's face as he contemplated the endless permutations without reaching a satisfactory conclusion.

"Tell them to park in a lot somewhere and keep beads on the hikers for the rest of the day. I still want to know where they're staying."

"Will do."

Rafalko cut the link and sat back. Perhaps he was getting worked up over nothing. New Oberon wasn't exactly a tourist destination, but there were always plenty of folks from the outlying settlements who enjoyed visiting Titania now and then. Many of them even wandered the surrounding woods, looking for native plants that didn't thrive where they lived. He'd heard there were a few species capable of giving humans a pretty decent high with few, if any, nasty side effects.

**

"It's getting serious," Savarese muttered. "Ten o'clock, just past that lurid bronze statue. Two specimens who seem out of place."

Charlam let her eyes drift toward a pair of fit-looking men in dark clothes who tried overly hard to seem as if they were out for a stroll. Both showed a slight bulge under the left arm, indicating they carried weapons.

"Like Sisters of the Void in a whorehouse," she replied in the same tone. "Now that we caught their attention let's find the most expensive restaurant in the area and eat lunch. I doubt—" Charlam paused. "Two more at one o'clock, across the avenue. As I was saying, I doubt they're either rich or refined enough to blend in with a posh noontime crowd."

"That's what I appreciate about you. Always combining the practical with the enjoyable."

"What can I say. It's a gift. If I recall correctly, there's a cluster of restaurants one block upriver from the plaza. Time for a leisurely stroll, I think."

The agents stood, stretched, and without glancing at any of the four watchers, ambled along the waterfront path, admiring their surroundings while surreptitiously keeping tabs on the cartel thugs.

"This looks nice," Charlam said when they finally stopped in front of a stone two-story building with large windows giving out onto the street. "Acheb's Delight. Let's see what the menu offers."

An unobtrusive screen came to life as they approached the door, displaying a list of dishes along with images and prices.

"Good thing we're on an expense account," Savarese said. "But the food looks tasty and the cost should keep them away. We might even talk ourselves out through the back door."

"Or we could eat, wander through downtown for the rest of the afternoon and get a room in a posh hotel for the night under our current identities, then slip away in the morning wearing our real faces."

"Works for me."

As expected, none of the cartel soldiers entered the restaurant, but when they left through the front door after a superb meal, both agents spotted them almost immediately.

"I'm disappointed," Savarese said as they turned a corner and headed away from the waterfront. "For all that the cartels are ferociously violent and capable of silencing witnesses with a single word, they're no great shakes at surveillance. I wonder whether the innocent visitors we're pretending to be would spot four thuggish men following them. If it weren't for the inevitable questions, I might consider amusing myself by complaining at the nearest police station."

They spent the next few hours visiting stores, trying on clothes, and browsing through various displays. The men never entered, and the agents never tried to vanish through a side door.

"Hotel?" Charlam finally asked when the sun was more than halfway to the horizon. "I think that's enough window shopping to last me a decade."

"Does the Titania Excelsior suit?" Savarese pointed at the local affiliate of the famous Commonwealth-wide luxury brand whose logo was barely visible above nearby rooftops.

"If they've not yet decided we're members of the harmless and idle upper crust, checking into the Excelsior should finally give them a clue. Certainly, let's break into the emergency funds and make a serious dent in our operating budget."

Charlam glimpsed the cartel thugs reflected in the Excelsior's windows as they entered the hotel. They didn't seem particularly happy, but to give them their due, the men remained within sight of the front doors until dark. When she looked at the street from their fourth-floor room after a quiet supper in the hotel restaurant, they were gone.

**

"So the pair are high-end travelers," Rafalko grunted after seeing the visuals brought back by Deyman's team. "Still strange that they went walkabout in the woods near here."

"Could be a coincidence, boss. They happen."

"I don't know. Send a crew back to the Excelsior before daybreak. Let's see what happens."

"You sure? We're getting a shipment tomorrow and need every hand on deck."

"The shipment isn't due until late in the day. Send two guys. A pair with brains and initiative." Rafalko gave his operations manager a hard stare.

"Sure thing." Deyman tilted his head to one side and considered his superior. "You seem tense, boss. Should I have a few specimens from the holding pens brought to your quarters?"

Rafalko considered the suggestion, but then remembered where the current batch awaiting shipment was headed. Wasting two or three prime heads of human cattle would put a dent in profits, and the cartel leadership got annoyed when crew appetites cost them too much. His preferred sort was worth a lot more than mechanical engineers in certain markets where those with particular tastes and a lot of money shopped for entertainment.

"Not tonight. Let's see what shows up in tomorrow's batch. Send a pair of guys to the Excelsior before the city wakes up."

"Done."

Rafalko cut the link and sat back with an irritated sigh. He didn't need distractions caused by what could be nothing more than dead leaves blowing past overly fine-tuned sensors. He still hadn't reported Goldie Neves' failure to his superiors. His people chose her as a prospect for the inner cadre, and she was his first failure.

Sending Goldie out on a cattle shipment to Kryani, the home world of humanoid aliens with peculiarly disturbing tastes deep in the Shield badlands, had been his decision alone. But ever since he'd wondered whether the cartel leadership would agree. They preferred to compartmentalize matters and might be happier if she'd died at his hands even if it meant a bit less profit.

But what was done was done, and no one ever returned from where the cartel sent them.

— Seven —

"Nice to know we can still shake a tail," Savarese said the next morning after they passed a pair of cartel watchers who showed no signs of recognition. Neither agent resembled the hikers who'd taken a room the night before, thanks to new faces and clothes worn inside out, so they showed different colors.

"They probably can't run one. Nevertheless, we should take our time and do a full circuit before heading home."

"Without question."

They reached the safe house unnoticed several hours and a lot of municipal transport rides later, but once inside, they still spent a good hour observing its surroundings for any sign someone followed them.

"Can we call it clear?" Charlam asked. "I want to look at the floater recordings."

"Sure. I wouldn't mind knowing whether this is in vain. It wouldn't be the first time bad intel made it back to HQ."

"Intel about human trafficking? Could be wrong, I suppose. Slavers are wily. But those gentlemen watching us as we enjoyed the good life yesterday were cartel, no doubt about it. I can smell carrion-eaters when I come across them. And satellite visuals of a private property blurred as if it were a military installation? We're not dealing with a monastery here. It's a target for Ghost Squadron if there ever was one."

Charlam retrieved her memory chip and tapped it against the living room's main display. After feeding her credentials to the display's controller, a distant building cluster surrounded by native forest appeared. She zoomed in on the compound until it filled the screen. Both agents studied it in silence for several minutes.

"Interesting," Charlam finally said. "There are two distinct parts. The one at the head of the access road is no different from any other large country home I've seen, albeit one with several buildings clustered around a central mansion. But look at the section behind it. What does that remind you of?"

"A small prison compound."

She tapped the side of her nose with an extended index finger.

"Precisely. Now, why would you build a prison compound behind the largest country estate on New Oberon? One with a courtyard capable of serving as a landing pad for sizable shuttlecraft?"

"Let's check the other signatures your floater picked up."

"First, infrared." She touched the controls, and the crisp image faded to blurry outlines filled by a riot of colors.

Savarese approached the display and pointed at the most intense hot spot. "That has to be the estate's power plant." He tapped the darkest spot. "And I'll wager that's a cold room for food storage."

"Big enough to drive a truck in." She studied the color patterns. "Plenty of warmth in the prison compound. At least double what's in the mansion and its outbuildings."

"And now, the life sign detector."

She tapped the controls again, and the colors vanished, replaced by bright spots.

"Holy moly. There are what? At least two hundred distinct life signs in those barrack blocks."

"Maybe even three hundred. I never heard of a country estate that required half a battalion's worth of staff."

"Humans held for transshipment."

Charlam nodded.

"I can't think of anything else. It fits with what the Constabulary undercover operative reported before vanishing."

Savarese ran splayed fingers through his hair.

"I wish we could keep sensors on that place and track changes in the life sign readings. But there's no way we can risk returning to the same spot as yesterday. Once is happenstance. When you're as paranoid as cartel goons involved in a nasty business, twice is enemy action."

"We could try sending the floater up from here. The tether should be long enough. We won't achieve anywhere near as good a resolution on the sensor readings, but it would be better than nothing. I doubt anyone will notice it. And even if a nosy neighbor does, we can always say we're bird watchers. Or whatever flying creature craps on statues around here."

"Do it."

Savarese resumed his study of the compound, lost in thought while Charlam reassembled the floater rig and took it up onto the bungalow's rooftop terrace, a flat space surrounded by privacy screens.

A few minutes later, she returned and said, "The floater is invisible from the ground. I can't even spot the tether past a meter or two. Are you done with yesterday's recordings?"

"Sure. Why?"

"I'll route the floater's sensor feed to this display. It'll be better than the control station's screen." He stepped away while she established the connection. Moments later, the life sign recording vanished, replaced by a distant view of hills to Titania's north, as seen from three hundred meters up. "It's at the end of the tether. Provided no low flying aircar or shuttle passes straight over the house, we should be okay. Now, let's focus."

Once the image stabilized and zoomed in on the Hogue estate, she stepped back.

"Not bad, except we can barely make out the prison compound."

"Definitely better than nothing."

Charlam flicked through the sensor's various modes, but the infrared and life sign signals weren't anywhere near as distinct as on the previous day's recording.

"At least we have a baseline with which we can compare future readings. It'll allow us to pick up changes."

**

"Boss, the guys watching the Excelsior didn't see the hikers come out yet. Either they left while no one was looking, or they're staying in for the day. Can we leave an eyeball to cover the hotel entrance and call it quits? There's a good spot across the street where it'll never be spotted. And the next time people we don't know show up, we can haul them in for a chat."

Rafalko leaned back in his chair, eyes never leaving Deyman's frog-like features, wondering whether he should worry that civilians fell off the grid so easily, or let the matter go. Even if they were cops, so what? No one made it within five kilometers of the estate without being spotted, and no one passed the front gate without vetting. Not to mention local law enforcement wouldn't step on Allard Hogue's property without the governor's permission.

"Your guys can set the eyeball on the hotel and come home. The ship's about to enter orbit."

"Roger that, boss."

Deyman raised a hand to his brow in a mock salute and left Rafalko's office. At least they would receive fresh meat in a few hours. Something to help distract him from running this place.

**

"Well, well, well. Come and look at this," Charlam said when the floater's sensor package alerted the control unit to a major event happening within its line of sight under the parameters she'd entered.

Savarese hurried into the living room and joined her by the display.

"Shuttles. Large ones. Capable of lifting forty or fifty people safely. More if you don't care about passenger comfort."

"I see four of them, so another two hundred inmates?"

"Why else would they land at Allard Hogue's place instead of the spaceport."

Charlam made a face.

"And no one on New Oberon wonders about all that private traffic? Charming."

"If one has enough money and influence, one can buy immunity from almost everything," Savarese intoned. "It has always been thus."

"Ghost Squadron can't arrive soon enough."

"Smack this one into the ground, and another will pop up elsewhere."

She turned to her partner and cocked an eyebrow.

"Aren't you Mister Sunshine?"

"Human beings treated as cattle out there bugs me to no end, especially since you and I can't do a damn thing about it until the cavalry arrives. Which means the people whose life signs we spotted could be on their way to short, hellish lives before then."

Charlam patted her partner on the shoulder.

"We can't save everyone, Gerold. Nobody can. Let's keep recording. In the meantime, how about you find the name of the ship that launched those shuttles. It should be listed by New Oberon Traffic Control as a new arrival. Then we send its particulars off to HQ, and the Navy will deal with it."

"Good point. I should have thought of that myself. I'm on it."

She gave him a wry smile.

"You were too busy worrying about strangers we can't save. Let's make sure Ghost Squadron prevents future victims."

An hour later, she stuck her head into the bedroom they'd designated as a primary workspace.

"The shuttles lifted. As far as the sensors can tell, it was a deposit, not a withdrawal. The intensity of the life sign and infrared readings doubled from the baseline."

"Meaning there's still a chance we — or at least Decker's lot — can do something about the people held by the cartel."

"Don't raise your hopes too high. Someone else might show up for a withdrawal before *Mikado*. Any luck tracking the ship?"

Savarese nodded.

"Yup. A freighter by the name *Frontier Magic*, whose ultimate ownership is hidden by a string of shell companies. I can't swim up that river with the resources at hand. Another job for HQ."

"Still more information than we had an hour ago. Any progress is good."

"Thanks for trying to cheer me up, buddy. I'll prepare a report and piggyback it on the local Marine garrison's regular subspace push. The sooner the analysts work on finding the ship's owners, the better."

**

Rafalko stood at the edge of the landing pad with Adra and watched as his people sorted the new arrivals according to their end-use and destination. It was a part of the job he enjoyed, not least because it allowed him to pick a few suitable candidates for his own pleasure.

Satisfying his needs in Titania was too risky. Getting caught might end with him strung up by colonial vigilantes. At the very least, Hogue would make the cartel put a new man in his place. Not that the organization's leadership cared about the proclivities of its senior members, but he enjoyed his job.

Once the cattle stood in orderly squares, staring ahead with the dull eyes of humans drugged into a zombie-like state, Rafalko, with Adra hard on his heels, slowly walked through the ranks. He inspected the new arrivals, checking the details listed on the manifest from the ship, to make sure they were in the right group. The Saqqa Cartel insisted on meticulous record-keeping, claiming it was the best way to maximize profits.

As he passed those who caught his eye, Rafalko pointed them out to Adra, who would see they were delivered to his quarters later that evening. And, with Rafalko's tacit consent, she made her selections, careful to avoid those with high value, such as technicians, engineers, and other specialists. She sometimes lost her self-control in the heat of the moment. But so long as they were low-value cattle, no one cared.

— Eight —

After her first day of imprisonment, Aleksa Kine had lost track of time, reality, and self under the influence of the drugs. Delivered in the food they ate and the water they drank, the mind-altering chemicals killed any thought of resistance. The very notion of escape became ineffably alien.

On the day of her departure, she'd meekly followed the herd as they were chivvied aboard shuttles and strapped into webbing seats. Part of her mind, that spark which kept a connection to her identity, screamed in protest, but no one, especially the Aleksa Kine who was now nothing more than human cattle listened. The twenty-year veteran of the Commonwealth Constabulary couldn't swim through the chemical fog, let alone rise above it.

Kine had remained conscious enough to notice their arrival on a starship's hangar deck, though she couldn't tell what sort of vessel it was. The same people who'd loaded them aboard the shuttles had led them through empty passageways and into a large compartment equipped with sanitary facilities and bedrolls. She'd heard the door slam shut and, imitating the other docile quasi-zombies, sat a bedroll at the urging of a loud voice whose owner remained unseen.

Days had passed without registering, though she'd felt the brief nausea of transitioning to and from hyperspace on more than one occasion. Food had been distributed once a day — tasteless ration bars and bulbs of water. Each time, the disembodied voice had urged them to form orderly lines while men appeared and took care of the distribution.

Kine couldn't even add one plus one in her drugged state, but she was vaguely aware her compartment didn't hold all of the captives and under other circumstances, might have concluded there were several such in the ship.

With no exercise, no entertainment, and unable to think clearly, the men and women around her had spent their time sleeping or sitting on their bedrolls, staring at the bulkheads, minds lost in a haze of distant memories.

**

Eventually, the same men as before led them back to the hangar deck and loaded them into the same shuttles. Ninety minutes later, Kine felt her craft slow to a halt, then drop until it touched the ground with a faint shudder.

When the aft ramp dropped, thick, moist air carrying the sulfurous stench of decay assailed her nostrils. After so long at a standard one gee, her body felt eerily lighter than it should when a guard prodded her into standing after undoing her restraints. Kine vaguely understood they'd reached their destination but couldn't begin to figure out where that might be.

She, along with those aboard her shuttle, was shoved into a single file once they stood on a rammed earth tarmac surrounded by a tall wooden palisade. If Kine's mind were clearer, she'd notice only four shuttles on the ground, compared to the eight that had picked them up on New Oberon and might wonder about the destination of the human cargo's other half.

At a barked order, her file shuffled off toward a low, flat-roofed structure built of pinkish stone. The other three files were moving toward similar buildings scattered around the tarmac's perimeter.

Once inside, other humans wearing strange clothing forced the captives to sit on the floor before shackling them to the walls with metal chains and manacles. The bare stone felt vaguely damp and exuded a miasma of mold mixed with rot, but Kine, a spectator to her own life, barely noticed.

With their captives restrained, the guards moved through the room and applied small adhesive patches against their necks. Moments after Kine received hers, the fog in her brain dissipated, and for the first time since Rafalko's men shoved her into the enclosure on New Oberon, she felt alive again. As did her fellow slaves. Because that's what they were now — human slaves on an alien world. Within minutes, the whimpers and cries began as others understood their fate.

"Awake, are we?" A rough voice asked in accented Anglic, cutting through the swelling noise. "Shut your yaps, my sweeties, or I'll give you a taste of my little friend, the cattle prod. Because that's what you are. Cattle."

Kine finally spotted the speaker as he walked through the middle of the room. A cadaverously thin human male with a pockmarked face, long, stringy gray hair, and an enormous nose. He wore a brown jerkin made of something that resembled leather over a bare torso along with gray knit trousers and sandals. And he indeed carried a long black stick in one hand.

"For those of you who've never heard of a cattle prod," he raised the implement, "this is a locally made shock stick used to control animals. And make no mistake, my lovelies, we are clever animals in the eyes of the Kryani, our owners. Even if they're only now discovering indoor plumbing, and we've known about it for over a thousand years. But they know animal control. This prod hurts. Don't make me or any of the other overseers use it by speaking out of turn, disobeying orders, or generally being an annoyance."

The veteran police officer in Kine recognized the man as someone who was either born without a shred of empathy or had it beaten out of him through brutality and deprivation. A survivor who knew no guilt, no shame, and no sin. He feared his masters and in turn, made his inferiors fear him.

"My name is Aldar," he continued, "and I'm your overseer until the boss sells you to approved buyers. Obey me, and you will fetch a good price. Disobey, and your price will be knocked down with every prod from my little friend. Our owners don't want to sell their merchandise at cut rates, and they know ways of disciplining cattle without causing too many physical consequences. Up here, though," he tapped his forehead with a grimy fingertip, "that's another story. Don't end up in the hands of a Kryani disciplinarian by resisting your overseers. We will speak with each of you in the coming hours, to confirm the ship's owners delivered what they claim. Be truthful. Do not hide things. Do not embellish. Lies cause my prod to spark."

Aldar paced back and forth a few times in menacing silence, studying the captives as if waiting for something.

"I was hoping one of you would mouth off so I could show the prod in action. Most shipments include at least an idiot or two who can't help themselves." He swung toward a young, dark-haired man whose face was a mask of terror. "Sorry, boy. I have to demonstrate on someone."

The prod touched the man's bare arm, and an unearthly scream filled the air as he convulsed and fought his restraints. Everyone stared, aghast, as the tremors subsided while he whimpered piteously.

"And now," Aldar said, "you know the price of disobedience. He'll recover, but the memories of your first shock never go away."

The overseers, five in all, filed through an open door at the far end of the room, leaving the captives in stunned silence, save for the cattle prod victim, whose moans were slowly fading. No one dared open their mouths during the hour it took for them to return. Most merely stared at the floor, wallowing in their misery. But a few, Kine among them, studied the others and their surroundings with alert eyes.

"Well now, my darlings," Aldar finally swept back into the room with his mates. Each carried a small tablet of obvious human manufacture. "Time to tell us who you are and what you're worth."

Kine tried to listen as five separate conversations at once started up, so she could get a better measure of where the captives came from and why the cartel abducted them. But she didn't hear much beyond them being a jumble of different professions and planets of origin.

Mostly they listed knowledge and skills that would be useful for a barbarian world trying to bootstrap itself from tribalism through an industrial revolution without developing a concomitant civilization.

Yet shipping humans across interstellar space didn't come cheap. Perhaps the Kryani paid with something that the cartel could resell at several times the cost of abducting and transporting victims. Something that hadn't come to the Constabulary's attention.

Aldar finally reached her. He glanced at his tablet, then at Kine.

"Name."

"Goldie Neves."

"What did you do for a living, Goldie?"

"I'm a mercenary. Mostly in private security work. My last job was with the Saqqa Cartel."

"And somehow you pissed them off enough to become merchandise. That doesn't speak well for your smarts. What's your age?"

"Thirty-nine."

"Health problems?"

"None."

"Do you claim any technical, medical, or scientific skills? Something the Kryani might find useful?"

"I'm a trained criminal investigator."

A snort of laughter escaped Aldar's lips.

"No call for that here. The clan chieftains make the rules, and their retainers enforce them. If a lizard says you're guilty, then no investigation is necessary to prove he's right. Savage bastards, the lot of them. Okay. You're a fighter. The Great Chieftain of Ruqint, who thinks he's this world's supreme ruler, even though he only runs a chunk of the largest continent, enjoys watching gladiator fights. Humans against humans, humans against Kryani, that sort of thing. We don't see a lot of human female fighters come through, which would make you an exotic pet. Someone to entertain him as he pits you against his champions. If you win, your value increases. And if you lose?" Aldar chuckled until he started wheezing. "You'll be invited to his table."

With that, he turned his attention on the next captive. Kine wanted to ask what Aldar meant but knew his reply would come via the cattle prod, so she bit her tongue.

Over the course of the day, individual captives were unshackled and marched out until only Kine, and one other remained. Then, fresh faces appeared, though not enough to take every vacant spot. Once his men had restrained the newcomers, Aldar entered, a cattle prod in hand, and surveyed his charges.

"You, my dears, are the unlucky ones — the dregs of the shipment. Since none of you have useful technical or scientific skills, your sole value is as entertainment for the high ranking Kryani mucky-mucks. And that means your future on this fucking backward planet is bleak. The Kryani often break their toys for shits and giggles. I'll let the boss look you over and see if he wants to recruit a couple of new overseers. He'll sell the rest as low-value pets, which means you'll land in the Grand Chieftain of Ruqint's stables. He has a big appetite for humans and buys what he can for his pleasure. Sometimes he even shares with the lesser chieftains, to keep them as happy, obedient allies."

Aldar resumed pacing.

"You'll stay in this room for the moment. We'll bring out bedrolls and food."

He pointed at a door that had so far remained shut.

"The sanitary facilities are in there. You'll enjoy running cold water and not much more. The shitters are holes in the ground. But the water comes from a well and is safe to drink. Or at least the local microorganisms leave human guts alone. Enjoy your time here. It may be the last reasonably comfortable, safe place you'll ever see. The lizards pamper those with useful skills. Pets? Not so much. Unless a Kryani decides he wants a human favorite. And even then."

As other overseers appeared, carrying thin bedrolls and ration bars, Kine wondered whether she should denounce herself as a cop in the hopes of being taken on by the slave market boss. Of course, such an admission could also mean instant death. Slavery was one of the worst crimes in the Commonwealth's law books, calling for automatic execution. And she was the law. At least back home.

In the end, she needn't have worried. When the boss, a greenish, leathery-skinned, humanoid reptilian, with a flat skull, bulbous eyes, and a wide, thin-lipped mouth entered the next morning, he didn't even look at the handful of women in the room. He immediately pointed at two of the biggest and strongest males. The sort who could handle heavy manual labor and, if need be, flatten uppity cattle without using a prod.

Aldar led them out, and the door slammed shut again, leaving the unwanted captives to their misery and fears.

— Nine —

"Colonel, you're right on time." Sandor Piech, sitting on the bridge's throne-like command chair, smiled over his shoulder as he heard the door open behind him. "We're making our final approach to New Oberon."

"Are we close enough to broadcast the signal for our advance team?"

"Sure." Piech nodded at the communications petty officer in the alcove to his right. "Jenks will set you up."

"Thanks."

Petty Officer Jenks gestured at Decker to take the vacant seat beside him.

"I just need a frequency and the message, sir."

Decker gave him a set of numbers, then said, "The message is as follows: 'rise and shine.' Put it on repeat until you receive a response that says, 'get bent.' Once they transmit that, you reply, 'foxtrot, oscar, alpha, delta,' got it?"

Jenks grinned at the Marine. "Unconventional code words, Colonel."

"So unconventional no one else would think of using them in a recognition signal. They'll reply with a data packet, encrypted. I'm the only one with the decryption protocol. It'll be the surveillance report on our target. Pipe it to my quarters, if you would."

"Sure thing, sir." A few moments passed. "Done."

"No chance your codes could be compromised?" Piech asked.

"Not even an iota. Agents memorize them and are conditioned against interrogation."

Decker didn't mention the existence of rare, but highly talented and utterly unfeeling artists who could break the conditioning. But few would work for criminal cartels. They were more apt to freelance or belong to the SecGen's security intelligence service.

Decker climbed to his feet.

"Sandor, please feel free to deploy the geosynchronous surveillance satellite over the target at your convenience."

"We'll do it the moment we pass through the right altitude. You still want me to ignore New Oberon traffic control?"

"We're guessing the cartel ships do so, based on experience elsewhere. If we can bamboozle the locals into thinking we're another one of those, so much the better because they won't ask questions."

"You're the mission commander."

"If we weren't heading for a regular parking orbit, I'd even suggest we go to silent running, but that might make sharp-eyed sensor techs curious."

"I wouldn't worry either way. According to the navigation notes, New Oberon doesn't boast an extensive orbital surveillance suite, which makes sense if the Saqqa Cartel corrupted the administration into ignoring its activities."

Decker shrugged.

"In which case, traffic control might think we're cartel and ignore us completely. Don't ask, don't tell. The motto of every corrupt organization throughout history. Did you query the local subspace relay for mail from home?"

"Not yet, sir." Petty Officer Jenks said. "I was about to do so." A pause. "I'm downloading an encrypted packet for the freighter *Gustav Pierson* from Universal Shipping Incorporated. I've piped it to your display, Captain."

Gustav Pierson was one of *Mikado*'s cover names, and Universal Shipping was Special Operations Command.

Piech glanced at the screen embedded in his command chair's arm, then entered his personal code to decrypt the message. After a moment, he looked up at Zack and gestured toward a vacant station to his left.

"Grab a seat. There's stuff here for you I can't read."

Decker did as Piech suggested, and, after a minute, he said, "It's from Hera. A copy of what the advance team sent home a few days ago. Visuals of the target area recorded by a floater from two different distances and the name of a ship whose shuttles landed approximately two hundred people at the Hogue estate, adding them to the almost three hundred that were already there. The ship's name is *Frontier Magic*, owned via twelve layers of shell companies by the Hogue family."

"Surprise, surprise. In business circles, they call that vertical integration. Sensors, see if there's a freighter in orbit whose transponder is broadcasting that name."

"Aye, aye, sir."

"I'm adding what the advance team sent to the mission data repository," Decker said. "My intelligence noncom will merge the floater visuals with what your satellite sees."

"Does the advance team confirm the target is legitimate?" Decker touched the controls.

"Look at the starboard secondary display, Sandor. What does that remind you of?"

Piech studied the visuals, then the infrared and life sign readings.

"A prison, or a holding camp. A place where the cartel keeps humans against their will."

"That's what the advance team says. Observe what happens when the shuttles land." They watched the video, then the life sign readings. "Too far for good resolution, but the population almost doubled."

"Yep." Piech nodded. "How do you want to play it?"

"Start by getting twenty-four hours worth of visual, infrared, and life sign data from the target area, and speak with the advance team. I'd still prefer seeing actual captives inside the Hogue estate, so no one can say later that we carried out the operation on spec. But if it comes to going in without a hundred percent certainty so we can save lives, that big cluster of life signs in a highly restricted area will do as evidence."

"Agreed."

Decker turned to Jenks.

"Still no response?"

"No, sir. Nothing."

"I should have asked before now. What's the time in Titania?"

Jenks queried the ship's AI before saying, "Twenty-three hundred hours."

"Hmm. They should be at the safe house so late in the evening, not gallivanting across the landscape. And even if they are, both carry receivers."

"You think they ran into problems?" Piech asked.

Decker shrugged helplessly.

"Operating in hostile territory without backup or support entails severe risks, as I know from personal experience. Hera and I experienced enough close scrapes that could have gone the other way when we were field agents. If we hear nothing by the time twenty-four hours are up, we'll assume something happened. Maybe we can send a team to check out the safe house. Radios break."

"They do."

"I'll be in the conference room with my people to review the data and start working on our operations plan."

"The moment we hear something, sir, you'll be the first to know," Jenks said.

Decker gave him thumbs up, then left the bridge.

"Any starships in orbit?" Piech asked his sensor tech.

"So far, I spotted four civilian freighters, all of whom I can identify from the Lloyd's Registry, Captain. *Frontier Magic* isn't among them."

**

"I think we need to send someone," Decker said the following morning after deciding Savarese and Charlam either couldn't or wouldn't answer. He glanced around the table at his command team. "If something happened, it would be better we know they were burned rather than assume the opposition is still fat, happy, and stupid."

Major Josh Bayliss nodded.

"Concur."

"They're conditioned against interrogation meaning the opposition wouldn't be wise to their true purpose on New Oberon," Captain Jory Virk, a tall, wiry, olive-skinned man with black hair and a youthful face said. "At worst, they'll think our people are Constabulary officers."

Sergeant Major Paavola grimaced.

"If they took Charlam and Savarese prisoner, then they're probably dead by now."

"Let's not borrow trouble. We'll send one of the command sergeants with a few troopers. They'll land at the spaceport, rent a vehicle, and go straight to the safe house. Once they've checked it out, it's back to the spaceport and *Mikado*. If the opposition has sensors in a wide perimeter around the target, there's no point in doing a ground recon. We'll plan with what *Mikado* can see from orbit."

Captain Delgado raised his hand.

"I believe one of *Mikado*'s shuttles has been configured as a Growler. It could take our team to the spaceport and scan the target during landing and takeoff. That would give us more than just high altitude and floater data."

"An excellent suggestion, Curtis." Decker glanced at Piech's image on the conference room's main display. He was listening in on the discussion from the bridge. "Can do, Sandor?"

"Sure. But with the pilot and a sensor operator, it carries only four passengers."

"Four it is."

"May I propose we task Q.D. Vinn?" Bayliss said. "He has the most experience working incognito in a civilian environment."

"Agreed."

Decker looked around the table again to nods of approval. Everyone knew about Command Sergeant Vinn and H Troop's involvement in two separate black ops under Decker back before Ghost Squadron's creation. The first rooting out Black Sword traitors inside Fleet HQ and the second stopping a coup d'état on Scandia.

"He's the best man for the job, sir," Captain Lucius Farnes, Vinn's company commander, said.

"All right. It's what? Early afternoon in Titania now?"

Piech nodded. "Just after fourteen hundred hours."

"I think we want to run the recon during daylight hours to avoid suspicion. How about we launch Q.D. and three of his people within the hour?"

"Done," Farnes said.

"Sandor?"

"I've already passed the order to prepare our Growler. It'll be ready when your team is."

"That leaves briefing Q.D." Decker turned to his operations officer. "Can you and Sergeant Nomura handle it?"

"Yes, sir. We have the safe house access codes, so there will be no need to break in, and Q.D.'s team will use their cover IDs to pass through entry control. It should be short and sweet. Do they go armed?"

"Definitely. New Oberon is a concealed carry jurisdiction."

"What about traffic control?" Piech asked. "And landing fees?"

"Your pilot can identify himself as belonging to the MV *Gustav Pierson* and pay the landing fees with our untraceable funds. Questions?" He paused. When no one spoke up, Decker said, "They leave in sixty minutes. Less if they're ready earlier. Thank you, everyone."

**

Landing at the working end of Titania Spaceport and passing through immigration on the commercial side turned out to be surprisingly easy. The bored customs officer didn't even ask about their business or what they carried. Command Sergeant Q.D. Vinn, a wiry, compact man in his late thirties with black hair, dark eyes, and an intense gaze, figured he and his troopers bore enough of a resemblance to cartel members for an easy ride through the bureaucratic niceties of arrivals control.

Finding a vehicle rental place took a bit longer since the nearest one was by the passenger terminal on the other side of the strip. But within twenty minutes of stepping off the unmarked Growler, they were on their way to the suburb where Savarese and Charlam's safe house hid among dozens of similar bungalows.

None of them spoke a word, conscious their car might be listening. They parked several blocks away, leaving only the driver aboard to make sure the vehicle didn't leave without permission.

Vinn and the other troopers approached the safe house via a circuitous route, alert for anything that didn't belong in this quiet neighborhood on a sunny late afternoon. From the outside, the safe house seemed unoccupied. Its doors and windows were shut, and there was no sign of the tethered floater mentioned in the agents' report to HQ.

After he and his men carried out a detailed visual inspection of the exterior, Vinn pulled a handheld battlefield sensor from his pocket and aimed it at the walls, using its electronic sniffer to look for life signs.

"No one's home. We're entering."

While the troopers watched his back, Vinn walked up to the front door and entered the access code. It slid aside without complaint. But instead of immediately stepping in, the sergeant scanned the opening and the foyer beyond, looking for booby traps.

Once they were satisfied, the three Marines entered. They cautiously went from room to room, searching for signs of Savarese and Charlam, or clues as to why they vanished, mindful that a cunning opponent could have left unpleasant gifts at random within the dwelling. They found nothing.

The spy kit was in its appointed hiding place, but the floater assembly, weapons, and ammunition were gone. If it weren't for those empty slots in the crate, Vinn might well believe the agents were never here. Crime scene sensors could probably pick up traces of their passage, such as strands of hair, skin flakes, and other biological markers. But his battlefield unit wasn't programmed for fine-scale work.

While they searched the house, they made extensive recordings of every room and every little corner, including the rooftop terrace. Perhaps running the visuals through Command Sergeant Nomura's intelligence analysis AI might reveal a detail the human eye missed.

Forty minutes later, they were back at the spaceport and an hour after that, aboard *Mikado*.

— Ten —

"What do you think happened?" Bayliss asked once Vinn and his troopers finished their verbal mission report and left the conference room.

Decker made a face.

"Search me. Unless the AI finds something in the visual record that Q.D. didn't notice, it'll stay a mystery. However, something that should be there but isn't could be a clue."

"The floater," Virk said. "Their report to HQ stated they would keep it above the safe house for a while, aimed at Hogue's estate hoping to collect more data."

"Exactly. The weapons and ammo being gone, I can understand if they bugged out. Taking the floater and nothing else from the spy kit? Why not take the whole box?" Decker exhaled. "Damn. Hazel and Gerold are among the last remaining old-timers, those who survived the Black Sword treachery. It would suck black holes if we had to put up commemorative stars in their names on the memorial wall. But that's how it sometimes goes."

"If the opposition took them, I'm sure we would see traces of violence in the house," Sergeant Major Paavola offered. "Yet that place looks like an army of housekeeping bots passed through."

Virk made a dubious face.

"Could be whoever is responsible for their disappearance scoured the place."

Decker raised both hands.

"We're not here to play detective, let alone crime scene investigator. They might have dropped out of sight voluntarily for a whole host of reasons and will resurface, eventually. It's the nature of the job. I'll report the situation to HQ once we analyze the visuals. It's time we planned the raid on Hogue's compound before a slaver shows up in search of human cargo."

**

"We're agreed, then?" Decker looked up from the three-dimensional topographic map projection of the target area covering the conference room table. "A long approach from two directions, dropping to treetop level for the last fifty kilometers. Erinye Company lands in the prison compound; Keres Company on top of the estate proper and Moirae Company on the southern perimeter as a backstop and tactical reserve, seeing as how the north side appears to be dense forest."

Though formally labeled Number One, Two, and Three companies, Ghost Squadron's troopers had suggested names from Greek mythology shortly after their first mission, names in keeping with the squadron's purpose. The Erinye were also known as Furies, three infernal goddesses of vengeance and retribution who personified conscience and punished crimes. The Keres were goddesses of violent death, particularly those related to the battlefield. And the Moirae were the three Fates, goddesses who were reputed to be the personification of destiny, the weavers of fate who determined when life began, when it ended, and everything that happened in between.

"Since this is a black flag mission," Decker continued, "those not in a cage are valid targets. We sweep through with extreme prejudice. Any victims of human trafficking we find we release on the main access road."

"Question, Colonel?" Captain Washburn Tesser, officer commanding Keres Company, raised a hand.

"Go ahead."

"About the last item. Traffickers often drug their victims to the point where they're about as sentient as bovines. If New Oberon is the Hogue family playground and by extension, the Saqqa Cartel's operating base, wouldn't it be throwing the victims back into the hands of cartel supporters? What keeps the bastards from rounding their victims up for outbound shipment once we're gone."

Decker straightened his back and frowned, annoyed with himself for not thinking about the problem.

"Good point, Wash."

His mind raced as he parsed the available options. *Mikado* could accommodate several hundred humans along with her crew and Marine contingent for a few short hyperspace jumps. But if Warrant Officer Aleksa Kine's trail led into the badlands, the Q-ship couldn't afford to bring so many passengers along for the ride. Her environmental systems wouldn't take the load for weeks at a time, nor would her food stores, which left the local Marine garrison as protectors for such a large number until a Navy transport arrived to repatriate the victims.

Even if the Saqqa Cartel had corrupted the entire New Oberon administration, police included, the Marines would stay clean, if only because the entire contingent stayed no longer than six to nine months before a fresh battle group replaced them. That wasn't long enough to turn even the most craven officer or noncom and make them cartel auxiliaries.

"We hand any rescuees to the local Marine garrison," Decker said. "Which means I'll identify myself to the commanding officer once we seize that compound, then ask him or her to run up there and take charge of the victims before we leave. I'll call home and have HQ send a naval transport charged with repatriating them."

Tesser nodded.

"That should do it."

"Anything else?"

"Sir." Captain Jory Virk raised his hand. "Could we borrow *Mikado*'s Growler again for the operation? Not only would it serve as a good airborne command post, but we could suppress any communications other than ours, just in case the cartel tries to warn friends who work for the colonial administration. I can ride it with Sergeant Nomura."

Decker turned to Piech.

"Sandor?"

"It's yours."

"Thanks. Last chance to raise issues I missed." When no one spoke, Decker said, "If anything comes up in the next few hours, talk to me. Otherwise, Jory will draw up orders. We launch in twelve hours when it's oh-three-hundred at the target. It puts us on the ground at oh-four-hundred — that magic time when the human body is at the lowest point of its daily cycle, and guards are half asleep if that."

Bayliss gave him a broad grin.

"The best time to tango with Ghost Squadron."

"My shuttles will be ready," Piech said. "Remember to invite Lieutenant Adjeng when you give out your formal orders."

"No worries. What will you call his flight this time?"

An amused smile appeared. "You choose."

"Let's keep it traditional. I proposed the operetta naming convention you Q-ships use to my company commanders and narrowly escaped a bloody mutiny." His quip drew scattered chuckles. "Condor Flight will be fine."

"Done."

"In that case, thank you. We'll regroup for orders in—" Decker glanced at Virk, who held up his right hand, index finger sticking out horizontally, "six hours."

**

Decker and Sergeant Major Paavola, both already in armor and full fighting order with carbines slung over their shoulders, walked through the Marine barracks, casually chatting with troopers as they prepared for the coming raid. It was a tradition and Decker's way of feeling out his squadron's mood and confidence now that every Marine knew the plan of action.

He found them in good spirits, ready to smite what they considered the most despicable people of all, those who callously profited from the misery of others by buying and selling men, women, and children without the slightest shred of empathy. Decker knew the Marines of Ghost Squadron considered this raid something they termed a righteous mission. One they would carry out for the sake of saving actual human beings and not to support a political goal they found far too abstract or worse yet, useless in the grand scheme of things.

"How are they hanging, Colonel," one of the men called out, smiling.

"Same as always, Benji," Decker replied. "One lower than the other."

"Nothing better than consistency for an easier life." Sergeant Benji Trimble swung his fighting rig over his armor. "And in a few hours, we'll make sure those cartel bastards are the consistency of mushy pulp."

"That's the spirit."

"By the way, Colonel, how is your daughter doing these days?"

Trimble, along with most of H Troop's Marines, had been part of the force that rescued Decker's only child on Scandia during the attempted coup d'état. He'd witnessed the reunion of a father and daughter after twenty years apart, thanks to his divorce from her mother.

Ever since, the Marines of H Troop kept track of her progress, especially since she'd shed her mother's last name in favor of her father's and joined the Commonwealth Marine Corps.

"Last I heard, Saga was gamely pushing through the basic platoon leader's course, but her course officer tells me she'll make it. I hope we'll be back on Caledonia when she graduates and receives her commission. I'd love to pin on her second lieutenant's diamond."

"And then off to the Pathfinders?"

"Perhaps as a liaison, but I doubt it. Saga is going to the Intelligence and Influence Operations School when she graduates basic. With her academic background, she'd be wasted in the infantry. Intelligence found itself short of smart officers who understand history and have solid, analytical minds after we cleared out those Black Sword traitors."

"Please pass along my best wishes the next time you speak with future Second Lieutenant Saga Decker. She's one tough cookie, just like her dad."

"Fortunately, she's much better looking than the colonel," Q.D. Vinn said over his shoulder, grinning broadly.

"I'm surrounded by comedians." Decker turned to Paavola. "Why am I always surrounded by comedians, Sergeant Major?"

Paavola put on a mock puzzled expression.

"Perhaps it's a natural phenomenon, sir? You know, some people follow their officers out of sheer curiosity to see what they'll do next. Maybe comedians end up under your command because they know you appreciate questionable humor when no one else will."

"And another comedian. It's not a natural phenomenon; it's a curse. See you on the hangar deck, folks." Decker and Paavola moved on to chat with the next group of Marines preparing for the mission.

Once they completed their tour of the barracks, Decker asked Paavola, "What's your feeling?"

"Our people are raring to go. I didn't sense a single doubter in the lot."

"That's my impression as well. Not every black flag operation is accepted with complete equanimity by everyone involved."

"Most of our people don't consider cartel thugs as being entirely human, Colonel, if you know what I mean."

**

When Decker entered *Mikado*'s shuttle hangar, Major Bayliss called the squadron to attention. Over three hundred feet stomped on the metallic deck, sending a dull thunderclap to echo off the bulkheads.

"At ease."

Decker stopped in front of Ghost Squadron's armored and armed Marines. If not for raised helmet visors allowing him to see alert faces, onlookers could mistake them for giant, dark, exoskeletal insects with outer shells covered by a stealth coating. Under the hangar's harsh light, their outlines remained reasonably clear, but in a darker environment, once they sealed their suits, the Marines would blend eerily with the background.

"You understand what we're about to do. The objective is saving every innocent life in that compound and eliminating those who hold them. We are on a mission of mercy but will show none to cartel members. This is why Ghost Squadron exists, and it's what we do best. If ever we adopt a motto of our own, I can't think of a better one than *force à superb, mercy à foible.* For those of you who don't understand archaic French, it means 'violence to the strong, mercy to the weak.' And that's what we're about to apply." He paused, then shouted, "Marines!"

"Oorah!" The battle cry would have deafened anyone not wearing a helmet.

"Mount up."

He waited until all but those who would stay behind climbed aboard *Mikado*'s shuttles, then joined Sergeant Major Paavola and Captain Washburn Tesser aboard the latter's craft. This was one of those operations where he wanted to be on the ground, at Ghost Squadron's sharp end, and not riding in the command post with Jory Virk.

Slavers had captured Decker long ago and sold him to an alien who specialized in janissary units made up entirely of humans. He had escaped with his unit's survivors after a disastrous defeat on a distant world and returned home but he'd nurtured a personal and deep-seated grudge against human traffickers ever since. This raid was personal to a degree few in Ghost Squadron, other than Josh Bayliss, could understand.

— Eleven —

When the last shuttle raised its aft ramp, a red light began to strobe, and the space doors, both port and starboard, opened. As Captain Piech and his hangar deck petty officer watched from the control room, the shuttles lifted off one by one and carefully made their way through the openings. When the last of them, *Mikado*'s Growler with Captain Virk and Command Sergeant Nomura aboard cleared the Q-ship, the space doors closed again.

All they could do now was hope no one saw the launch. Once Condor Flight entered its spiraling downward path, the shuttles would be invisible to New Oberon traffic control satellites and ground stations.

Piech made his way to the combat information center, where he would wait until Ghost Squadron and *Mikado*'s shuttles returned — hopefully safe and sound. The moment he entered, the sensor petty officer of the watch glanced over his shoulder.

"I'm tracking Condor Flight, sir, but barely. They'll be invisible to anyone else."

"Good."

Piech took the command chair from the officer of the watch and settled back, eyes on the tactical hologram where thirteen small blue icons were circling a reasonably accurate representation of New Oberon. A malevolent red dot marked the Hogue estate north of Titania where, in an hour, all hell would break loose.

"Sir." The sensor tech raised his hand. "I'm tracking a sloop-sized civilian ship inbound from the hyperlimit whose configuration matches that of a vessel on the BOLO list."

"What is the reason for the BOLO?"

"Piracy. Naval units are to stop and seize."

"How close is the match between that ship's configuration and its BOLO listing?"

"Too close for coincidence, sir." Side-by-side pictures of the same vessel appeared on a starboard secondary display, with technical data such as size, emissions signature, and more beneath each. "The left image is from the BOLO. The other I just took."

"I'd say there's no doubt about it," Lieutenant Monique Dulay, *Mikado*'s combat systems officer, said after studying the images. "That emissions signature alone is a close enough match for any judge to issue a search and seizure warrant."

"How recent is the advisory?"

"A few weeks, sir."

Dulay turned to Piech.

"That might explain why the crew made no modifications to blur its electronic identity."

"Or they suffer from overconfidence because they're protected."

Piech scratched the side of his face, thoughts racing. Was it here to pick up the people held on the Hogue estate? Or drop off more human cargo? Or was its purpose unrelated to the Saqqa Cartel's operations?

The order for naval units to stop and seize vessels didn't cover Q-ships because they relied on their civilian identities when carrying out special missions, such as the current one. He could legitimately ignore the pirate, though he would report his presence in any case. Of course, the irony of the situation was that between special missions, Q-ships such as *Mikado* lived to suppress piracy on the frontiers.

"Designate the pirate — what's the name listed in the BOLO?"

"*Sargon's Spear.*"

Piech made a face.

"Overly dramatic for a manky tub, but pirates do enjoy highfalutin names. Designate *Sargon's Spear* as Tango One."

"You plan on seizing it, sir?" Dulay asked.

"If we can do so without jeopardizing Ghost Squadron's raid. I figure by the time Tango One is in orbit, the Hogue estate will be no more. We'll see what orbital path he takes and then creep up on him by slowly shifting our orbit. If we can recover the shuttles before then, good. Otherwise, they can wait for a little while longer before coming aboard."

"Or we make Tango One stand down and divert one of Colonel Decker's shuttles to take it on the way back."

"That too. We'll play it by ear, as usual."

A few minutes passed in silence, then Jenks, the communications petty officer of the watch, raised his hand.

"Captain, Tango One is transmitting on normal radio bands, but not in clear. I'm running the encryption through our library."

"He's clearly not talking to New Oberon Traffic Control. Listen for the reply and pinpoint its source."

"Both the pirate and *Mikado* are within the Hogue estate's line of sight right now." Dulay gestured toward the tactical projection.

"I understand we're tracking a pirate on the BOLO list," Lieutenant Commander Hallie Cotto, Piech's first officer, said from the bridge.

He glanced at her hologram hovering by his right elbow. Cotto possessed a knack for always staying abreast of events, even when she wasn't standing watch.

"You heard correctly. With any luck, we'll find out momentarily who his correspondent on New Oberon might be. He sent an encrypted message over normal channels."

"Which means we can rule out traffic control or any arm of the colonial government. Or at least any honest arm."

"My money is on the Saqqa Cartel," Dulay said.

"And you'd be right, Lieutenant." Petty Officer Jenks turned around to face Piech. "Sir, a reply on the same frequency and with the same encryption protocol just came from the Hogue estate. And that protocol is not in our library, sorry."

Piech waved his apology away.

"What they're saying to each other isn't as important as knowing Tango One is indeed a cartel asset. And that means it just became part of the mission profile."

Dulay made a face.

"The transmission indicates someone's awake, which isn't good for Ghost Squadron."

"Duty crew, nothing more. They wouldn't do a prisoner transfer in the middle of the night. Not if the New Oberon government closes its eyes to regular shuttle traffic between visiting starships and the Hogue place. That means most of the goon squad guarding the estate will be asleep and ripe for the picking."

**

Lieutenant Colonel Zack Decker, sitting in the jump seat behind the lead shuttle's pilot, Lieutenant Rhada Adjeng, ran through his mental checklist, looking for something, anything he and everyone else overlooked. No plan covered every possibility or every contingency, especially not when unpredictable civilian thugs protected a target. The cartels hired every sort of sociopath humanity produced in its worst nightmares.

In contrast to properly organized and trained military forces, their reactions were almost impossible to predict, which meant adapting on the fly if they didn't crumble under the first strike. And hardened criminals seldom did so. Not when they made themselves guilty of crimes for which the death penalty applied. Better to fight and die than face execution, summary, or otherwise.

The troopers in the passenger compartment behind him were also lost in their thoughts. A few might wonder whether this mission would be their last. Others were contemplating the morality of killing a cartel cockroach in cold blood after he surrendered or while he lay on the ground, injured during the fight. But most focused on the chance to save defenseless people and nurtured their anger at those who would sell them to anyone with enough money and insufficient scruples.

"Message from *Mikado* on the reserved channel, sir." Adjeng's voice snapped Decker out of his contemplation.

"What is it?"

"A ship on the Fleet BOLO list for piracy is about to enter orbit. It exchanged encrypted communications with the Hogue estate. Once you declare the ground mission complete, Captain Piech will seize it, perhaps with your help, if the timing works out. So far, he doesn't know whether that pirate is here to deliver human cargo or pick it up."

"Understood. We'll do what needs doing. Let me know when and if the pirate launches shuttles. Should I be called upon to act as a boarding party, I will place Ghost Squadron under Captain Piech's operational control."

"Acknowledged."

Another joker in the deck. But as a wise man once said, no plan survived contact with the enemy. On the other hand, this new arrival might open the door to interesting opportunities if they took it as a prize. Provided it didn't carry victims. Otherwise, the pirates might imitate the slavers of old and toss their captives through the nearest airlock, hoping to show a boarding party they were clean. Not that it would work, but criminals of this sort were cunning rather than intelligent.

Decker watched their progress on the pilot console's main screen and saw they would momentarily drop to the deck before splitting into two groups, one which would come at the Hogue estate from the east and one from the west. He forced himself into a calming trance that would chase away his trepidation. It was a trick Naval Intelligence taught him when he first became a field agent. Decker couldn't influence events until they landed and worrying needlessly during the last thirty minutes of flight was counterproductive. Events would unfold as directed by the Fates, the Moirae of Greek mythology.

Adjeng startled him by announcing, "We're kissing the treetops and splitting into attack groups, Colonel."

Decker glanced through the nearest porthole but saw nothing, not even a distant glow from Titania, let alone the Hogue estate. This low, they should escape sensors focused on aerial threats.

"Thanks."

He fell back into a trance until Adjeng's voice roused him once more.

"Five minutes."

"Hmm?" Decker's eyes snapped open. "Right. Five minutes. Thanks."

He turned his attention on the pilot console's main display and saw it now showed a large-scale view of the target and Condor Flight's relative position.

"Still nothing stirring?"

"If something were, *Mikado* would call, Colonel."

"Right."

Nerves. He used to be as cool as interstellar space while going into a situation with his partner Hera Talyn when it was just the two of them. But being responsible for the lives of over three hundred Marines put a different spin on things, not to mention the innocent souls held in the estate's prison compound.

"I'm not picking up aerospace defense tracking signals," Adjeng said. "Maybe there's nothing, or what's there is dormant. Either way, it's good."

Finally, a faint glow outlining distant hills reached Decker's eyes via the porthole on his left. Titania. Then an even fainter glow ghosted through the forward windows.

"Three minutes and still no tracking signals. Reducing forward momentum to prepare for landing." A pause. "The Growler is blanketing every frequency except ours."

They crested one last low hill standing between Decker's half of Condor Flight and their destination.

"Target in sight. One minute."

There it was — the Hogue estate, or more accurately, the Saqqa Cartel's slave-trading station, bathed in the soft light of floating globes.

As always, the last sixty seconds went by at hyperspeed. Decker felt his shuttle touch the ground, then heard the aft ramp drop before a low, "Go, go, go," came through his helmet's earpieces.

The unearthly howl of an alarm siren shattered the still night air as Ghost Squadron's Marines raced from the grounded shuttles to their designated objectives.

— Twelve —

With unerring precision, the troopers of Erinye Company ran toward their objectives inside the prison compound — three barrack buildings and the windowless block separating the prison from the estate proper. The doors were, of course, locked. But each member of Ghost Squadron carried a dozen small doorbuster explosive packs, and within moments, a crackle of low power detonations filled the air. No sooner did the sound fade than a remote weapon station rose from concealment atop the windowless block and turned a multi-barrel automatic plasma gun toward the Marines.

Before it could open fire, one of the shuttles spat instant death and destruction across the prison yard with a twenty-millimeter topside gun, chewing up the remote weapon station and the building's upper story along with it. No sooner did the shuttle stop shooting that Captain Delgado and First Sergeant Hak heard loud shouts followed by gunfire coming through an open barracks door. They jogged over to see what was happening, but Command

Sergeant Rolf Painter, who led A Troop, stepped out before they could enter.

"It's secure now, Captain. A couple of cartel cockroaches had themselves an oh-dark-thirty rape party with prisoners. They met their maker a few moments ago. Sadly, at least one of the kids they were assaulting won't survive short of entering a trauma center's stasis pod within the next few minutes. Harvey Lytak is staying with her until she goes. The local garrison will have their hands full providing medical care."

"Crap."

"Yeah."

More gunfire sounded from the windowless block's ruined entry, followed by the dull crump of flash-bang grenades. B Troop, backed up by C Troop, was practicing high-speed house clearing drills, but with live ammunition.

"What about the other prisoner barracks, Rolf?"

"No cartel cockroaches. Plenty of people."

"Thanks." Delgado flicked on his radio transmitter. "Niner, this is One-Niner, objective alpha secure. Going through objective beta now, over."

"This is Niner," Decker's voice filled his ears. "Acknowledged. Out."

Delgado turned to Hak. "Let's see how B and C Troops are doing."

**

A pleased smile danced on Decker's lips as the grounded shuttles took out one cartel remote weapon station after the other, chewing up the estate's main and secondary buildings. Keres Company's troopers blew open outer doors and streamed in, tossing flash-bangs left and right before shooting their way into each room. Windows lit up with bursts of plasma fire while the shouts of surprised cartel guards rang out.

"Niner, this is Two-Niner, objective gamma is a guards' barracks. Estimate fifty-plus inside." Gamma was one of the estate's outbuildings.

Decker paused while he decided, then said, "Withdraw from gamma. Make sure no one comes out. Condor Flight, if you'd be so kind as to flatten objective gamma with your twenty mike-mikes?"

Adjeng replied almost instantly.

"Turning available guns on objective gamma and awaiting the order to open fire."

Decker thought he detected a hint of glee in the Navy officer's voice.

"Condor Flight, this is Two-Niner, my call sign is clear of gamma. Enjoy the turkey shoot."

Moments later, five plasma streams split the night, converging on the rectangular, two-story, timber-clad building with the red tile roof and chewed through the walls as if they were made of paper. Screams came from within as anything flammable struck by the plasma combusted with vigor, and more than one cartel thug tried to escape via one of the four ground-floor doors only to be cut down by merciless Marines.

"Two-Niner, this is Two-One, we hold their security control center." A pause. "And I'm told we got here before they could destroy their data banks."

"Excellent."

Before Decker could reply, another voice piped up.

"Two-Niner, this is Two-Three. Objective delta turns out to be the personal quarters of the cartel's higher-ups. A few of them are still alive. I wish I could say the same for their victims." Command Sergeant Clayburn Knudsvig, who led F Troop, sounded sick. "Niner should see this."

"Niner is on his way," Decker replied. He nodded at Sergeant Major Paavola. "Clay has a strong stomach. Whatever he found must be bad."

Objective delta was the outbuilding across the courtyard from objective gamma, now entirely engulfed in flames. One of F Troop's Marines ushered Decker inside and pointed at a staircase leading to the second floor.

"Clay is waiting for you upstairs."

He found an ashen-faced Knudsvig in the wood-paneled hallway who said, in a voice trembling with barely suppressed rage, "The suite at the end of the corridor is where the head cockroach, Rabmag Rafalko, lets his freak out. He has a thing for children. The bastard's still alive but barely. I stopped my guys from slitting his throat on account you might want to ask him a few questions before he dies. The other suites, not as bad, but we're still talking deeply perverted psychos."

Decker followed Knudsvig into the main suite where he found an unclothed, whipcord-thin, olive-skinned man with a prominent nose and a hairless skull shackled and on his knees. One of F Troop's Marines was pressing the muzzle of his carbine against the back of Rafalko's head.

"Back here," Knudsvig pointed at an open bedroom door.

Decker stuck his head through the opening and felt nauseous at the sight of three small, lifeless bodies. Rafalko had cruelly abused them before they died. He turned back toward the kneeling cartel thug while a blinding white rage replaced his earlier nausea. He didn't even hear Paavola cursing when the sergeant major looked inside the bedroom.

"What sort of animal are you people?" The words came out in a low growl, not much different from that of a Parthian male carcajou protecting his cubs. "Never mind. I don't want an answer."

"Who the fuck are you?" Rafalko asked in the strangled tone of a man who'd suffered throat damage during an uneven fight with the Marines, damage unlikely to be accidental.

"An angel of the Almighty, come to smite servants of evil."

"You don't know with whom you're messing."

"The Saqqa Cartel? And how will it stop me? I already destroyed most of this estate, and I'm taking your victims with me. Good luck to your bosses if they want to rain retribution on us. We do the hunting around here, as they'll learn soon enough. I want to ask you just one question. Where is Goldie Neves?"

A painful laugh scraped Rafalko's tormented vocal cords.

"Long gone, asshole. She's about to become a plaything for the Grand Chieftain of Kryani. And he plays just as hard as I do."

A leaden weight settled in Decker's guts. Kryani was one of the alien techno-barbarian worlds deep inside the Shield badlands, well beyond acknowledged Commonwealth space. And its inhabitants were reputed to be among the worst humanoids in the known galaxy. Brutal and greedy, they considered every other species beneath them, even those whose civilizations were more advanced than theirs.

And theirs was a society akin to eighth century Earth with every single one of that era's worst elements combined, but one which boasted a faint patina of modernity thanks to unscrupulous traders. It made for a bad combination. Fortunately, they were still far from developing the ability to build and maintain starships and could only buy tech from visiting off-worlders.

"Why did you send her to Kryani?"

"What's it to you?" Rafalko asked with a sneer. Decker rapped him on the head with his gauntleted fist. "She failed the loyalty test. Too damn squeamish for my crew. Could even be a fucking cop."

"Could? You mean you didn't even try to find out?"

"If the bosses ever heard I almost let a cop into the inner cadre, I'd be the one on my way to Kryani. No evidence means no harm, no foul. Besides, they condition undercover cops against interrogation, and that means lost profits if she died. The bosses love their profits."

Decker took a step back and switched on his radio.

"Two-One, this is Niner. Confirm the cartel's database is intact."

"Looks like it," Command Sergeant Faruq Saxer replied moments later. "We see a lot of accounting and inventory records."

"Look for the name Goldie Neves."

"Wait one."

While Saxer ran the search, Decker drew his sidearm, a Shrehari blaster identical to the one he'd liberated during a raid on a Shrehari corsair base many years ago. The original was long gone, taken by criminals who came to an ugly end. But he eventually found a replacement for what his partner and most of his friends called Zack's hand artillery, on account of the blaster's size.

"Niner, this is Two-One. We found her. She's on the manifest for a shipment to the Grand Chieftain of Kryani out in the Shield badlands. It left here three weeks ago. The analysts will go nuts with these records. There's enough to build a complete picture of the cartel's human trafficking operations. And we captured hundreds of hours of video."

"Good. Take a copy, then retrieve the hardware. Niner, out."

Decker stared down at Rafalko.

"Nice of your lot to be so meticulous. That means I don't need what's in that diseased mass of protoplasm you call a brain. Come to think of it, there was bunch of nasty bastards on pre-diaspora Earth who enjoyed enslaving others and murdering them in job lots. They also kept meticulous records, which helped the good guys hang them. But we won't bother with the legal system."

He raised his blaster and stroked the trigger. A smoking hole appeared where the bridge of Rafalko's nose used to be. The cartel sub-boss keeled over, dead.

"And the other top parasites, Clay?"

"Knudsvig gestured toward the hallway.

"If you'll follow me."

A brutish woman, this one fully clothed, was kneeling on the floor of a smaller, less luxurious sitting room.

"According to the file, this one goes by the single name Adra. There's one dead guy — adult — in her bedroom."

"What the hell is wrong with you critters?" Decker asked as he met her bloodied but defiant stare. "Sampling the merchandise is one thing. But killing people for shits and giggles?"

"There are always a few useless ones in every herd," she replied in a raspy voice hinting at throat damage similar to Rafalko's. "If you can't sell 'em, you might as well enjoy 'em."

Decker raised his blaster. It coughed once and Adra collapsed, her face ruined by the plasma bolt.

"Kill the rest, Clay. Anyone who considers humans to be cattle shouldn't breathe the same air we do."

"With pleasure."

The fight was over less than ten minutes after Condor Flight landed, and every cartel member on the Hogue estate was dead. Now came the tricky part.

After a quick inspection of the prison barracks and a headcount confirming there were four hundred and seventy-two surviving victims, some with injuries, all of them drugged, he returned to Lieutenant Adjeng's shuttle.

"Please link me with *Mikado*."

In a matter of moments, Captain Piech's face appeared on the pilot console's main display.

"And?"

"We're done. Out of the hundred odd cartel goons that were alive just before we landed, none survived. But we now have almost five hundred people in need of protection and care on our hands. Can you raise the CO of the Marine garrison now and link us, Sandor?"

"Sure thing."

"Tell him a Code Excalibur is calling."

Decker wrenched off his helmet while waiting and stared through the cockpit window as E and F Troop set fire to the remaining outbuildings. Meanwhile, D Troop stripped the main house of anything the Fleet could use to destroy the Saqqa Cartel and find its victims. The latter would mean heading out into unclaimed space, where species who envied and hated humans held sway. He pondered his next move when Adjeng's voice drew his eye back to the display.

"We have a link with Lieutenant Colonel Lea Brozek, commanding officer of the 22nd Marine Regiment's Battle Group Oberon," Petty Officer Jenks said. "Are you ready to accept?"

"Put her through."

The face of a square-jawed woman with short black hair, dark eyes, and the look of someone still partly asleep appeared on the screen.

"I'm Lea Brozek. And you are?"

"You understand what a Code Excalibur is?"

"Sure. Hush-hush Special Forces mission."

"Are you ready to copy and verify my authorization?"

"Go ahead."

"Two, delta, epsilon, five, tau, omega, three, three."

"Roger. Let me check my book." She looked away for almost a full minute. When her eyes rose to meet his again, she asked, "What can I do for you, sir?"

"We just raided the Hogue estate, which has been serving as a holding station for a human trafficking operation with tentacles that reach far beyond the Commonwealth sphere." When her eyes widened in shock, Decker said, "The Saqqa Cartel, to be precise. Well connected, well protected, and with plenty of friends inside the colonial government. We recovered four hundred and seventy-two victims, a number in dire need of medical care. I can't take them with me. Our mission is not over yet and I can't hand them to the colonial government, because they'll be victimized again so that Hogue and his cronies can evade responsibility."

"What do you mean by victimized again, if I may ask?"

"Killed, made to disappear. Re-enslaved. That sort of thing."

After a pause, Brozek nodded.

"Understood."

"Good. I'll reach back to my HQ for a naval transport, but it will be days at best before it arrives. That means I need someone to care for the victims and protect them from the cartel until then. You're it, Colonel."

"What are your orders, sir?"

"Send enough transport to the Hogue estate to lift these people in one go. By air is preferable and it has to be within the next hour. The victims and my unit must vanish before first light."

"My battle group includes a gunship and transport company. Between them, they can lift everyone at once. And now, I'm going to call an unplanned alert and bring the battle group to full combat readiness. Say one hour until my aircraft land?"

"That'll work. Thank you, Colonel. My troopers will help with the loading and stand guard while it happens."

"If you don't mind, I'll come out there myself."

"I don't mind. We'll be waiting for you."

"In that case, Brozek, out."

— Thirteen —

"Code Excalibur?" A burly woman in black Marine battledress, fighting rig and helmet asked as she came down a Warthog gunship's aft ramp. She wore a lieutenant colonel's oak leaf wreath and diamonds on her collar and carried a carbine slung over her shoulder.

Decker, who stood by the windowless block's gaping doorway, raised a gauntleted fist.

"Over here. Thanks for getting this operation going so fast."

"What can I say. I'm a softy for humanitarian missions and a hard ass at getting Battle Group Oberon into action. We can always use more practice." She nodded toward the eastern horizon. "First light in thirty minutes. That should be enough."

Decker raised a fist and shouted, "Start loading." He turned back to Brozek. "My second in command is a wizard at this stuff. While they're doing that, I'll show you what the Saqqa Cartel was up to in this building, so you gain an appreciation of the evil we wiped off the face of the universe tonight."

He led her to the torture rooms and explained what used to happen there, leaving out no detail until Brozek's face took on a greenish tinge. When he showed Brozek the prisoner pens and where Rolf Painter's troop had discovered a rape in progress — they'd left the bodies — he heard her hiccup as she fought a bout of nausea.

"We found worse than this in a building used by the local cartel leadership. It's one of the two you saw burning brightly as you came in."

"And no cartel survivors?"

"None."

"I can't think of a bunch who deserves summary execution more than this lot." She stopped to look at him. "I know I'm not supposed to ask a Code Excalibur any questions, but please tell me you're just getting started. Look, there are plenty of rumors on New Oberon about strange happenings here, and the power of the Hogue family, but the colonial administration operates on a don't ask, don't tell basis. The governor and his clique, including the planetary police force, keep both the Constabulary detachment and my unit at arm's length. This planet is probably the rottenest place I've ever garrisoned."

"We're only starting the clean up, so don't expect things to change for a while. And be ready for pressure from the government to hand over the victims."

"They can pound sand. I own the most impregnable piece of land on the planet and the biggest guns."

Decker clapped her on the shoulder.

"Shoot anyone who gets cute."

"What will you do with the estate?"

"Once everyone is clear, my ship will drop kinetic penetrator rods right on top of the main house. It should make a nice five-hundred-meter-wide crater."

"Rods from God. Love it. And won't that piss off Allard Hogue? The man's a smarmy, self-important asshole who behaves as if he owns the planet."

The first of Battle Group Oberon's transport aircraft lifted off in a howl of thrusters, loaded with docile men, women, and children who couldn't quite understand what was happening thanks to the drug-induced haze that dulled their senses. Then, one after the other, the rest rose into the pre-dawn air and headed south, until only Brozek's remained.

"That's me, sir. For what it's worth, you're doing the Almighty's work. Godspeed and good hunting." She drew herself to attention and saluted. Decker returned the gesture with a solemn nod.

"Thank you again, Colonel."

As she left, Bayliss and Paavola signaled him furiously, gesturing at the last of *Mikado*'s shuttles in the prison yard.

"Time," the former shouted. "The countdown to the kinetic strike has started. Orbital mechanics being what they are."

All around the estate, shuttles were lifting in good order, headed away from Titania. Once Brozek's Warthog cleared the top of the windowless block and vanished, Decker jogged to where his second in command and sergeant major waited.

"We're the only ones left," Bayliss said. "*Mikado* is less than five minutes from launch."

"Then we'd better bug out."

They marched up the ramp, which closed the moment Decker entered the aft compartment. He went up front to sit behind the pilot, one of *Mikado*'s petty officers, while Bayliss and Paavola settled in among the Marines of Erinye Company. Without warning, the shuttle rose under full military power before banking to starboard and speeding off after the rest of Condor Flight.

Decker tapped the pilot on the shoulder. "Let *Mikado* know we're clear."

"Will do, sir." A few moments later. "The strike is on its way."

"Can you keep a visual on the target?"

The pilot nodded.

"I'll put it on my console display. I don't need it right now."

He touched a control surface, and the forward view vanished, replaced with that of dark, undulating forest outlined by a hint of pink on the far horizon. As they gained altitude, the encroaching light of day strengthened, until a bright flash erupted from where the Hogue estate once stood. A half-dozen two-meter-long tungsten rods launched from orbit had struck the ground at terminal velocity, releasing enough energy to destroy what remained of the cartel's way station on its human trafficking highway.

**

"If the folks aboard Tango One noticed us, they're staying remarkably quiet." Lieutenant Monique Dulay glanced over her shoulder at Sandor Piech. "No sign they're powering up for either fight or flight."

Piech nodded without taking his eyes off the holographic tactical projection. *Mikado* had gone to battle stations shortly before firing the penetrator rods. And now that her part in the ground raid was over, he intended to seize *Sargon's Spear* by slowly closing the distance between them while both orbited New Oberon at the same altitude.

"What are you thinking, Captain?" Lieutenant Commander Cotto asked. She was once again present in the CIC via holographic projection from the bridge, where she occupied the command chair whenever *Mikado* was at battle stations. "I see a gleam in your eyes."

"My gut tells me they don't know about the BOLO. They're acting far too confident for pirates who should exude paranoia from every pore. I figure a boarding party con might be the best way. Let's quietly turn into our naval alter ego, the intrepid patrol frigate *Zhukov*, and inform *Sargon's Spear* we will inspect them under the applicable interstellar transport safety regulations. Except we send fully armored and armed spacers along with the inspectors."

"I always love a good con," the first officer replied in an approving tone. "With one modification. I suggest we use the Marines from Colonel Decker's squadron headquarters who didn't take part in the raid as the boarding party's muscle. They may carry out administrative functions in the course of their regular duties, but every one of them is an experienced Special Forces trooper. If you want, I can alert Warrant Officer Kondou, who's the most senior of them aboard now."

"Do it."

"You want Torrance to lead the boarding party?" She asked, naming *Mikado*'s second officer, Lieutenant Torrance Toh.

Piech gave the question a few moments of thought. He rotated the assignment among his officers so each could practice boarding potentially hostile starships. But this one could turn nasty and Toh was not only *Mikado*'s senior lieutenant, he was also the one with the most experience and the greatest professional maturity.

"Yes. Call both to the conference room right now and tell the hangar deck to prepare a shuttle. Then hand the bridge to the officer of the watch and join us."

"Aye, aye, sir."

Piech turned to Lieutenant Dulay.

"Unmask and prepare our *Zhukov* beacon, but don't activate it yet." He stood. "The CIC is yours."

"Sir."

Piech didn't wait long before Lieutenant Toh and Warrant Officer Kondou entered the conference room. Before he could speak, the latter said, "My people are suiting up. They're happy at the chance to do some ass-kicking for a change."

"When is the last time you carried out a boarding party mission, Warrant?"

"Simulated? A few weeks ago. For real, it's been about eighteen months. The same applies to the others, more or less. If the pirates aren't expecting two dozen armored Marines to appear on their hangar deck as if by magic, it'll be over in short order."

Piech heard the quiet confidence in Kondou's tone and nodded once.

"Good. Lieutenant Toh, who does this for a living, will be in overall command, but since we're supposed to be conducting a routine inspection, he and the crew members who'll accompany him won't be armored, just armed. And since we plan on taking that ship, I'm sending more of mine over than if it were just an inspection. I don't want to waste time shifting a prize crew afterward. Ghost Squadron is on the way back as we speak."

"If there's shooting, we'll put ourselves in front of them, sir. No worries. I figure this will be a shock and awe operation. Even pirates know they're beat once a troop of Marines in full fighting order makes it aboard, especially if they think they're not yet on anyone's shit list."

"All right." Piech went over the mission parameters, then said, "I'll let you and Torrance work out the details but be ready to go in thirty minutes."

Toh and Kondou glanced at each other.

"We'll be ready in fifteen," the former said.

"Even better. Thank you."

When he returned to the CIC, Dulay rose from the command chair and returned to her station.

"We're fully unmasked and functioning as a patrol frigate, but still nothing from Tango One."

"Light up the beacon. Bridge, bring us within five kilometers of Tango One, and give them the standard safety inspection hail."

Piech sat back and studied the tactical projection, which now focused on a small arc of New Oberon's orbitals and showed his ship visibly closing with the target.

"Bridge to CIC, there's a Captain Ahmeti of the freighter *Sargon's Spear* on the link. He's asking why we want to inspect his ship."

"Put him on." A craggy, leathery-skinned face beneath black hair appeared on Piech's command chair display. Deep-set dark eyes on either side of a large, hooked nose stared back at Piech.

"What is it you want with me, Navy?" Ahmeti asked in a heavily accented Anglic.

Piech gave him a bored smile.

"I'm Commander Sergei Lermontov. This is a routine safety inspection visit, Captain. You know how it is. HQ gives us a quota and you fit the profile. This month, we're doing independent frontier traders."

"Picking on us little guys, eh?"

"I'm sending a boarding party under my second officer via shuttle. It's in your best interest to cooperate with him. The inspection shouldn't take more than an hour. If we find nothing in contravention of interstellar transport regulations, I will issue a compliance certificate good for one year. Show it to the next naval vessel that stops you, and it's a get out of jail free card."

Ahmeti shrugged, though Piech could see unhappiness mixed with annoyance in his eyes.

"Fine. We'll cooperate."

"Thank you, Captain. Much appreciated. You wouldn't believe the grief some of your colleagues give us, even though they know we can use as much force as necessary."

"He who has the biggest guns makes the rules."

"Exactly." Piech tapped the side of his nose with an extended index finger. "We'll be five kilometers behind you for the duration of the inspection, so feel free to look us over. Was that it?"

"You won't find anything wrong with my ship, so you'd best prepare that certificate. Ahmeti, out."

The pirate's face vanished.

"So far, so good." Piech took a deep breath and exhaled loudly. "And since he didn't argue, he's running in ballast, meaning we needn't worry about civilians."

"The bugger's just as wary as any other captain about to receive a naval inspection team, Skipper," Cotto's hologram said. "But I didn't sense he figured we'll seize him and his crew on suspicion of piracy. Otherwise, I would expect his drives to light up just about now in the hope of making a clean escape thanks to his ship's smaller size."

"Or he figures the cartel's backers can spring him from the brig before anything gets in front of a judge."

"Perhaps." Cotto paused, then asked, "What will we do with our prize afterward? I doubt Colonel Decker would approve of a detour to the nearest star base so we can drop it off."

"That thing is a sloop. We'll land it on Fort Lysander's main parade square and let someone else deal with the problem."

"Colonel Brozek might not agree."

"Tough."

— Fourteen —

The back of *Mikado*'s administrative shuttle was cramped with the twelve spacers of the prize crew and twenty-four Marines in armor, but the flight over to *Sargon's Spear* was mercifully short. As they nosed through the hangar deck's open space doors, Kondou gave the signal for his troopers to shut their helmet visors. Lieutenant Toh, who was with the pilot in the cockpit, waited until the space doors closed and the inner airlock opened to admit Captain Ahmeti before climbing out of his seat.

"All right, folks. Time to take ourselves a prize. Wait for my orders."

Toh opened the starboard front door and stepped out. He drew himself to attention before saluting Ahmeti.

"Permission to come aboard, Captain."

Ahmeti returned the courtesy with a brief dip of the head.

"As if I have a choice."

"I brought additional personnel, subject matter experts in various domains to help us do this faster. Perhaps you could

127

assemble your department heads so they may guide my folks through various parts of your ship."

Ahmeti scoffed.

"Department heads? What do you think this is? A corporate luxury liner? I have twenty crew members."

"Then perhaps your first and second mates, as well as your chief engineer, will suffice." When Ahmeti hesitated, Toh said, "Sir, I'm just trying to make this as easy as possible on both of us. Trust me; we don't enjoy doing safety inspections any more than you enjoy being on the receiving end of them. But pass this one, and as my captain said, he'll give you a certificate exempting this ship from inspections for a year."

"Very well." The words came out in a grudging tone. Ahmeti raised a communicator to his lips. "Piotr, Harry, and Lee to the hangar deck. You're giving the Navy a tour of the ship."

"Thank you, sir."

Three men with faces just as villainous as their captain's showed up in the hangar deck a few minutes later. After noting the holstered blasters on the men's hips, Toh gestured at the shuttle, and nine of the eleven noncoms assigned to the prize crew came through the starboard front door. They joined Toh and the pirates by the airlock

"Each of your officers can take three of mine around while we chat, Captain."

"What is this?" A suspicious Ahmeti asked when Warrant Officer Kondou and one of his Marines exited the shuttle.

"Protocol, sir. Whenever we land in a civilian vessel or on a civilian tarmac, a pair of the ship's Marines must stand guard. Since the order comes from HQ, I can't do anything other than obey. You know how it is."

If Ahmeti noticed neither of the armored figures wore rank or unit insignia, he didn't react, though his narrowed eye followed the pair as one took position by the shuttle's nose, the other at the aft end. Both carried their carbines casually slung over their right shoulders, barrels pointing downward.

Toh gestured at the inner airlock, hoping the pirates would leave it open.

"Shall we, sir? I wouldn't mind seeing your bridge. Small, fast traders such as yours fascinate me because of how the designers cram so much functionality in every nook and cranny."

Ahmeti nodded at his officers to go ahead, then made a follow me gesture with his hand. When they reached the pirate's cramped bridge, Toh looked for anyone or anything monitoring the hangar deck, but the only crew member on duty was at the helm console, looking bored. Toh reached into his pocket and tapped his communicator three times, telling Kondou the rest of his Marines could disembark and fan out through the ship.

"Nice setup, Captain." Toh walked to the front of the compartment, where he turned and faced Ahmeti and the helmsman. "Neat. Everything a bigger ship has but in miniature. She must be a charm to sail."

The helmsman, who'd been studying Toh, put on a weak grin that seemed rather nervous.

"No complaints, Mister Navy. You want to hear real thunder, stand on a spaceport observation deck, and watch us land."

Before Toh could reply, two Marines entered the bridge, weapons ready. Ahmeti and his helmsman turned when they heard boots on the metal deck.

"What the fuck?"

"Hands on top of your heads," one of the Marines growled. "Make a false move, and you die."

When they complied, the other deftly snapped restraints on their wrists.

"Kneel."

As they did so, Toh met Ahmeti's furious gaze.

"Captain Ahmeti, *Sargon's Spear* is on the Navy's list of ships known to engage in piracy. You and your crew are under arrest, and this ship is now our prize." He felt his communicator vibrate three times, the signal that Marines had joined the three fake inspection parties. "I now control your ship."

"Bullshit. This is piracy. There's no evidence we did anything illegal. Your captain will pay for this outrage."

A cold smile crept across Toh's face.

"Actually, the sale of your ship as a prize will pay our captain, and the rest of us, a handsome little bonus. As to evidence, we overheard you communicate with people on the ground who engage in human trafficking. I daresay we'll find your holds equipped to feed and transport slaves.

Oh, you've hidden the evidence in case something like this happened before you could pick up your cargo, but we know what to look for, and where."

When he saw the expression of alarm on Ahmeti's face, Toh's smile broadened. Gotcha.

"That human trafficking operation has been put out of business permanently, so if you're hoping the Saqqa Cartel or its backers will bail you out of the brig, forget it. Everyone connected to the New Oberon end of the business, including you, will be cut loose. The only thing a judge needs is proof you carried human trafficking victims on this tub, and it'll be goodnight Irene because the Commonwealth government still executes slavers."

Warrant Officer Kondou stuck his head through the open bridge door.

"The crew is accounted for and shackled. They're in one of the holds. A few tried to resist and earned themselves nasty bruises but nothing permanent, unfortunately."

Toh pointed at Ahmeti and the helmsman.

"Add them to the lot. I need to organize the prize crew."

He found the communications console and opened a link with *Mikado*.

"So?" Piech asked the moment his face appeared on the main display.

"It's ours. Twenty-one crew, all taken alive. I've not walked through it yet, but there's no doubt they were transporting people for the cartel. Ahmeti's not good at keeping a straight face when he's under stress."

"Excellent. Well done, indeed. I'll let you settle in. Ghost Squadron's shuttles are on final approach. Once I speak with Colonel Decker about his intentions, we can figure out what to do with our prize."

"Could we please name this thing something other than *Sargon's Spear*, even if we end up landing it in Fort Lysander later today?"

A mischievous smile tugged at Piech's lips, and Toh raised a restraining hand.

"It need not be from The *Mikado* either, sir. Not if you're thinking about one of the hyphenated character names."

"Would I do that to you?"

"In a hyperspace second, Captain."

"Your temporary command shall henceforth be known as *Katisha*. It's the least comical name of the bunch. You're welcome. Call me when you're ready to sail her."

"Yes, sir. Thank you, sir."

"*Mikado*, out."

Petty Officer First Class Wermuth, who'd come aboard as helmsman-designate, entered the bridge moments later.

"They're damned slavers alright, Lieutenant. We found where they hide the slaver gear and rations between jobs. Too bad we didn't catch them in the act. I'd have enjoyed watching the bastards swim through vacuum."

"I may still find enough evidence in the ship's logs for summary execution. But right now, we need to make sure we can sail this thing and, if necessary, land it."

"When's the last time you landed a sloop, Lieutenant?"

"In real life? Never."

"Me neither. This could be fun."

"Or the captain could find people who've done it before and send them over."

Wermuth snorted.

"Why? I'm game if you are."

— Fifteen —

"Want to see it again?" Piech asked after showing Decker video of the penetrator rods vaporizing the Hogue estate on his day cabin's main display.

"Sure. A thing of beauty, that was." The Marine raised a coffee mug emblazoned with *Mikado*'s crest. "And good shooting too. Right in the middle of the target. Rods from God, indeed."

"I prefer to call it a holy cleansing. The Lord High Executioner in action, so to speak." Decker had given *Mikado*'s captain a thumbnail sketch of the horrors they'd found. "Here's to a righteous strike. What's next?"

"Ever heard of a little place called Kryani?"

"Way out in barbarian space?"

"At its darkest heart, buddy." Decker took a healthy swallow. "This could use go-juice."

"You realize it's not quite noon yet, ship's time."

"For those of us who stretched our legs, the sun is barely rising."

"Even worse. *Mikado* has the autonomy to visit Kryani, return home, and keep a good safety margin in the bargain. It's just a matter of plotting our course and heading out. Will you check with HQ before we sail where the Senate forbade us Navy types to go?"

"Check with HQ? Not really. Tell HQ? Sure. This is a Naval Intelligence-sponsored mission, and the head of the Special Operations Division expects me to go wherever necessary. Besides, it won't be the Commonwealth Starship *Mikado* and 'A' Squadron, 1ˢᵗ Special Forces Regiment who'll be violating the rules. What is it you call yourself again when you're undercover?"

"The merchant starship *Althea*."

Decker nodded.

"Right. It'll be the merchant starship *Althea* carrying a mysterious military outfit known only as Ghost Squadron, who'll head to Kryani. And when we operate under our cover identities, neither of us officially exists. In effect, a nonexistent vessel carrying a phantom ground unit will leave the Commonwealth sphere, and there are no rules against that."

Piech gave the Marine a look of resigned exasperation.

"If you're trying to make my brain hurt with your spook stuff, it's working."

Decker grinned at him.

"Story of my life. I used to be the man of a thousand faces, none of them my own. Now, I'm the commanding officer of a squadron whose missions never happened, in spite of the fresh crater where the country estate of New

Oberon's wealthiest citizen once stood. Spooky stuff is normal."

"For you, perhaps. And I used to think sailing a Q-ship into troubled parts of the Commonwealth was pretty daring for a Navy officer. We should discuss the future of that slaver ship we captured while you were smiting cartel garbage."

"Take it with us to Kryani."

"Why would we do that?"

"Think about it. If the cartel routinely ships humans there, we will be liberating more than just Warrant Officer Kine."

"Provided we arrive before something nasty happens."

Decker made a face at Piech.

"Keep a positive attitude, will you?"

"Fine. I'll be as positive as I can. And you think we might need *Katisha*—"

"Is that what you're calling her?"

"It's a fitting name since she's *Mikado*'s prize. As I was saying, you think we might need her?"

"To repatriate others of our species enslaved by the Kryani? Absolutely. We don't know how many the cartel sold there. But I'm sure it'll be more than your environmental systems can manage. Survey *Katisha* and if she's fit for a long trip — she should be, considering she was here for a pickup — give her enough crew, and I'll send over enough Marines who can handle her weapon systems. That way, we can bring home as many as we can save. What do you say?"

"Hard to argue with that sort of logic. Besides, Torrance Toh didn't sound particularly enthusiastic at trying to land the thing on Fort Lysander's parade square. But we will give Colonel Brozek the prisoners. We can't bring them with us on a round trip to Kryani, and they're not eligible for summary execution."

"I won't argue with you on that point. I'm sure—"

The chime of the day cabin's intercom cut off Decker's next words.

"Bridge to the captain. Colonel Brozek is calling from Fort Lysander."

"Speak of the devil. Put her through to my day cabin." Piech gestured at Decker to hide his mug with *Mikado*'s crest. Seconds later, the commanding officer of Battle Group Oberon appeared on the main display.

She nodded.

"Gentlemen. I just wanted to let you know a storm is raging down here. The colonial administration is spinning in ever-tightening circles. At this rate, it'll vanish up its own ass by noon. The New Oberon police are in an uproar and can't figure out how a gaping hole replaced Allard Hogue's country estate. In the meantime, word got out I'm housing over four hundred victims of human trafficking inside my perimeter, and the governor is demanding I release them into the government's care after telling him where I found them. Hogue was with the governor when he called, which should tell you something. Of course, I told him to pound sand. Politely. Fort Lysander is on lockdown until the ship you promised shows up and takes my guests. This is one of those times when I really enjoy the fact Commonwealth military installations enjoy extraterritorial status and are therefore out of bounds to planetary governments."

"The ship we promised is the naval transport *Pachino*, and she's somewhere in interstellar space on a course to New Oberon as we speak. Call it four days tops until she's in orbit," Piech replied. "I received confirmation an hour ago."

"Will you be able to keep the locals away until then?" Decker asked.

"Yes. At gunpoint, if necessary. The New Oberon commissioner of police, whom I didn't quite accuse of turning a blind eye to human trafficking on his patch, and I already exchanged harsh words. Once matters settle, I'll be sending a full report to my regimental commander, suggesting he rotate the battle group at once rather than at the end of a full six months. After this, I don't dare let any of my Marines off base on liberty."

"You're expecting police harassment?"

"Oh, yes. It's hard to convey how insane things are here right now. Your actions terrified a lot of people. And those who aren't scared are speechless with rage."

A grimace creased Decker's face.

"Sorry about that. If it were possible for me to take care of the victims without involving you, I'd do so."

Brozek made a dismissive hand gesture.

"No need for apologies. I don't regret helping you, especially not now that we're treating the injured and listening to their heartbreaking stories as the drugs wear off.

This is why we Marines exist, right? But I don't mind saying Fort Lysander feels under siege right now." When Decker opened his mouth to speak, she added, "Don't worry. We have what we need inside the berm, and because you probably wiped out most of the cartel thugs on New Oberon, I doubt anyone will try to attack. Anyway, I thought you ought to know about the situation."

"Thank you for calling, Colonel. And once again, we deeply appreciate your help. My CO will write to yours and formally commend you for your actions. And since we have you on the link, can I ask for one more favor?"

"Name it."

"We seized a pirate ship. It arrived during the night, Titania time, to pick up the unfortunates you're protecting. We took twenty-one prisoners who will enter the justice system as soon as Fleet Security processes them. But our mission isn't over, and we're about to head off in a completely different direction with that pirate ship under a prize crew. We'd appreciate it if you took the prisoners out of our hands since we can't hold them in our brig for what could be weeks or even months. They'll leave aboard *Pachino*, so it's only for a few days."

"With pleasure, sir."

"Thank you, Colonel. An unmarked shuttle broadcasting a naval beacon will land in Fort Lysander within the next ninety minutes."

"We'll keep an eye out for it. Was there anything else?"

"No."

"In that case, Godspeed and good luck with whatever you're doing next. Brozek, out."

Her image faded from the display.

Piech turned his gaze on Decker.

"Did you expect to stir up a political hornet's nest?"

Decker held up his hand, palm facing downward, and wiggled it from side to side.

"Yes and no. When we carry out a mission, we normally wipe out the target and leave little to no clues behind, hence my unit's nickname. However, this time, we needed to do something for the people we rescued, and that left a trace which, right now, ends at Fort Lysander's main gate. But it'll eventually lead the cartel's backers to blame the Fleet for carrying out a police operation without the New Oberon government knowing — a clear violation of the law. Except they can't complain about much more than that. I doubt they'll even go so far because it would raise uncomfortable questions about why the local police did nothing until an unacknowledged military operation took care of a known cartel problem. Perhaps it's a good thing the New Oberon government and upper crust are scared. They ran the planet their way for so long that the first sign of someone coming in with a big broom makes them go stupid. And stupid is easier to beat."

Decker drained his mug and stood.

"I'm holding a hot wash with my people in fifteen minutes. Then, I'll finalize the mission report for transmission to HQ. I'll tell Captain Talyn at the same time that we're heading for Kryani, where the cartel shipped

Warrant Officer Kine. How about you sort out the prize crew and work on the navigation plan in the meantime? We could conceivably break out of orbit later today."

"Only if you don't plan on waiting for a reply from Caledonia."

"I don't. I assume you intend to report the pirate's seizure?" When Piech nodded, Decker asked, "Will you wait for a reply?"

"No."

"Good. Because someone might get cold feet after this morning's performance hits the news nets. Best we're in interstellar space if that happens."

"Then you'll want our first jump to be long enough that we come out of FTL beyond the range of any subspace array."

Decker winked at Piech.

"Now you're thinking like me. By the time we're once again close enough to retrieve our messages, it'll be over and done."

"Better we ask forgiveness than permission, right?"

"It always worked for me. Well, there were a few missteps along the way, but here I am, a lieutenant colonel who enlisted as an eighteen-year-old private, rose to chief warrant officer and took his commission as a major."

Piech made as if he was choking on his coffee.

"A few missteps? Buddy, I've been speaking with Josh Bayliss, and your fuck ups were things of beauty. Of course, it makes your later successes that much more impressive."

"Why thank you kindly for saying so. And don't believe everything Josh tells you. He's as much of a tall tale spinner as any old-time Marine who was commissioned from the ranks."

"Speaking of tales, I've meant to ask, but what are those unusual names you gave your companies? I thought the Corps numbered them."

"You mean Erinye, Keres, and Moirae? I'm trying to start a new tradition in the 1st Special Forces Regiment. Instead of boring old numbers, I'd rather we use names drawn from mythology or history that personify our missions. Ghost Squadron collectively went with ancient Greece. The Erinyes were three infernal goddesses of vengeance and retribution who punished crimes. The ancient Romans knew them as the Furies. The Keres were goddesses who personified violent death, and the Moirae were the three Fates who controlled the thread of life of every mortal from birth to death."

Piech's eyebrows climbed up his forehead.

"Interesting. And disturbingly apt for your line of business."

A grin lit up Decker's face.

"That's the point."

— Sixteen —

According to Warrant Officer Aleksa Kine's internal clock, now that a drug-induced fog wasn't obscuring it, almost a week passed before the outer door opened to admit Aldar for the first time since he'd grouped those without technical or scientific backgrounds in a single room. Two overseers accompanied him. He ordered his captives to strip off their coveralls and stand with their backs against the wall. Once they'd complied, the overseers shackled their wrists and ankles.

"In a few minutes, the Great Chieftain of Ruqint's beastmaster will honor you. He comes to replenish his lord's kennels with new pets. Behave yourselves, or you'll feel a tickle from my little friend here." Aldar hefted his cattle prod. "With any luck, he'll take the lot of you."

Within moments, the slave market boss who'd picked the two largest men from the reject group, as Kine thought of herself and the other captives, ushered in a newcomer, another Kryani. He wore more ornate clothing than the boss, and sparkling gems adorned his flat, reptilian skull.

The two aliens spoke with each other in a sibilant hiss that grated on Kine's nerves. The visitor stopped in front of each shackled human and studied him or her with bulbous, unnerving eyes. He invariably groped arms and thighs with his four-fingered hands, as if testing muscle tone. When he reached Kine, he subjected her to the same treatment. She didn't flinch because she expected to feel rough digits tipped by black claws on her skin.

But when the Kryani's long, narrow tongue flicked out to lick Kine's cheek, she closed her eyes in disgust, grateful that the wall prevented her from involuntarily backing away. The tongue left a slimy, wet streak on her face, and when she breathed in through her nose, an unexpected odor of rotting meat almost made her gasp. She reopened her eyes only to stare into the being's mouth and noticed rows of sharp teeth designed by nature to rend flesh. The Kryani turned his head and said something, then moved on to the next captive.

"He especially finds you appealing," Aldar murmured as he passed her. "The lizards are nuts about human females."

Kine forced herself not to speculate what that might mean. By now, her imagination was running rampant, and nothing, not even the worst scenarios seemed impossible. Both non-humans finally left, but Aldar and his mates remained behind.

"We'll cut you loose so you can put your clothes on again. I know at least one of you will go to a new home soon." Aldar leered at Kine. "That flick of the tongue never lies."

With the captives unshackled and dressed, the overseers left them to speculate in silence about their fate. Several hours later, they returned, and Aldar announced, "He bought the lot of you, thank the gods. Leave your bedrolls right there and line up facing the door. You're headed for the high mucky-muck's palace. I won't wish you good luck. You've had none since the cartel took you prisoner, and that will not change no matter how long you live."

A large ground vehicle with a sizable windowless box behind an open-air cab waited outside. The cab sat on a large cylindrical assemblage of metal parts that spewed black smoke from a tall, thin stack near its front end while clouds of hot water vapor escaped through vents on each side as it idled.

Two soot streaked Kryani stood at the controls and watched with dead reptilian eyes as the human captives approached. The stench was such that Kine wondered about the nature of the fuel burning in what surely was a steam engine's firebox. She'd seen various iterations on some of the more hardscrabble outer colonies during her career, but none of them burned anything that exuded such a nauseating odor.

Aldar's men shoved them into the box, and when the last of the captives was aboard, they slammed the sheet metal doors shut with a loud clang. The vehicle lurched into motion, and more than a few of them lost their footing. With no seats or handholds visible in the faint light streaming through multiple air holes, Kine carefully lowered herself to the floor and sat with her back against one of the sides. The others quickly imitated her.

Whether the primitive truck owned something as simple as a suspension, Kine couldn't tell. Her rear end quickly became numb from endless bumps testifying to equally primitive roads. She couldn't hear anything above the machine's overwhelming noise and the constant, buzz saw vibrations from its drive train and didn't try to speak with her fellow pilgrims on the road to an alien hell.

At that moment, Kine surprised herself by wishing she'd kept the religious faith of her youth. Belief in the Almighty might help her face a future that seemed destined to be brief and brutal. But twenty years of police work, seeing the worst humanity could offer, had stripped any notion of a higher power from her soul. Witnessing the seven deadly sins in action and practiced with gusto taught her there was no redemption in this universe, let alone salvation.

She felt the steam truck turn this way and that at irregular intervals. Then, the vibrations and the pounding of its cylinders decreased at it slowed, though they went on for a while longer before grinding to a halt. The doors opened to let in both light and a dank miasma. A bald human head peered in.

"Last stop on the train to perdition, children. Everyone off. I'm Harko, the Grand Chieftain of Ruqint's principal non-Kryani slave. He's the top lizard on this planet. You can consider me his head of human resources."

A choked chuckle erupted from his throat, quickly replaced by a deep cough. When it cleared, he spat on the ground.

"As far as you're concerned, my word is law. I'm the only human in the palace who can communicate with our owners. The language is a bitch to learn and worse to speak. It practically rips up your throat's lining. If any of you are quick learners, do let me know. I wouldn't mind sharing the pain. Now climb out and line up."

They were inside a spacious barn-sized structure built from what resembled wood. Thick pillars buttressed the high ceiling while enclosures ran along both longitudinal walls. Tall windows provided the only lighting, though Kine saw torch holders everywhere.

The primitive truck lurched backward and chugged out through the open door, leaving clouds of soot and steam behind.

"Welcome to the ass-end of the universe," Harko said when the noise faded. "This is the human cattle building, where our sort lives. As rejects from the industrialization project, your sole use is to entertain his nibs. And when you're not doing that, you'll do physical labor under my supervision. Since this place has lower gravity than what most of us are used to, the labor will include stuff lizards can't or won't do by hand. Hint — the lizards do most things by hand. Only the rich and powerful can afford machines and modern stuff such as electricity.

"The enclosures you see are your barracks. That's where you spend the night, locked up, so you don't try anything stupid. And those cattle prods you saw at the slave market? We got 'em as well." He pointed to the far end. "Latrines are out through that door, as are the water troughs where you'll wash. Food is what the locals eat. It doesn't taste particularly good but has enough nutrients to keep humans alive, with nothing that'll make our sort sick. Other than sick of eating the same thing every damned day for the rest of our lives, for damned we are."

Harko surveyed the new arrivals with deep-set eyes beneath beetling brows.

"You can ask questions here. In fact, you'd better ask about everything and anything, so you don't fuck up. Our lords and masters will kill us for the slightest reason since we're only animals to them. Oh, if a random lizard kills the great chieftain's slaves, he'll pay for the damage, sure, just as you would back home when you run down a farmer's cow. But nothing more."

Kine raised a hand and Harko focused on her.

"What's your name?"

"Goldie Neves, boss."

"We don't use last names around here, Goldie. Don't need 'em. You got a question?"

"What's the average life expectancy for our sort?"

"Depends on how useful or amusing you are. Me, I speak their language and run herd over the human slaves. That means my life expectancy is pretty good, under the circumstances. If you're wondering about yours, the only thing I can say is live one day at a time. Worrying about tomorrow is a mug's game because there might not be a tomorrow if that's the grand chieftain's wish. I know it sucks, but that's the hand fate dealt you. Play it to the end.

"And if you try making that end happen yourself, don't miss your shot. Our owner doesn't tolerate self-terminating pets and generally inflicts as much pain as he can on survivors in the belief it'll teach us suicide is not a way out. Yeah, they don't understand how we think, mainly because they don't care. The Kryani consider themselves superior to any other species, and no amount of evidence showing the contrary will change their minds. Not even the fact our species operates faster than light starships. They don't even understand the concept of light speed, let alone how vast the universe is. Anything else, Goldie?"

"Plenty, boss. But maybe now is not the time."

"Talk to those who've been here a while. They'll be back from their daily work soon. They can tell you how it is. For now, you'll sleep in enclosure ten." He indicated a door painted with the human numeral. "When and if you end up on a work crew, you'll shift over to their enclosure. Go grab a bedroll and wait for the evening meal call."

— Seventeen —

A nattily uniformed aide with a braided gold cord hanging from his left shoulder ushered Rear Admiral Kos Ulrich, Head of the Special Operations Division and his chief of staff, Captain Hera Talyn, into the office of Admiral Darius Kruczek, the Chief of Naval Intelligence. Kruczek, a wizened, seventy-something, gray-haired man who'd joined the Navy before Talyn was born, gestured at the chairs in front of his desk.

"Sit. I understand you received Colonel Decker's mission report."

"Yes, sir." Ulrich nodded.

"Good. Because once you've apprised me of its contents, we're going across the hall to Grand Admiral Larsson's office where you will give him chapter and verse. The news nets heard of events on New Oberon, and as you might expect, rumors, half-truths, and outright lies are stacking up. Word may not have reached Earth yet, but when it does, there will be a political storm. Now, what happened?"

Ulrich gestured at Talyn to speak.

"Sir, as you know, Warrant Officer Kine's last report mentioned she saw and heard evidence of Saqqa using the Hogue estate as a waypoint for human trafficking. She was right. During their raid on the place, 'A' Squadron freed four hundred and seventy-two victims from confinement. The cartel maltreated many of the survivors and drugged all of them to ensure docility. 'A' Squadron found another six dead, killed by guards for sport and sexual gratification, including three children."

Kruczek's dark, bristling eyebrows rose in surprise at her words.

"Good lord."

"Over a hundred cartel enforcers died during the raid, but 'A' Squadron recovered the estate's entire database intact. The Saqqa Cartel keeps meticulous records, and we should close a lot of missing person cases over the next few weeks. They also kept extensive video records of them harvesting organs from live victims, engaging in torture to teach cartel enforcers the finer art of interrogation without drugs, and murdering victims as an initiation rite for members inducted into the inner cadre.

"Warrant Officer Kine was one of those slated for such induction. But she refused to kill the man designated by the cartel and was shipped out as a slave to Kryani, a charming barbarian kingdom in the rough part of the known galaxy. Unfortunately, the video evidence also showed the cartel attempting to interrogate Chief Warrant Officer Hazel Charlam and Lieutenant Commander Gerold Savarese, two of my officers assigned as Colonel Decker's reconnaissance team on New Oberon. They were captured when a local police surveillance unit spotted the floater watching Hogue's estate and reported it to their cartel friends. Since both were conditioned, they died under interrogation. The New Oberon police are as dirty as it gets, and we should consider its leadership a prime target for elimination."

When she paused, Kruczek gave her an encouraging nod. "Noted. Go on, please."

"Faced with almost five hundred innocents on his hands, many of them needing medical care, Decker enlisted the CO of the local Marine garrison, a Lieutenant Colonel Lea Brozek, of the 22nd Marine Regiment's Battle Group Oberon. He identified himself as a Code Excalibur, so while Brozek knows he's Fleet, she can legitimately say she doesn't know who carried out the raid. In any case, Brozek ran an airlift between the Hogue estate and Fort Lysander just before daybreak, using her integral aviation assets. The surviving victims are now under Battle Group Oberon's protection until the transport *Pachino* arrives. Once aboard, they'll head to Starbase 51 for debriefing and repatriation."

"Under Battle Group Oberon's protection. An interesting choice of words, Captain."

"Sir, as soon as the last shuttles cleared the Hogue estate, *Mikado* obliterated it with a kinetic strike from orbit. A few hours later, the New Oberon government got word of Brozek's Marines rescuing human trafficking victims from the property of the planet's wealthiest man, one who owns the governor and his administration. The commissioner of police ordered Brozek to surrender the victims, but Decker warned her they would vanish if the governor's minions took them from her. She therefore refused and told them in so many words that no one was entering Fort Lysander without her authorization and that she would open fire on anyone who tried."

"A brave officer."

"An officer who, thanks to Colonel Decker, saw enough evidence of what was going on at the estate with the full connivance of senior local officials and decided her unit was garrisoning hostile territory. I suggest Brozek and her battle group be replaced by a fresh unit as soon as feasible. They'll stay inside their fort so cartel operatives can't carry out reprisals. New Oberon is already unstable enough. We don't need running street battles between off-duty Marines and local goons."

"Or we could remove the entire colonial administration and senior police ranks," Ulrich suggested. "Which would allow the complete extirpation of cartel influence in that star system."

"A logical thought, Kos, but I doubt Earth will do something that drastic. Colonial governors are invariably friends of powerful senators or the Secretary-General himself."

A cruel smile lit up Ulrich's face.

"I wasn't planning on asking for permission from Earth. The New Oberon police, in particular, needs a good cleansing."

"I'll take the notion under advisement."

"Shortly after 'A' Squadron launched, a ship which figures in the Fleet BOLO list as a known pirate showed up, presumably to pick up the victims Colonel Decker saved. *Mikado* boarded and seized it without casualties, put a prize crew aboard, and handed twenty-one pirates to Colonel Brozek for safekeeping until *Pachino* arrives. Colonel Decker intends to use the ship, which they renamed *Katisha*, for the next phase of the mission. Captain Piech raised no objections."

"I can imagine what Colonel Decker intends with that prize. Please continue."

"*Mikado* sent us petabytes of data which still require analysis. I'm sure we will find evidence that discredits the Hogue family and ties it to cartels, human trafficking, and slavery. It should also prove the New Oberon government and its institutions are irredeemably corrupt and in need of wholesale renewal."

"If we, and by we, I mean Grand Admiral Larsson, make the evidence public. Remember the Hogues control one of Arcadia's two Commonwealth Senate seats, and Senator Graciela Hogue is one of the Centralist faction's leading lights. What Colonel Decker discovered could well be the political equivalent of a massive antimatter explosive device, destructive and unpredictable."

Talyn inclined her head.

"Understood, sir. But the news is already leaking, and someone will connect the events, which will lead them to Hogue, the colonial government, and ultimately to Arcadia. From there, it's a small step to the Centralist faction. At best, we can work to stay ahead of events so we can shape them in a way that will advance our plans."

Kruczek glanced at Rear Admiral Ulrich.

"She's learning fast, Kos. Maybe we can move up your promotion to deputy CNI. We'll discuss it when the current — I don't want to call it a crisis, but it may well become one — blows over."

"And that brings me to Kryani, sir."

"Proceed."

"*Mikado*, now under her cover identity as the freighter *Althea*, and the prize ship *Katisha* are well on her way to that barbaric backwater. By now, they're light-years beyond the Commonwealth sphere. Are you acquainted with the Kryani, sir?"

"Vaguely. A humanoid species whose society combines the worst aspects of our various civilizations circa the eighth or ninth century with industrial technology bought or stolen from unscrupulous merchants. They epitomize the term techno-barbarians."

"That's the bunch. They're not developed enough to maintain, let alone reproduce the technological artifacts they buy, hence the demand for human slaves. It seems the Saqqa Cartel became one of their suppliers. Or at least a supplier of the grand chieftain who nominally runs the largest and most powerful clan, and controls interactions with traders. With the data Decker retrieved on New Oberon, we'll know soon enough how many victims they shipped into that particular heart of darkness."

Kruczek didn't immediately reply, though his eyes remained on Talyn.

"We always knew," he finally said, "that some of the most powerful families in the Commonwealth were financing illegal ventures. Proof at least one of them is involved in the most despicable trade of all could cause a tsunami strong enough to shake the peoples' confidence in their political leaders on a scale not seen since the last Migration War."

"I'd say shatter what little remains among the citizens of the outer star systems, sir. Most human trafficking victims come from their worlds. Those living in the core systems don't and won't care. That's what makes this so dangerous. The last Migration War pitted the same two segments of humanity against each other, except now, the population on the Out Worlds rivals that of the core systems, and both groupings hold the same number of Senate seats. If this spirals out of control, we could face another civil war, except it would kill billions more than the last one. Hence the need to shape events so we don't face such an outcome."

Kruczek cocked an amused eyebrow.

"She's definitely ready for your job, Kos. Yes, indeed, Captain. But how we stay ahead of events and mold them to our specifications is Grand Admiral Larsson's decision." He glanced at the antique clock on a sideboard. "And we're expected in his office in five minutes. Was there anything else?"

"That was it, sir. In broad strokes. Details will be forthcoming as the analysis proceeds."

"I trust you put a top-secret special access designation on it?"

"Of course, and we're processing the data on a segregated network which has no physical connection to any other."

Kruczek stood.

"Shall we share this joyful news with the grand admiral?"

**

Larsson, a tall, lean, gray-haired man in his late sixties, studied Talyn with intense dark eyes once she finished essentially repeating what she'd told Admiral Kruczek earlier. The commander-in-chief of humanity's military forces pursed his lips in thought, then exhaled slowly through his nostrils.

"I've always been fascinated by examples of how small matters can turn into events capable of changing history. A wrong turn in a motorcar. Written orders lost by a courier. Our past is replete with them. Perhaps we're facing one of those events and we don't know it yet. A Constabulary warrant officer, working undercover on a criminal matter goes missing. We send in our best at the Constabulary's request and blow a slaver cartel wide open. And that cartel is abetted by the family which essentially owns both the New Oberon and the Arcadia governments, never mind the former is a federal colony supposedly controlled by Earth.

"It raises serious questions about corruption at the very heart of the Colonial Office. When this finally percolates through the news nets, outrage will explode in the outer sectors. And we're only talking the Hogues for now. Who knows what else will pop up once pressure increases; how many Centralist senators turn out to be thoroughly corrupt? The Out Worlds are already at loggerheads with the core and Earth over the issue of star system sovereignty. It could become one of those events that causes half of our species to reconsider its relationship with the other half."

"Hera recommends we shape events in a way we believe will avoid repeating the mistakes that led to the last Migration War," Ulrich said.

Larsson nodded sagely.

"Staying ahead of problems is always a good idea. The question is, in what direction do we push to keep the Commonwealth from sinking into a fratricidal war? And once we know what that is, will we be able to remain in control without causing unwanted second and third-order effects, a skill our political leaders never mastered?" He turned his eyes back on Talyn. "Tell me, Captain. How should we use the tempest triggered by that Special Forces squadron you unleashed on the Saqqa Cartel and New Oberon?"

Talyn glanced at her superior and long-time mentor.

"Privileged platform, Hera," Ulrich said. "Speak your mind. Nothing we say here, today, will ever reach anyone else's ears."

"We know where the current situation is heading, sir. The rift between the outlying sectors and the Commonwealth's core is growing. No one on Earth cares. They want to play power games and wallow in what they perceive as their moral superiority. If the Fleet sides with the Out Worlds to support star system sovereignty and encourages a split, we might establish military superiority over the core without fighting, especially now that you're reducing the units stationed there to mere placeholders. Then, after the new political entity consolidates it could systematically absorb the older star systems one at a time on its terms while avoiding the mass casualties that birthed our current political system, since it would englobe the old Commonwealth core."

"And how would we accomplish this?" Larsson asked after a long pause.

— Eighteen —

"Sir?" Firmin Yelle's cultured voice cut through a silence punctuated only by the ticking of the antique clock sitting on an equally ancient sideboard, flanked by busts of men who'd been dead for centuries.

Secretary-General of the Commonwealth Brodrick Brüggemann, humanity's head of state, looked up from his desk, frowning at the interruption. A portly man of sixty, with thick, wavy dark hair, penetrating eyes and a fleshy face, Brüggemann was an Earther born and bred. He had served as one of Earth's two senators before winning the SecGen's mantle thanks to a tidal wave of promises, political payoffs, and backroom maneuvers.

The Commonwealth Senate elected Secretaries-General from among its members, which was fortunate for someone of Brüggemann's caliber. He made up for his lack of charisma by ensuring his supporters were well rewarded.

"What is it, Firmin?"

Yelle, who'd ridden Brüggemann's coattails into the Secretary-General's office, bowed his head in apology.

"*Mes excuses, Monsieur le Secrétaire général,* but disturbing news just came across from the Colonial Office about an incident on New Oberon."

Brüggemann, who'd left Earth to visit the other human worlds only a few times during his life, and not once since becoming Secretary-General, felt a surge of irritation at hearing the name of a distant and unremarkable colony. His job would be so much easier if not for the petulance of the outer star systems.

They constantly demanded Earth respect their petty little sovereignty instead of working toward the greater good. Then there were the colonies agitating ceaselessly for independence, even though they were singularly unsuited to govern themselves. If only they would be more cooperative, as the Core Worlds were, he could make this a better Commonwealth for everyone.

"And?"

"Governor Theroux reports that an unidentified military unit attacked the country estate belonging to Allard Hogue, of the Arcadia Hogues. They killed every single employee and destroyed the property with a kinetic strike from orbit."

"Pirates? Someone with a grudge? The Hogues have plenty of enemies." Including many in the Senate's Out World faction, as Brüggemann knew only too well from his time as a senator. "Why did the Colonial Office think I needed to know right away? It could have waited until the weekly cabinet meeting."

"Because the local Marine Corps garrison, a battle group deployed by the 22nd Regiment, removed over four hundred people from the estate, supposedly the victims of human trafficking and is keeping them under guard inside Fort Lysander. The commanding officer refuses to allow colonial officials inside and has cut Fort Lysander off from the rest of the planet. She almost outright accused the New Oberon police commissioner and Theroux's administration of aiding a criminal cartel. Governor Theroux believes the people sheltering in Fort Lysander could be illegal migrants or worse. But he has no way of finding out because the Marines won't bow to his authority as your representative on New Oberon."

Brüggemann bit back an angry remark. He was the chief executive of humanity's interstellar government. Yet he couldn't simply reach out, tap Grand Admiral Larsson on the shoulder and ask him what the hell was going on, let alone make him order the Marine commander on New Oberon to stand down.

Grand Admiral Kathryn Kowalski made sure of that late last century when she redefined the Armed Services' relationship with the SecGen's office in a de facto constitutional coup d'état. Besides, Larsson was dozens of light-years away and would answer subspace missives from his nominal superior at his own pace.

But what was Allard Hogue doing on New Oberon that attracted the Fleet's attention? And yes, it had to be Fleet, because Brüggemann knew the local Marines wouldn't have cooperated with the attackers if they were anything else.

Were the Hogues financing a cartel engaged in human trafficking? Surely that family wasn't so arrogant it climbed into bed with organized criminals, believing itself above the law?

Once Out World politicians got a whiff of what happened, there was no telling how it would play out. Damn the Fleet and its growing tendency to intervene where it had no legal right. Attacking and destroying a privately owned piece of property because of a matter that belonged to the police was outrageous.

"Summon the defense and colonial secretaries to my office now, Firmin."

"*Oui, Monsieur le Secrétaire général.*" The aide bobbed his head and withdrew.

Brüggemann rose from behind his desk and went to the tall windows overlooking Lac Léman and the mountains beyond. Geneva was where humanity first attempted to unite under the League of Nations centuries ago. The attempt ultimately failed, as did its successor, the United Nations and that successor's offspring, the United Nations of the Stars. It ended with the First Migration War shortly after the initial wave of interstellar expansion founded colonies that almost immediately chafed under Earth's rule.

The UNS was replaced by the first Commonwealth of Stars, which in turn gave way to the Commonwealth of Sovereign Star Systems after the Second Migration War. But throughout it, Geneva remained, if not at the heart of humanity's attempts to become a single entity, then at least the main stage on which many global, and then interstellar dramas played out. And the venerable building in which he held court, once called the Palace of Nations, became the Palace of the Stars, though its core complex, at least outwardly, remained virtually unchanged by the passage of six centuries.

Brüggemann was shrewd enough to understand small events could sometimes entail major consequences. One of the Commonwealth's great families which virtually owned one of their star system's two Senate seats getting involved with a human trafficking cartel? That could easily upset the delicate balance of power between Core Worlds grown complacent and Out Worlds growing in power and influence. Especially since it was certain the victims recovered on New Oberon came from outlying sectors.

Gertrud Weyden, the defense secretary, arrived first. A senior bureaucrat with the vanity of her social class and enough family money to pay for the finer things in life, she was a perfect fit for her position. The commander-in-chief of the Armed Services acknowledged only the Senate as his civilian superiors, not the secretary of defense. And so, her role was reduced to that of a comptroller overseeing the defense budget, which hardly kept her occupied. Though Kowalski had tried, the Commonwealth executive at least retained control of the purse even though it lost control of pretty much everything else.

Blond, slender, and of middle height, Weyden wore the face of someone who used artificial means to stave off the ravages of age. She was much older than Brüggemann and the other secretaries, though she pretended otherwise.

Weyden flounced into the office with her usual fake smile and irritating energy.

"I hear there's a problem on New Oberon?"

He gestured at the antique upholstered chairs surrounding an equally ancient coffee table.

"Take a seat. We'll discuss the matter when Raimundo gets here."

The moment those words left his mouth, Raimundo Nauta, the colonial secretary, walked in with an air of concern on his broad face. Another career bureaucrat, but with real and challenging responsibilities, he was, in most ways, Weyden's complete opposite. Intelligent, without vanity, and desirous to make a difference, Nauta was one of the more respected cabinet members.

"I know, Brodrick. I should have delivered the news in person, but since you're preoccupied these days, I thought it best if Firmin passed along the message and let you choose the time of our inevitable meeting." Nauta took a chair next to Weyden's.

"What the hell happened on New Oberon?" Brüggemann sat across them and, elbows on the armrests, joined his splayed fingers in an affected pose.

Nauta shrugged and repeated almost verbatim what Firmin said, adding, "We don't know more than that. Rick Theroux isn't the Almighty's gift to colonial governance, but he's no idiot either. If he thinks the Marines landed on Allard Hogue's estate and freed a bunch of people held by a cartel before a Navy ship in orbit flattened it, then I'd say that's what happened. Except there's no proof. The only evidence that ties the attackers to the Fleet is the 22nd Marine Regiment's Battle Group Oberon taking charge of those imprisoned at the estate. And they're not on speaking terms with anyone."

"I realize that. And I also understand Grand Admiral Larsson isn't the sort of fool who'd launch an operation on a federal colony without political authorization if he didn't have evidence of serious criminal doings which might affect interstellar security. That being the case, we should take this matter seriously. It's happening out there, no matter how hard the Constabulary and local authorities try."

A frown creased Brüggemann's forehead.

"Tell me, Raimundo. How is it that the entire colonial administration didn't know about human trafficking in its own backyard, something of enough magnitude that the damn Marines came from afar and stomped it out? Are they that incompetent, or are Theroux and his people, down to the lowest ranking New Oberon police constable either in the cartel's pay or under its thumb?"

Nauta gave him a helpless look.

"As I said, Rick's not an idiot. But he is chummy with Allard Hogue and got the job thanks to Graciela Hogue. He was her nominee for the post."

"You're saying someone corrupted a colonial governor to the point where he ignores what is in effect slave trade happening in his jurisdiction? Do you understand what that means? What news of this getting out will do to Commonwealth politics?"

"I do. Those considerations occurred to me the moment I read Rick's report. There's no getting around it. This is bad. Really bad. Once the Navy picks up the victims now under Battle Group Oberon's protection and repatriates them, presumably after a thorough debriefing by both Naval Intelligence and the Constabulary, word will spread faster than an antimatter explosion."

"Did the Marine contingent's commanding officer on New Oberon actually suggest she thought Theroux and the police commissioner were in the cartel's pocket?"

"I saw a recording of the conversation. She did. Diplomatically, to be sure, but her meaning was clear. And she told the police commissioner if anyone breached Fort Lysander's perimeter, she would open fire."

"A lowly Marine lieutenant colonel doesn't enjoy such autonomy," Weyden said in a high-pitched voice tinged with outrage. "How dare she threaten public officials of the Commonwealth government?"

"If I knew those running the colony I'm supposedly defending are in league with the worst sort of criminals, Gertrud," Brüggemann replied in a patient tone, "I wouldn't mince words either. Nor would I neglect my security. Cartels can field combat troops."

"I suppose we should try to stay ahead of the news," Nauta suggested in a dubious tone.

"And how pray tell, will we do that when the Fleet is in control of events? Larsson won't listen to Gertrud, the Senate in plenary session, or me if he's dealing something of the sort."

"Find another grand admiral?"

Brüggemann turned his eyes on Weyden, irritated at her inability to understand the military mind. If it weren't because his nomination as SecGen came with a few 'suggestions' on cabinet appointments he'd have dumped her long ago.

"A replacement who would do our bidding will find him or herself ignored by the Armed Services. And anyone whose orders would be obeyed won't do what we want unless our orders coincide with the Fleet's agenda. Please keep up with how the military thinks nowadays, Gertrud."

"How about I replace the colonial administration wholesale?" Nauta asked. "Say every non-native New Oberonian on the civil side and the senior ranks of the police who are appointed by my office? When word gets out, we can state that regrettably yes, bad things happened, but see — we're already cleaning house."

"You'll do that, and more. Revoke New Oberon's permission to police itself and ask Public Safety for a Constabulary battalion on an emergency basis. They'll take charge of policing and ride herd on the locals. Call it a temporary measure until you're sure the cartel is no longer in control."

Nauta inclined his head in a gesture of obedience.

"Of course. An excellent suggestion. May I inform Public Safety you gave the order for that Constabulary battalion?"

"You may. But cleaning up the colonial government still doesn't help us with the Hogue issue. That's where the real problems will come from once his name and connections to the case are made public."

"Just order him shot," Weyden suggested, surprising Nauta. "And tell the rest of the clan they're next if they raise a stink. Isn't that why the Secretary-General of the Commonwealth has his dedicated security intelligence service? Sic your *Sécurité Spéciale* on him. Once the newsies announce his death, the family can distance itself and blame everything on dear sociopathic Allard."

Brüggemann cocked an eyebrow at her.

"I didn't know you were so bloodthirsty, Gertrud. And we will not speak of extra-judicial assassinations again, understood."

"Sure. Understood."

She bobbed her head respectfully and missed the gleam in Brüggemann's eyes. Nauta didn't, but he held his peace. If the SecGen decided Allard Hogue would meet his maker in the name of a greater good, it would happen. And since the penalty for slavery was death, Weyden's suggestion didn't seem as outlandish as it first appeared.

Brüggemann climbed to his feet.

"Thank you for coming so promptly. Raimundo, let me know when you've dispatched a new colonial administration. Gertrud, please make Grand Admiral Larsson aware my office does not condone the Armed Services carrying out unauthorized police actions inside the Commonwealth, and that I'd be grateful if he refrained from overstepping his constitutional bounds."

"For all the good it will do," Weyden muttered before pasting an insincere smile on her overly taut face. "Certainly, Secretary-General."

— Nineteen —

"*Katisha* is right where she's supposed to be, Captain," the sensor petty officer of the watch reported once humans and artificial intelligences recovered from the usual disorientation triggered by transitioning between hyperspace and the normal universe.

"Good. And are we where we're supposed to be?"

"Pretty much dead on, sir," Lieutenant Jill Corzon, *Mikado*'s navigator replied. "That bright orb gracing our main display is Kryani's sun. It matches the navigational data we extracted from *Katisha*'s computer core."

The pirate ship's database was a treasure trove of information on alien worlds in this part of the galaxy, data accumulated by those engaged in nefarious activities. Unfortunately, it didn't contain detailed lists of victims and their destinations. The cartel was smart enough to make sure a random naval inspection wouldn't uncover anything so incriminating.

"Let's find the planet, shall we?"

"Already doing so, Captain."

"Good. Signals, raise Lieutenant Toh."

A few moments later, the command chair's display came to life with Toh's face.

"Excellent station-keeping, Torrance. How are things on your end? Are *Katisha*'s systems behaving?"

"Nothing Chief Bukari can't handle. The previous owners took reasonable care of her. I've sailed worse pirate tubs than this blackbirder."

"And the Marines?"

"Going a little stir crazy, but we'll live. Mind you, we learned a few things from them I probably shouldn't repeat in polite company. Just a word of warning. Don't go near a bored Marine who's holding a deck of cards in his hands."

Piech chuckled at the rueful expression on his second officer's face.

"Noted."

The bridge door opened with a soft sigh.

"Are we there yet?"

Piech glanced over his shoulder at Zack Decker.

"Almost."

"And found it," the sensor petty officer raised his hand. "On screen now."

The image of a bluish-brown marble covered here and there by scraps of white cloud replaced that of its sun.

"The picture fits with the rest of the navigation data," Corzon said. "I'm preparing the inward jump now."

"There you go, Zack. We'll arrive in — Jill?"

"Thirteen hours."

"Good. I'm running out of new parkour routes that won't annoy your crew, so my people are getting just a bit bored."

"Do you want to switch out the contingent in *Katisha?* We can spare an hour or two."

"No. Let's not spare an hour or two. It might mean the difference between life and death for Warrant Officer Kine and anyone else sold to the Kryani grand chieftain."

Piech nodded.

"In that case, we'll go FTL across the heliopause as soon as our drives finish cycling. Any messages for your troopers before I let Torrance go?"

"No."

"Torrance, you're about to receive the navigation plot from Jill. Sync up and let her know when your drives are ready."

"Understood."

"*Mikado*, out."

Decker nodded at the main display with Kryani's image.

"Can we obtain a recording of whatever your sensors pick up? I wouldn't mind us studying the place while we're on the inward leg."

"There won't be much detail, sir," the sensor petty officer said, "but sure. It'll be in the mission repository."

"Thanks, and I know we won't see much detail but absorbing what we can of a target helps us visualize the mission and gain focus. It's a Special Forces Zen sort of thing. We enjoy meditating on the enemy's fate ahead of time."

"Is that your version of putting a hex on the opposition?" Corzon asked.

The Marine winked at her.

"Sure. Call it the Ghost Squadron magic."

**

"Well, well, well. There's a ship in orbit, and it's of human construction — a fast trader judging by the configuration. I'm running the image through Lloyd's Registry. Maybe we'll get a hit," Lieutenant Adjeng said once the first scans of Kryani from its hyperlimit passed through the CIC's tactical AI. "I wonder whether it's another cartel slaver."

"It doesn't matter what the damn thing is," Captain Piech replied. "If that's a shady trader selling the Kryani stuff they shouldn't be, he's just as liable for seizure as a blackbirder."

"Another prize?" Decker asked from his seat at the back of the CIC.

"Sure. We can handle crewing one more merchant ship for the return to Starbase 59. Taking jokers of that sort out of commission is our regular job, Zack. Carrying you fine Marines around from one target to another is a secondary duty. Mister Adjeng, please designate that ship as Tango One."

"Need heavy metal on the boarding party?"

Piech glanced over his shoulder at Decker.

"I was hoping you might offer."

"Another con?" Lieutenant Commander Cotto asked from the bridge. "They'll be shocked as hell if they suddenly spot a Navy frigate on their six offering a one year get out of jail free card in return for a safety inspection."

"No. I'd rather we give the Fleet plausible deniability with operations beyond the Senate-imposed limits. I think brute force is the way for this one. We'll call ourselves privateers, box him in with our two ships and threaten instant death. If he surrenders, we'll promise to drop the crew off on a safe world or hire them on ourselves."

"And if he'd rather fight back?" Decker asked.

Piech shrugged dismissively.

"Then we only bring one prize home, not two. Seizing scummy starships is fun but policing the star lanes by turning them into wreckage does the same job."

"I'll just point out that if there are more than four or five hundred humans down there who need rescuing, that second hull will come in handy, Skipper," Cotto said.

"Point taken, Hallie." Piech took a deep breath. "I'll try a con first. Make him believe we're Saqqa Cartel. Should that not work, then I'll use brute force."

"Agreed," Cotto replied.

Decker nodded.

"Seconded."

"In that case, let's turn into the most fearsome privateer on the Commonwealth frontier. Unmask, then go silent. Tell *Katisha*. Jill, plot a single burst at sublight that'll put us into orbit undetected so we can sneak up on him and see if he'll surrender quietly."

"I doubt the bugger circling that shit hole is keeping much of a watch. Besides, Kryani isn't putting out a lot of radio waves — most of them are damn weak, to begin with — so I figure orbital traffic control is nonexistent," Adjeng said. "We go up systems ten klicks from his six, and the crew will die of fright."

Decker chuckled softly.

"I love your crew's bloodthirstiness, Sandor."

"As I said, this is what we do for a living most of the time. And we're damn good at it."

"So are my Marines for seizing hostile ships, strong-points or pretty much anything else. A troop should suffice, right?"

"If it's a regular merchant, we're talking two dozen aboard, tops. So yeah. A troop in tin suits will do the trick. We just need to get them aboard, and that's where my guns come in."

"How long?"

Piech glanced at the tactical holographic display, then at the telemetry on a side screen.

"Seven or eight hours, since we're coasting. Less, if the bastard lights up. At that point, we'll convince him accelerating away will only mean a flight of anti-ship missiles coming up his drive nozzles. Unless they're fanatics with a death wish — and those belong to a small circle of socio-political nut jobs with quasi-religious delusions — it usually convinces them staying alive and showing up in court on charges of piracy is the best course of action. Especially if they have friends in low places."

"Such as the Saqqa Cartel."

"Yep."

"Not this time. With what we recovered at the former Hogue estate, any federal judge on the take will run for cover."

"I love your self-confidence, Zack. I really do. But the Hogues of this galaxy are beyond anyone's reach. As a cynical man once said, rules are for little people."

"We're already rewriting that rule book, buddy. Two or three years ago, HQ wouldn't have let us attack the Hogue estate even if we obtained proof of the cartel using it for the slave trade. They would have left the matter in the Constabulary's hands, and good luck with the search warrants and the chain of evidence, let alone a legal system twisted in favor of organized criminals who pay quarterly dividends to their backers. No more. That's why SOCOM stood up Ghost Squadron. We're just fanning a small breeze at the moment, but it'll strengthen fast, while we do the things our Constabulary cousins can't do, and our elected officials won't do, to keep humanity safe."

Piech cocked a questioning eyebrow at the Marine.

"What do you mean?"

"When the Devil whispers in my ear, *you cannot withstand the storm*, I whisper back, *I am the storm*."

— Twenty —

"Goldie!" Harko's voice echoed across the barn where she and the other human slaves languished between work assignments.

"Boss."

She climbed from her bedroll, muscles aching after days of hard labor repairing the palace's outside walls and shuffled out of her work group's enclosure to where Harko stood, arms akimbo. Her stomach cramped without warning, and she almost doubled over.

Kryani food might be digestible by humans and give those of her species the necessary nutrients for survival, but every meal left her feeling bloated and fighting off cramps while the tasteless goo they ate passed through her digestive system.

"What's up?"

"You. The grand chieftain has decided he wanted you to show him your fighting skills. He's fascinated by the whole concept of warrior women. Kryani females are breeders and not much else. They sold you as a fighter, which to their eyes, is exotic as hell. I hope that wasn't a lie."

Kine shook her head.

"I was in the private security business."

"A mercenary, eh? Any good at hand-to-hand, or with knives, fighting sticks, that sort of thing?"

"I'm trained in a few of the unarmed martial arts and can handle myself with non-powered weapons." Like all Constabulary members, especially those working undercover missions, she could have added if she weren't still keeping the truth to herself. "When will this blessed event occur?"

"Tonight. I'm bringing you to his nibs' arena in a few hours."

"Who am I fighting?"

Harko shrugged.

"Not a clue. Whoever his nibs wants. A Kryani, a human, a critter. Oh, don't worry, you'll be given about as fair a chance as anyone on this plugged lavatory of a planet. The chieftain's beastmaster bought you for entertainment, and since the lizards don't mate in the same way we do, fights are it. Our lord and master won't want his newest pet to die on the first attempt although I could be wrong. Still, there's nothing we can do but obey. Just make sure you fight as if you mean it. If he sees you trying to lose on purpose and get killed, it's the torture room and no second chances. They consider attempting death by gladiator the same as an attempted suicide."

"Understood. Besides, I'm not the sort to just up and die. Where there's life, there's hope."

A mirthless cackle escaped Harko's lips.

"There may be life here, but no hope. Rest up."

Kine returned to her bedroll, mind spinning.

"What's going on?" One of her groupmates asked.

"I'm to give the big boss a demo on how human females fight."

The man winced.

"Ouch. Try not to lose, okay. You're a good egg and work hard."

"Why? What happens with losers?"

"Not a clue, but we never see them again. If Harko knows, he isn't telling."

"Sounds ominous." Kine stretched out.

"Dying in the ring or when an unsecured stone falls on your bare noggin — dead is dead. At some point, you figure you'll never see home again. That's when a quick, painless death becomes the preferred outcome for just about anything."

When Harko called for Kine again a few hours later, her groupmates gave her encouraging thumbs up, but she saw in their eyes that they wouldn't be surprised if she vanished as others before her had.

"Follow me," Harko said when she joined him under the barn's high, curved ceiling. "I'll watch the fight along with the lizards, since none of them speak Anglic and wouldn't know how to tell you what they want, even with gestures."

"So, you've seen fights before?"

"Yep. Every single one since the lizards put me in charge of human resources."

"What happens with the losers?"

"If you lose, but his nibs wants to see you fight another day, you come back with me. Otherwise, his soldiers will take you away and you'll never see me again. And no, I can't tell you what happens when they take you away. No one ever came back to let me know."

Something in his voice made Kine the police investigator believe he was lying, that he knew what happened to humans who lost in the ring or otherwise displeased the Great Chieftain of Ruqint. But did she truly want this knowledge ahead of time?

They emerged from the barn into an early evening fog that turned every outdoor lamp into a blurry blob. Harko led her to a section of the palace she'd not visited yet, a single-story building apart from the main complex. Light spilled out of tall windows set at regular intervals, and she sensed life within, non-human life. They entered through a small side door and took a flight of stairs into the building's basement where mold-covered stone walls dripped with moisture. The stench of rot and death was strong here, and Kine fought to keep from retching.

"We'll go into the ring from here," Harko said. "When we stand in front of the great chieftain, we will show our submission by placing both our hands on our necks in this manner." He raised his in a chokehold. "Don't ask why. Just do it."

"Okay. Then what?"

"He tells me who you'll fight and with what so I can translate. After that, your opponent will come through the ring's opposite entrance. His nibs will order the start of the bout. Even though you won't understand the language, you'll know when that happens."

Harko took her up another flight of stairs and into a circular pit approximately ten meters wide. Its stone walls were a good two meters high and sand covered the rammed earth floor. Both humans stopped in the center and looked up at a richly adorned Kryani who could only be the Great Chieftain of Ruqint himself.

"And salute," Harko murmured.

They placed their hands around their throats for a count of three.

"Release." Harko turned on his heels and vanished back the way they'd come. A metal door slammed shut behind him, cutting off any route of retreat.

Unsure whether it was permissible for a slave to stare at her owner, Kine looked away, glancing at the rest of the spectators, two dozen of them, including the beastmaster who'd licked her with his long, narrow tongue. All stared at the captive with expressionless, bulbous eyes that unnerved her beyond anything she'd ever experienced. Here and there, tongues flicked out, as if tasting her scent, but none of them spoke.

Movement from the ring's other entrance caught her eye. A Kryani wearing what looked appeared to be a leather harness and nothing else stepped out onto the sand. Kine assumed it was a male because of Harko's comment concerning females, though she couldn't see any secondary sexual characteristics identifiable by human eyes, let alone overt genitalia. He turned to face the great chieftain and made a gesture of submission as well, but instead of grabbing his neck, he placed both four-fingered hands on his hairless, leathery chest.

The sibilant sound of swishing parchment paper filled the air as the great chieftain's jaw moved. Kine spotted Harko stepping out of the shadows from the corner of her eyes.

"The Great Chieftain of Ruqint orders a claw-to-claw fight between the champion of his personal guard and the alien animal before him."

Kine's heart sank. Champion of his personal guard? Granted, she was quicker and stronger here thanks to the lower gravity, but the Kryani was as tall as she was, and though his reach was shorter, his claw-tipped fingers would be dangerous weapons.

"He commands you to fight well and prove your worthiness as one of his pets. Since you are defective and lack claws, he allows you a knife." Harko raised his arm and a shining blade, almost thirty centimeters in length, attached to a bone handle landed on the sand beside her. "Pick it up and hold it above your head to show your gratitude."

Kine did as he told her. The knife didn't feel balanced, and its grip seemed to be shaped for Kryani hands, but she couldn't fault the keen edge or sharp point.

A harsh sound came from the chieftain. Kine recognized it as an order and instinctively adopted the knife-fighting posture she'd been taught years ago, eyes on her opponent who seemed rooted to the spot as he studied her stance.

Kine could usually read her human opponents when she practiced martial arts, but this strange being gave off no clues as to his mood or his intentions. When he finally came at her, both arms outstretched, perhaps intending to hook his claws into her arms, Kine moved out of his way, her speed compounded by the planet's lower gravity. The Kryani skidded to a halt and reoriented himself.

Though she felt nothing for the being in front of her, no sense they were fellow intelligent beings, Kine couldn't push herself to attack and draw first blood. She was still a cop beneath the grimy slave coveralls.

Sand crunched beneath her sandals as she shifted every time her opponent charged. The chieftain's voice reached her ears, and it didn't take Harko's translation to tell her he was unhappy at seeing a dance when he wanted a fight.

Kine's opponent charged again, but this time, she used her greater reach, lengthened by the blade to swipe at his right arm before shuffling aside. A startled hiss erupted from his half-open mouth when blood welled from the deep cut.

As if galvanized by the pain, he came at her with greater vigor than before, and Kine lost her balance trying to avoid his claws. The Kryani pounced. She rolled away just as his outstretched fingers raked her right arm, drawing blood. A rumble of what might be approval filled the air above her. Kine doubted it was because of her last-second evasion.

The wounds stung more than they should have, and she briefly wondered whether those claws were coated with venom. Both fighters climbed to their feet, watching each other intently. For a moment, Kine hoped the chieftain would call an end to the bout, now that each of them bled in equal measure. Yet both he and Harko remained silent.

The Kryani seemed to know only one move. Charge with claws leading the way. Perhaps they fought by grappling. Those pointy teeth would do wonders at ripping out an opponent's throat. Use the claws to hold on, then chew until the other guy chokes on his gore.

He came at her again, but she let her instinct take over and crouched a fraction of a second before he made contact. As he flew over her, she raised the knife and plunged it into his abdomen. Momentum took him beyond her, but instead of rebounding, the Kryani remained still, blood gushing from the deadly wound.

Kine slowly stood and stared at her opponent. A rustle of alien speech filled the air, rising with each wave until it threatened to assault her sanity. She turned toward the chieftain and stared at him defiantly while the alien warrior let out one last gasp, then seemed to deflate as life left his body. The chieftain raised a hand, and the noise ceased instantly. He hissed for a few seconds, then stared at Harko.

"Our lord condemns you for killing his champion and ending the bout before its time," the overseer said. "You shall be taken from here and placed in the pens until you become the most honored presence at our lord's next feast."

Kine caught the beastmaster sticking out his tongue again, and she fancied she saw a hungry look on his flat face but knew in the same instant she was anthropomorphizing.

"What does that mean?" Kine asked.

Instead of answering, Harko turned on his heels and vanished into the shadows. At the same time, one of the ring level doors opened, and four Kryani dressed in identical jerkins and harnesses and carrying crude chemical propellant weapons emerged. Two of them seized her, one on each side, their claws digging into her biceps, and yanked her toward the dark opening.

The soldiers half carried, half dragged Kine to a part of the palace complex Harko said was out of bounds for humans on pain of instant death. Knowing she was fated to die, Kine didn't bother struggling. There would be no escape on this alien world.

They took a stone ramp and entered a basement door that stood open to the evening air. Almost immediately, a stench of blood and offal assailed her nostrils. She found herself in a long, narrow, low-ceilinged room dominated by several large wooded tables bearing dark stains. Various bowls, pots, and cutting implements hung from hooks set into the stone walls or dangling from blackened ceiling beams.

A Kryani wearing a stained leather apron appeared as if by magic and, after taking a brief look at her, headed for the back of the room where he opened a door. The soldiers dragged Kine through it, pushed her against a damp, moldy wall and snapped metal shackles dangling from the ceiling on her wrists, adjusting their length so her arms were extended almost vertically above her head, and her feet barely touched the floor.

The soldiers left and once they were alone, the aproned Kryani walked up to Kine and examined her closely. She almost gagged when his rotten breath washed over her. A tongue flicked out and left a slimy trail on her left cheek, but she forced herself to stare into the alien's soulless eyes.

He uttered a sound resembling a grunt and produced scissors from his apron. He cut off her clothes until she hung there, naked. After tossing the coverall remnants aside, the Kryani stepped back, studied Kine for a few more seconds, then left the cell. He returned after a brief interval, carrying a container with several attachments sprouting from its upper surface. He placed it on the ground near her, deployed a short length of hose, and pulled a pump handle upward. When he rammed it down, a stream of cold water hit Kine's face, making her gasp.

The stream played over her body, top to bottom, back to front until it trickled off to nothing. After the last few drops vanished into the drain at the center of the room's floor, her captor stepped close and his tongue touched her skin once more.

The Kryani grunted softly, stowed the hose and carried the container out of her cell. He returned a few minutes later, loosened her chains so she could sit, but no more, then left. With the door closed, her cell was plunged into darkness, and the fears she'd been suppressing all evening bubbled to the surface.

No one ever accused Kine of owning an overactive imagination, but at that moment, she thought she knew what her fate would be. And though everyone heard apocryphal stories of dire rituals on alien worlds, none had ever been confirmed beyond a doubt. Perhaps her final moments would prove one of the most horrifying was true.

— Twenty-One —

Secretary-General Brodrick Brüggemann looked up when he heard Firmin gently clear his throat by the open office door.

"Yes?" He put down his reader.

"Senator Hogue begs for five minutes of your time, *Monsieur le Secrétaire général.*"

Brüggemann swallowed a sigh of irritation. He already knew what she wanted and couldn't muster enough energy to discuss the finer points of Commonwealth law with her. News of the New Oberon incident was spreading as predicted and had become the subject of debate in the Senate a few days earlier, with the expected Core Worlds-Out Worlds split, only it was more acrimonious than ever.

Though many privately pointed the finger at a rogue Armed Services unit for carrying out the raid on the Hogue estate, no one was foolish enough to say so openly, let alone on the Senate floor. And so far, Brüggemann's administration was keeping the focus on criminal cartels.

Surprisingly, the Fleet was doing so as well instead of pointing out the cartels could only operate with such impunity because of political corruption on New Oberon and elsewhere. Even more astonishing, Grand Admiral Larsson had shared a summary of the Fleet's findings with him. Of course, Larsson was following his own agenda, as Brüggemann well knew. But if their goals coincided for once, so much the better.

The matter of human trafficking victims coming from the Hogue family's New Oberon estate wouldn't go away, and Brüggemann could only hope against hope they found a way to deal with it that wouldn't deepen the crisis. The estate itself was gone, along with the supposed cartel enforcers who worked there, and the Fleet's evidence was too tainted for a court of law. But the court of public opinion would look for justice.

If Allard Hogue could make a good case he was unaware of cartel activities because he never visited and left matters in the hands of his trusted, and now sadly vanished manager, it might raise enough doubt to avoid a formal investigation. But if incontrovertible evidence surfaced, things would get ugly. Allard might well threaten to expose the colonial administration's corruption should he find himself in front of a judge, which would reflect badly on the Commonwealth government as a whole.

And his cousin, Senator Graciela Hogue, who understood the ramifications should they not prevent the legal system from connecting her family with the Saqqa Cartel, wanted to make sure that would never happen. Brüggemann checked his calendar, knowing their conversation was inevitable.

Besides, Hogue and her colleague from Arcadia were among those who voted to install him as the Commonwealth's head of state, and he couldn't just brush her off.

"Tell the honorable senator it would please me to receive her at fourteen hundred hours today."

"I shall do so right away, *Monsieur le Secrétaire général.*" Firmin bowed his head before withdrawing.

At the appointed time, he ushered Graciela Hogue, a short, plump fifty-something woman with a face permanently set in a disapproving frown, into Brüggemann's office.

"My dear Brodrick. Thank you so much for receiving me at such short notice."

"For you, anything." They exchanged patently false smiles and a limp handshake before Brüggemann indicated the coffee table and its circle of chairs. "Please, sit. Can I offer you something?"

"If you still have some of that delightful Blue Mountain, then I accept."

"I do. Firmin, ask the kitchen to send up the necessaries."

The aide bowed his head and vanished while they settled across from each other.

"You look well, Graciela."

"As do you. The strain of your high office barely shows."

"How are your children?"

"Prospering. My eldest, Yannik, has been commissioned into the 2nd Marine Regiment and will come to Earth. We're very proud of him. He joined the Corps under his late father's family name, so there wouldn't be any favoritism."

"Commendable, though I should think he performs splendidly under any name."

"How kind of you to say so, but yes. My son is incredibly smart and talented. Much more so than those grubby officers you hear about causing no amount of trouble in the frontier sectors. Such as that deplorable colonel on New Oberon who insinuated my cousin Allard was guilty of a capital crime. And only because she rescued people who should not be there in the first place. Never mind an evil entity destroyed our property and murdered every single employee retained by the estate's manager. What is the Commonwealth coming to?"

Brüggemann sat back, placed his elbows on the arms of the chair, and joined his hands at the fingertips while studying Hogue.

"The Commonwealth, Graciela? Or your family? That a human trafficking cartel used your New Oberon estate as a transfer point to slave markets on alien worlds is, at this point, beyond dispute. The victims were interviewed, and the slavers coming to pick them up were captured by the Navy."

When he saw her rear up in outrage, Brüggemann raised his right hand in a signal to stay silent.

"This leaves us with only two options. One, Allard didn't know what was happening at the estate because he placed his confidence in the wrong property manager. This would mean he's incompetent and cannot be trusted to oversee an ice cream stand, let alone exercise surreptitious control over the administration of a federal colony. Oh, yes. We're cognizant of his activities on New Oberon since the day my predecessor once removed forced Arcadia to surrender it. The new governor and his staff will not tolerate any interference by the star system you represent, nor will the Constabulary battalion on its way there as we speak. Please make your friends and family aware Arcadia's influence, be it ever so benign, is no longer welcome."

A smile briefly crossed Brüggemann's face when he saw Hogue press her lips together in annoyance.

"The other option," he continued, "is that Allard was not only aware but actively supported the cartel in return for a lot of money. Since he's the apple of Elize's eye, I'm sure the rest of the Hogues are on good terms with the cartel as well. Is it possible one of the most powerful Arcadian families has fallen on hard financial times? Or is it mere greed?"

"I resent your implication we would support the practice of slavery, Brodrick. Take care with your words."

"Or what? Come now, finish your threat so we can discuss the next steps. But remember, the facts are not in question. The Navy has the evidence it needs, though it was obtained in a manner precluding prosecution."

When she refused to speak, contenting herself with a hard glare, he shrugged.

"We cannot allow this matter to become a major point of contention between the Core World and Out World factions in the Senate, the government and the population at large. And that means more must happen than just replacing the administration and police on New Oberon *en masse*. Allard messed up. Badly. He didn't keep a tight rein on the senior cartel man running the New Oberon operation. An undercover Constabulary officer sent to investigate became a victim in turn, which led to a rescue attempt by the Fleet, though its participation will never be officially acknowledged or confirmed. Should the raiders have flattened your family's estate and killed everyone within save for the trafficking victims? Probably not. But most Commonwealth citizens would applaud if they knew the truth."

"Will they?"

"We want to avoid that, my dear. However, it means Allard takes the fall and exonerates your family, or the stench of guilt will surround every Hogue, ending your career as a senator. I prefer the former to the latter. It would save the Centralists and me from a nasty confrontation with Elize when your peers eject you and demand a representative from Arcadia who is not related to anyone named Hogue."

"I'm sure I don't understand what you mean."

"You do. I can see it in your eyes. One does not become a Core World senator without a ruthless streak ten parsecs wide. Publicly disavow Allard and arrange for him to take his own life as atonement. Or to escape justice. It may not create a credible gap between the cartel and the Hogues of Arcadia, but there's no better path available."

"Elize will never allow it," she replied, naming the Hogue family matriarch, a redoubtable centenarian who was the real power on her home world.

Brüggemann shrugged dismissively.

"In that case, Elize can deal with the consequences. The wealthy and powerful might escape punishment for committing any of the seven deadly sins, but abetting slavery isn't among them, especially when the trade sends humans to alien worlds as chattel. You want me to make this go away? Sorry, I can't. No one can. It's time to enter damage control mode. I'm putting the matter in your hands, Graciela. It would be best if Allard left this life on his terms or those of the family rather than by an assassin's hand. Once he's dead, you, as Senator Hogue, will publicly repudiate Allard and offer your star system's apologies for not noticing such evil at the very heart of Arcadia's most prominent clan."

The casual way in which he spoke those dire words finally seemed to penetrate her shell of denial because she visibly paled.

"Nothing will save Allard, but you can at least minimize the fallout. And I suggest you do your best because what friends you still claim in the Senate will quickly disavow you lest they too become tainted." At that moment, Firmin entered with a tray holding a porcelain coffee service and a steaming pot. "Ah, the Blue Mountain. Wonderful."

Hogue stood in a jerky motion and said, "My apologies, Brodrick, but I won't stay for coffee. If you'll excuse me."

"Certainly."

Brüggemann didn't bother rising or offering his hand. He merely watched Firmin escort her out of his office, then poured himself a cup, happy at how the meeting had unfolded.

Judging by her reaction, she knew what was going on before the Marines raided her family's New Oberon estate. Perhaps it was time the *Sécurité Spéciale* took a good look at the entire clan's financial situation. If they were filling the coffers through illegal schemes, that evidence might come in handy if ever there was a close vote in the Senate.

— Twenty-Two —

Decker entered the hangar deck to see off Clayburn Knudsvig's F Troop, who'd won the honor of escorting *Mikado*'s boarding party. His troop finished with the best score in the simulated battle run competition during the trip to Kryani.

"Ready, Clay?"

Knudsvig stomped to attention, his armored boot raising a satisfying thump that echoed off the bulkheads.

"As always, sir. Those fuckers won't know their own mothers' names when we finish with them."

F Troop, formed in three ranks beside the boarding party's shuttle, stood easy, helmet visors open as they waited for the order to load up. The naval component, also in combat armor this time, was in a cluster on one side, going over Lieutenant Dulay's instructions one last time. As next in order of seniority among the ship's space warfare officers after Torrance Toh, Dulay would become the target's prize master once they seized it. If they seized it. Sometimes, it only took a desperate crew member who knew he faced summary execution and tried to take everyone with him.

Decker clapped Knudsvig on the shoulder.

"Good hunting."

He nodded at Dulay as he crossed the hangar and headed for his battle stations post in the CIC.

"How are we doing?" Decker asked when he entered and dropped into a seat at the back.

"He's still orbiting fat and happy," Piech replied over his shoulder. "We're about to slip in behind him. He can't run anymore."

Decker and Piech watched the tactical projection intently for a few minutes until Lieutenant Adjeng raised a hand.

"We're within effective engagement range, Captain."

"Thank you. Bridge, time to go up systems. Mister Adjeng, raise shields and pound Tango One with our targeting sensors at maximum strength."

"Aye, aye, sir."

"I'd love to be on that bastard's bridge right now," Decker said.

"*Katisha* is lighting up."

Piech nodded in reply. He knew Torrance Toh would keep a close eye on *Mikado* and do as she did within seconds.

"Shields are up, targeting sensors are pounding, and weapons systems are ready to open fire, sir."

"Signals open a link with the tango. Audio only."

"Tango One has raised shields and is powering weapons," the sensor tech reported.

Almost a minute passed before a rough voice came over the speakers.

"Who the fuck are you, and what do you want?"

"I'm your worst nightmare," Piech replied. "You heard of the Saqqa Cartel, right?"

The man at the other end didn't immediately reply. His next words, when they came, sounded tentative.

"Yes. Are you—"

"Saqqa? You bet. And you're in our territory. We own Kryani."

Another pause, then, "No one told us."

"What are you doing here?"

"Trading. We're independent merchants who go where regular traders won't."

"And what, pray tell, is the nature of your merchandise?" Piech's tone took on a menacing hint of impatience.

A few seconds of silence again.

"Weapons."

"Are you insane? Selling weapons to the Kryani? Especially without the Saqqa Cartel's approval?"

"We're talking chemically propelled slug throwers only. The lizards can't fabricate blaster and plasma rifle ammo, let alone power packs."

"Slug throwers can still kill a man who's not wearing combat armor, sunshine. Tell me you didn't deliver your load yet."

"My captain is on the ground right now with our shuttles and the cargo. They're dickering with a human slave who works for some local great chieftain."

"Wonderful. Meaning you're the first mate?"

"Yep."

"Tell me, Mister First Mate, you're delivering these weapons on behalf of someone. Independent traders rarely dabble in old-fashioned ordnance for primitive species."

"Um. Yeah."

"Who?" Piech spat out the word.

"Our client pays well to stay anonymous."

"My guns don't know the meaning of anonymity. Tell me who, and I'll make sure they don't send hapless civilians into a Saqqa-controlled star system again. Stay silent, and you'll see a single warning shot crease your hull. It'll leave a nice black streak that can't be removed short of entering dry dock."

"The Confederacy of the Howling Stars," he finally said in a resigned tone.

Piech and Decker exchanged a surprised glance. The Confederacy of the Howling Stars, founded by disaffected veterans of the war with the alien Shrehari Empire over seventy years earlier, was a ruthless criminal organization, but not nearly as ruthless as the cartels which had sprung up along humanity's frontiers in more recent times.

The Howlers, as they were colloquially known, didn't engage in piracy or human trafficking, or any other activity for which the penalty was death, especially those entailing summary execution if caught in the act. And they operated mostly in the Rim Sector, on the other side of the Commonwealth sphere.

"How the hell did the Howlers decide selling weapons to primitives such as the Kryani was a good idea?"

"Hey, we're just the delivery service."

"And what are you getting as payment?"

This time, the first mate paused for a longer period.

"Drugs. Stuff that grows on Kryani and gives humans an incredible high. They told us police sniffers can't detect it."

Decker nodded. The Howlers were up to their necks in the illegal drug trade. And if they sourced this stuff far from their normal hunting grounds, it meant the Saqqa Cartel was probably taking payment in drugs as well for the humans they brought here.

"That stuff belongs to Saqqa, which means you face a problem. You can't run, and you can't hide. The only thing you can do is take a shuttle ride."

"What?"

"If you and your crew want to live, you'll do exactly what I say. The Saqqa Cartel's rule is one chance at redemption. Fuck it up, and instant death ensues. Here's how it'll play out. Your ship now belongs to the cartel, as a penalty for entering our territory. We will offer everyone aboard the chance to join Saqqa once we return home. Those who'd rather not will leave the Shield Sector and never return on penalty of death. However, in the meantime, you'll be my guests while I put sworn cartel members aboard your former ship."

"You can't just steal our ship. That's piracy." The first mate's outraged tone didn't quite mask an undercurrent of fear.

"Would you rather die?" When he didn't reply, Piech said, "Everyone aboard will cram into a shuttle with their personal effects. You'll launch that shuttle and settle into orbit five kilometers below us, where we can keep our guns on you. And we will check with our sensors to make sure you obey. Once we're in control of the ship, I will take your shuttle aboard and settle you in our guest quarters. Any false moves, any attempt at sabotage, the slightest bit of resistance, and you will die. No second chances. If you've heard of the Saqqa Cartel, you'll know we don't screw around."

"What about my captain and the three others who are down there with two of our shuttles?"

"They can land in my ship and join you. Or stay on Kryani and go native. I don't much care," Piech replied in a bored tone. "Now, what'll it be? Life and a chance to work for the Saqqa Cartel? Or death? My guns are ready, and my trigger finger is itching."

Piech glanced around the CIC. Everyone was watching him with either an amused smile or a broad grin — especially Decker, who gave Piech an appreciative nod and thumbs up.

"How do I know you won't just kill us?"

"Because I'm a man of my word. If you don't cooperate, I *will* kill you. That's a promise."

The sincerity in Piech's tone seemed to work because the trader's first mate said, "I guess Fate has fucked us with her fickle finger. All right. Give me half an hour to make sure everything is on automatic and launch the shuttle."

"How many will be aboard that shuttle?"

"Nineteen. We're twenty-three in total. What do I tell my captain?"

"Since your captain has probably been listening in on our conversation from the get-go, you need not say anything. Right?"

"Sure." Resignation weighed heavily in his reply. "The landing party is stuck negotiating with the lizards for a while longer anyway, so no worries."

"Leave your hangar deck's space doors open and disable the access codes on your various interlocks so my folks don't need to dick around, which would annoy me. Making them dick around will not help your cause when it comes time to join Saqqa."

"Understood. Can I ask what your name and that of your ship are?"

"Sure. I'm Sergei Lermontov, and my ship is *Althea*. How about you?"

"Fridolph Lazaro, of the fast trader *Pallantis*."

"Well, Fridolph Lazaro, you made the right choice. If you join us, you could enjoy a prosperous future. Perhaps our superiors might even give you a command of your own. And depending on the choices your captain makes, that command could be *Pallantis*. By the way, what is your captain's name?"

"Magdalene Bustos, though she prefers to be called Mag."

"Make sure Mag understands she's welcome aboard *Althea*, provided she behaves. And call us when you're ready to launch."

"Will do."

"*Althea*, out."

When Jenks nodded to indicate he'd cut the link, spontaneous applause broke out in the CIC and on the bridge.

"If the Navy ever becomes boring, you can reinvent yourself as a thespian, Skipper," Lieutenant Commander Cotto said. "That was a remarkably chilling performance."

"Let's just hope Lazaro or Bustos do nothing stupid."

Cotto chuckled.

"No worries. If you gave us the chills, imagine how they feel?"

"Like crapping their pants," Decker said. "I'll organize an armored troop for the hangar deck to receive our guests and search them thoroughly. We wouldn't want to find out the hard way they're carrying nasty surprises."

— Twenty-Three —

"There he comes." Lieutenant Adjeng nodded at the main display showing *Pallantis* as she disgorged a large civilian shuttle through her aft-facing space doors.

"Nineteen separate life signs aboard," the sensor tech added. "I can't pick any up in the ship, and no anomalous energy readings either."

"I'm painting it with our targeting sensors. Their detectors should be screaming right now. Pucker factor twelve and climbing."

"He's playing it safe," Decker said.

Piech glanced over his shoulder.

"I doubt we're dealing with hardened criminals or suicidal fanatics. The traders out here might skirt a lot of Commonwealth laws, but only because we can't enforce them. There's a lot of profit in exporting restricted items to more primitive worlds, such as chemically powered firearms and other bits of technology a society on the cusp of industrialization might desperately want." He tapped the controls in his command chair's armrest. "Captain to the boarding party, you're clear to go. Take care."

Dulay's voice came on at once.

"Acknowledged. We're launching."

"CIC, out."

Several minutes later, one of *Mikado*'s unmarked combat shuttles appeared on the main display as it carefully lined up with *Pallantis*' open space doors. It nudged its way through the force field keeping the air in and vanished from view.

"Mother Goose, this is Gosling One; we are disembarking."

The view from the CIC shifted to Lieutenant Dulay's helmet pickup and showed her walking off the shuttle's aft ramp on a narrow hangar deck with four parking spots, three of them empty. Piech, Decker, and the rest of the CIC crew watched as Dulay approached the airlock, cycled it, and stepped in with a squad of armored Marines. They saw her looking at a control panel.

"I'm closing the space doors." Shortly afterward. "There. She's buttoned up. I'm opening the inner airlock door."

F Troop's Marines cautiously passed through and fanned out to check every single compartment, first with handheld battlefield sensors, then with their own eyes. Almost half an hour passed before Dulay's voice came over the CIC speakers again.

"Sergeant Knudsvig reports the ship clear of life and traps. I'm heading for the bridge."

Piech glanced at the first officer's hologram, hovering by his elbow.

"Please bring our guests aboard, Hallie."

He turned to the sensor tech. "Find those shuttles on the ground and see if we can pick up Warrant Officer Kine's tracker signal."

"You figure we should prevent them from handing over the bang sticks?" Decker asked.

Piech shook his head.

"No. The Kryani are welcome to plug each other with lead slugs until the universe collapses. I want to see the shuttles from a good distance, in case *Pallantis'* former captain does something unwise."

"Mother Goose, I control the ship," Dulay reported. "Did you wish to change her name, or will we stay *Pallantis?*"

"Since I suspect you'll be annoyed at me if I pull a name from our favorite comic operetta, *Pallantis* she remains."

"Thank you, sir. Commanding the good ship *Pooh-Bah* isn't high on my list of life goals."

The sensor tech raised his hand.

"Sir, the shuttles fired their thrusters to lift. Designating as Tango Two and Tango Three." A pair of red icons appeared in the tactical projection, now dominated by a representation of Kryani. "They were smack dab in the center of a large settlement. The largest on that continent."

"Probably the great chieftain's capital," Decker said. "Concentrate your search for Warrant Officer Kine's tracker in that area to begin with."

"Aye, aye, sir."

"Hangar deck to the captain."

Piech touched his seat's embedded controls. "Captain here."

"The shuttle from the prize is aboard, sir," the hangar deck petty officer in charge said. "They're disembarking without giving the Marines any grief. But if you want to cram a few more cargo shuttles of that size in here, it could make launching Ghost Squadron a little iffy."

"We'll make them land in *Pallantis*, then ferry the prisoners over," Piech replied after a few seconds. "And send the one already here back to its mothership."

Cotto's hologram raised a hand.

"I'll handle it and let their former captain know where to go, Skipper."

"Thanks." Piech touched the controls, and one of the side displays came to life with a view of the hangar deck. He let out a snort of surprise.

"Your people are thorough. Is having them strip naked necessary?"

A sly grin played on Decker's lips.

"With a bunch of shady traders such as that lot? Probably not. Our sensors can pick up any weapons or other nasty items. But it puts the prisoners in the right frame of mind. There's nothing better than a bit of exposure in front of armored troopers to make you feel vulnerable and submissive. If they were pirates or slavers, we wouldn't allow them to put their clothes on again."

"Colonel." The sensor tech raised his hand. "Your call was right on the money. I believe we're picking up a Constabulary tracker implant at the center of that large settlement, just about where those shuttles lifted. The signal is damned faint, but since this place doesn't produce much by way of electro-magnetic emissions, I don't think it's a phantom. I fed the location to the mapping database."

"Excellent. Now see what you can pick up in terms of human life signs anywhere on the planet, please."

"Will do. It'll take me one full orbit, at least, sir."

"Thanks." Decker turned to Piech. "When we have Captain Whatshername in the brig—"

"Magdalene Bustos, who prefers the diminutive Mag."

"Right. I want my intelligence noncom, Command Sergeant Nomura, to interrogate her about conditions on Kryani, about who bought the guns, where she picked them up, her relation to the Howlers, that sort of thing. Not only is it part of his job, but good practice. Don't worry. We won't harm a hair on her head. I expect she'll spill everything except what might get her in even more trouble with the Howlers."

"So long as he doesn't let on we're Fleet."

"He won't, and I'm sure the Saqqa Cartel has its own intelligence gathering network, so it'll seem natural. But our guests will eventually find out once we dock at Starbase 59 and hand them to its chief security officer."

"Not if I arrange for us to stay incognito. Everyone there will play along if I ask them nicely. And should we rescue people on Kryani besides Warrant Officer Kine, it'll help keep the upcoming political shit storm from exploding in everyone's face. Especially if they don't speak of gallant Marine Corps Special Forces troopers and a Navy frigate well beyond their authorized area of operations."

Decker nodded. "True. But Kine gets to know since she's almost one of us."

"That's your call, but for what it's worth, I'll see her berthed with my crew rather than among any others you pick up from that benighted planet."

"I expected no less. Let me warn Nomura so he can prepare a suitable interview compartment."

**

Command Sergeant Kaori Nomura, a lean, hard-faced, black-haired man in his late thirties looked up from his reader when the door to the vacant cabin he'd chosen as the interrogation room opened. One of Ghost Squadron's troopers in unmarked battledress uniform and a woman wearing a merchant spacer's dark blue tunic with four gold stripes on the collar stepped in.

"Captain Magdalene Bustos, I presume." Nomura gestured at the empty chair on the other side of the table he'd set up in the middle of the compartment. "Please sit."

"Who are you?" She asked in a low, gravelly voice.

"My name is not important. Only my function matters, and that is asking you questions, then recording your answers."

Nomura studied Bustos as she reluctantly took a seat after glancing at the stony Marine behind her. She appeared to be in her fifties, with the seamed face of someone who spent most of her life in space. A shoulder-length bob of thick, wine red hair framed angular features sculpted with a hatchet and left to weather under the onslaught of cosmic radiation. Dark eyes beneath arched brows on either side of a long, beaked nose stared back at him with a mixture of anger and defiance.

"What makes you think I'll cooperate with damned pirates who stole my ship and imprisoned my crew. Not to mention seized my outbound cargo."

"Ah, yes. The drugs. We'll discuss them in due course. Are you *Pallantis'* owner-operator, or merely her captain?" When he saw her lips squeeze together, Nomura said, "Cooperation will make sure you live long enough to find a new command somewhere far from the Shield Sector, Captain."

"I'm a part-owner, okay. *Pallantis* belongs to a private consortium. I hold twenty percent of the shares."

"And is that consortium related to the Confederacy of the Howling Stars?"

"Fridolph spoke more than he should. But then he always was a talker. The Confederacy owns twenty percent as well."

"What about the rest?" When she didn't reply, Nomura allowed himself a frosty smile. "Let me guess. Commercial interests, perhaps even shipping companies who need a hull they can send into places few sane merchants go. It's a common theme along the frontier. I dare say even the large conglomerates such as ComCorp own a small fleet of supposedly independent traders to handle less than legal business."

The minute tightening of the skin around her eyes told him he'd hit the target, or at least come close.

"No matter. Once we finish analyzing *Pallantis'* database, we'll find them. Now, let us discuss your reasons for being here. I understand you offloaded a consignment of chemically propelled slug throwers. Please describe these weapons, state how many you delivered, and with how much ammunition."

After another defiant silence, Bustos shrugged.

"We dropped off a thousand modern copies of a pre-diaspora rifle design from Earth called the Martini-Henry, along with one hundred thousand twelve-millimeter cartridges. Don't ask me for details. I don't know a damn thing about the weapons or the ammo."

"Who did you deal with on Kryani?"

"A human slave by the name Harko. He works for the head lizard who runs most of this planet."

"Any idea how the Howlers set up the deal?"

Bustos shook her head.

"Not a damn clue. Ask them if you can. I guess it wasn't through the Saqqa Cartel. Otherwise, I'd still be in command of my ship."

"Tell me more about Harko."

"What's to tell? He's a nasty looking character who speaks lizard and lords it over the other human slaves. When he checked the merchandise — crate by crate no less — he handled the rifles as if he knew how they worked, which is why it took us so long. I suppose he could be a weapons instructor."

"Please describe the place where you landed."

"Rammed earth tarmac. A parade ground, maybe. There were enough Kryani around who resembled soldiers. You know, all wearing the same clothes and harnesses and carrying spears topped by long, serrated metal blades that'll tear out a sophont's guts and leave it howling in agony. The tarmac is at the center of a big, walled-in complex of buildings. Call it a palace, if you want, with stone structures everywhere, a few up to four stories tall. It didn't seem to be a tourist destination if you get my drift. We were too busy getting the transaction sorted while keeping one hand on our blasters in case the lizard soldiers tried to harpoon us."

"How did it go?"

"Human slaves unloaded my shuttles, one crate at a time. Harko checked each before his people carried them into the largest building's basement. Or at least through a door below ground level accessible by an incline. The same humans then carried the outbound merchandise aboard my shuttles."

"Did you check what they loaded?"

Bustos nodded.

"Before the trip, they gave me a handheld sensor with a pre-loaded chemical profile in its memory. I scanned every box to make sure the contents matched the profile."

"No issues?"

She shook her head again. "None."

"Let's discuss your port of departure and intended destination after leaving this star system."

— Twenty-Four —

Decker, who'd been watching the interrogation from *Mikado*'s conference room along with Piech and Ghost Squadron's senior leadership cadre, picked up the handheld battlefield sensor his people retrieved from Bustos' shuttle.

"I never thought to see the day a Fleet-issue, highly restricted Mark Thirteen, would be used for drug analysis. Will wonders never cease?"

Bayliss made a face.

"We know the bad guys are pilfering our supply depots thanks to corrupt Fleet personnel. Why not grab some Class Five items along the way? Considering they stole a few hundred kilos of MHX-19 compound a while back and getting that out of an ammo bunker normally requires a three-star's signature…"

"Maybe for our next mission, we ought to clean out the depots," Sergeant Major Paavola suggested.

Bayliss let out a wistful sigh.

"I wish."

"And what about those drugs?" Piech asked. "They're aboard *Pallantis* now. I'd rather we didn't smuggle them into the Commonwealth. In spite of my willingness to indulge you phantom Marines, I draw the line at trafficking."

Decker thought for a few seconds.

"Make a full record of the load, seal one container and stow it in *Mikado*'s evidence locker so we can give the Constabulary labs a decent sample for analysis, then space the rest."

"Done."

"All right." Decker tapped the tabletop with his fingertips. "I think we heard everything germane to our upcoming excursion planet-side from Captain Bustos. Kaori's remaining questions will deal with issues the analysts back home can ponder. We know Warrant Officer Kine is still alive and in the same location where Bustos handed a thousand large caliber slug throwers to a bunch of primitives. I don't think a twelve-millimeter copper-jacketed lead bullet will penetrate our armor, but at close range, it could be enough to knock a trooper off his feet and send a shock wave through his body. A direct hit on the helmet visor might be even worse, and we can't assume the Kryani aren't yet able to use that sort of weapon. This could be a follow-on shipment, which means they might already own primitive breech-loaders and be familiar with firearms."

"At least the Howlers didn't jump right over the chemical propellant era and sell them plasma guns," Captain Curtis

Delgado remarked. "Mind you, any of them who fire at us with those bang sticks once won't ever do so again."

"Glad you think so. Erinye Company has the honor of rescuing Warrant Officer Kine and any humans held in the great chieftain's fortress."

Delgado grinned at Decker.

"Hurray for us. On behalf of my gallant troopers, I accept the honor."

Decker touched at controls embedded in the table's surface. A map of Kryani's main continent appeared on the main display.

"The red marks show concentrations of human life signs. Since our sensors can't necessarily detect individuals from this altitude, there may be more in other locations. I want *Mikado*'s Growler to fly a reconnaissance pattern at a lower altitude, beginning with the main continent."

A low whistle escaped Captain Washburn Tesser's lips.

"That's a lot of separate locations."

"Which is why I intend to disperse Keres and Moirae companies by troops, including those in *Katisha* and *Pallantis*. We don't know what command-and-control system the Kryani use, but I doubt it's efficient, so we can probably stagger our strikes with no one ambushing us when we hit follow-on locations. That means once Erinye Company clears the palace and loads Kine and every other human there into *Pallantis*' shuttles — two should suffice if the life sign tally is correct — it'll disperse by troops and seize three more targets. Same for the other companies. Once each troop clears a target and ships the humans off in

Katisha and *Pallantis'* shuttles, it'll head on to its next assignment, and so on until we've done everything possible to recover all humans on the planet. I will coordinate the execution from *Mikado*."

"Picking up everyone could take a while," Captain Lucius Farnes of Moirae Company said.

Decker nodded.

"Up to a day, I think. But I don't want to leave anyone behind. Once we clear the surface, I plan on us selectively destroying every site which shows signs of advanced technology through kinetic strikes from orbit. That should return the planet to the level it would be without humans stupidly giving them knowledge when they're not yet particularly civilized. We can't afford another humanoid species with barbarian instincts roaming the star lanes and plundering what they need from more advanced societies. In any case, that's my concept of operations. The floor is open for discussion. Once we agree, Jory will draw up orders and start the countdown to launch."

Decker glanced at Captain Virk, who gave him a nod of agreement.

**

After the command conference broke up, leaving company commanders to issue their warning orders and the operations officer to draft the detailed plan, Piech invited Decker for a coffee in his day cabin.

Once they sat facing each other across the former's desk, cup in hand, Piech said, "I asked Hallie to work with both prize masters and figure out how many human bodies our three ships can carry home if we push hard up against the most extreme safety limits. Depending on how many people each of those life sign clusters represents, it could be tight. And that's without knowing if the Growler will pick up added ones. Hallie ran a few scenarios based on numbers, and they range from workable to impossible. Did you consider a situation where we can't take everyone aboard?"

"What do you think? None of my people brought it up during our discussion, but we're worried about the possibility. It's one of those things where they'll vote to stay here, dig in and wait for another ship so captives can take their places in *Mikado*."

"Would you? Stay here and wait until we can send another ship?"

"Sure. Find a spot close to potable water we can defend against any number of Kryani. Take enough ammo and rations with us, then wait. If need be, forage. They must feed their human slaves something our species can digest. And there seems to be plenty of backcountry where the locals can't attack us in massive numbers at once."

"Let's hope it doesn't come to that. If need be, I can let the prizes travel at their best speed in tandem, overload *Mikado* with rescuees, and push into the highest hyperspace bands. That way, we might reach Starbase 59 before our environmental systems collapse and we run out of rations.

She may not look like it, but her drives are more capable than those of *Katisha* or *Pallantis*. And when we run out of berths, I'll turn the hangar deck into a dormitory with gym mats and spare blankets. The folks you aim to pick up won't mind if it means going home."

"No, they won't."

"Another question. What about the collaborators? People such as this Harko who are the Kryani's trustees? There will be more of his sort there, captives who sold their souls for extra privileges and an easier life."

Decker gave Piech a sad look.

"People often do bad things to survive. Not everyone is a Warrant Officer Kine, who deliberately put herself at mortal risk, so she didn't compromise her values as a cop. I figure there aren't many with that sort of intestinal fortitude. It's an old story. If you want to see one of its worst manifestations in human history, read up on the concentration camps of Earth's Second World War. They used people called kapos — prisoners who oversaw other prisoners, often with inhumane brutality. The winners tried many of them after the war and executed some for crimes against humanity. But in later years, they were also seen as victims, which begs the question, how can I condemn the Harkos? If they wish to come with us, we'll let them. The judge advocate general's branch can decide whether they should be prosecuted or set free."

"Provided they're not torn up by the others during the trip home. You know, summary justice."

"It'll be our job to make sure that doesn't happen. If we can separate them from the rest before the urge for vengeance comes to life."

Piech snorted.

"Our noble attempt at riding to the rescue could become messy before everything is said and done, I think. In keeping with most things in this life and this universe."

"In every life and every universe."

Mikado's captain took a sip of coffee while studying Decker over the rim of his mug.

"Just out of curiosity, and I'm aware it's your call and yours only, what rules of engagement are you giving Ghost Squadron?"

"Shoot to kill for the preservation of human lives. If the Kryani don't engage and let us recover our people, they won't suffer casualties. If they attack, they'll die."

"You know they won't let you just waltz in and take what they consider their property."

A cruel grin lit up the Marine's face.

"That's their problem, not mine."

"Good thing the bleeding hearts on the Core Worlds who've experienced no alien predation in living memory can't hear you. Otherwise, they'd try to see you cashiered on charges of violating the Kryani's sophont rights."

"Which are fiction anyway."

"An idiot senator will come up with the idea any day now under some twisted logic such as if enslaving another sentient species is part of their culture, then who are we to kill them over it." Piech took another sip. "But enough about our so-called betters. I want to offer you my CIC as a command post for the operation. I'll watch from the bridge. Bring whoever you need, and I'll leave you my signals, sensor, and combat systems watchkeepers."

Decker inclined his head in gratitude. "Many thanks. I accept with great pleasure."

"And I'll deploy a few satellites, so you don't lose track while we're on the other side of the planet. Better that than rising to a geostationary orbit, in case someone needs precision fire support."

"Did I ever mention how much I enjoy working with you, Sandor?"

"No, but I would appreciate a favorable mention in your after-action report, which will no doubt land on the grand admiral's desk, considering what we're about to carry out in total violation of our political masters' restrictions."

"Consider it done." Decker drained his mug. "And thank you. I should join Jory and help him put together the mission orders. Not that he's the sort who makes mistakes. On the contrary. Otherwise, he wouldn't be squadron operations officer, which technically makes him third in the order of command after Josh Bayliss. But it'll speed things up, and the sooner we free our fellow humans from alien bondage, the better."

"Enjoy."

The Marine found Captain Jory Virk, Command Sergeant Kaori Nomura, and Major Josh Bayliss in the conference room, hard at work teasing out the most effective mission sequence based on his concept of operations.

"Come to heckle or help?" Bayliss asked when Decker dropped into a chair.

"Which one would speed up things?"

"The first option. There's nothing that inspires your loyal troopers to improve their performance more than you ragging on them."

"How about news we'll get the ship's CIC as a command post for the duration of the operation? And a few satellites to allow us uninterrupted contact with the ground while staying in a low enough orbit for fire support if things go pear-shaped?"

Virk's face brightened, and he gave Decker a silent thumbs up.

"See," Bayliss said in a grave tone, "that's called helping. If you wanted to heckle, you'd be wondering out loud why none of us thought to ask."

"I didn't ask. Sandor Piech offered."

"Mighty nice of him. I'll retract some of the mean things I've said about the Navy. If you want to help, look at the preliminary phasing and tell us if it works."

— Twenty-Five —

When he saw Decker was about to come through the hangar deck's inner door, Major Josh Bayliss, called out, "Ghost Squadron."

The assembled officers and command noncoms snapped to attention. Some commanding officers only called their company commanders to formal orders. But having been an enlisted troop leader, Decker understood how vital it was that the warrant officers and senior sergeants heard the same thing as their captains and could seek answers directly from the man who formulated the plan.

Decker strode across the deck to where they stood, facing the large screen used to post instructions for arriving and departing shuttles.

"At ease, everyone."

The screen came to life with an image of Kryani's principal continent.

"I'm sure by now, you've memorized our area of operations."

Red splotches appeared.

"Those," he gestured at the display, "mark the locations of confirmed human life signs. When I say confirmed, I don't just mean by *Mikado*'s sensors but also by her Growler, which finished crisscrossing the main continent at an altitude of twenty thousand meters. It is now checking out the minor continents, where *Mikado*'s sensors didn't detect human life signs, just to make sure. The good news is the Kryani are keeping their slaves in a few locations, probably under the control of local chieftains who answer to the top boss. That's his capital, outlined in green. That's where our main target, Warrant Officer Aleksa Kine, is being held. It stands to reason the planet's top rulers are keeping human slaves to themselves. They represent a way of bootstrapping a preindustrial society into the space age without undergoing that boring and lengthy process we call developing a civilization."

Decker's sarcastic quip earned him a round of appreciative chuckles.

"The not so good news is that the Growler's granular scans show there may be more humans on the ground than *Mikado*, *Katisha*, and *Pallantis* can carry for the time it will take to reach Starbase 59. But rest assured, we will leave no one behind, even if it means Ghost Squadron spends half the trip living in tin suits to ease the stress on *Mikado*'s environmental systems."

Decker saw nothing but approval in the eyes watching him. They were inured to hardship and understood the welfare of defenseless civilians came first.

"This mission is dubbed Operation Magic Carpet. Ghost Squadron, attention to orders." He gestured at Command Sergeant Nomura. "Please go ahead with the enemy situation."

"Sir." The squadron's intelligence NCO ran through what they knew about the Kryani, their weapons, especially the Martini-Henry rifles that Erinye Company might face in the great chieftain's palace. He finished with detailed aerial views of each target location on the main screen. "There are copies of the aerials on your tablets."

He stepped back and nodded at Decker.

"The friendly forces section is short and sweet, as always," the latter said. "*Mikado* will be available for air support while she's within line of sight of your objectives, but I would prefer you rely on your shuttles' integral armament if you need something with a larger caliber. Since I'm setting up the squadron command post in *Mikado*'s CIC, a simple request to call sign zero will suffice if fire and brimstone become necessary. That brings me to our formal mission statement."

Decker paused to let his eyes roam over the assembly.

"Ghost Squadron will raid the marked objectives in a phased attack and rescue every human held by the Kryani. Execution. My concept of operations is as follows."

He described the phased extraction of humans from each location, one after the other. As he spoke, the red blotches changed color to represent each of his three companies: gold for Erinye, silver for Keres, and royal blue for Moirae.

"We will achieve our end state when the humans on Kryani are aboard our three ships, and Ghost Squadron returns to barracks. Any questions so far?"

When no one raised a hand, Decker gestured at Captain Virk, who walked them through the detailed tasks and sequencing. He ended with the coordinating instructions, which included the vitally important timetable. After running through the logistics and command-and-control paragraphs, Decker gave them a few minutes to look through the orders and prepare for questions. He wandered off to one side with Bayliss and Paavola while the company commanders clustered with their first sergeants and troop leaders to discuss their parts in the overall scheme.

"It'll be a hell of a thing," Bayliss said in a low tone. "Our first large-scale recovery of unarmed civilians. If the Kryani are faster and have better communications than we expect, it could become bloody, fast."

"I'm not so much worried about the operation itself," Decker replied. "Our people can handle anything the Kryani throw at them. It's the civilians. How many will we recover, and in what condition will they be?"

Paavola shrugged. "We play it by ear, sir. Nothing else we can do. *Mikado*'s medical personnel will take care of the worst cases."

"With a sixteen-bed sickbay."

Bayliss clapped his old friend on the shoulder.

"At least they'll be alive and on their way home, Zack. That's the important thing."

After running through questions and confirming everyone present shared a common understanding of the operation, Decker dismissed his officers and command noncoms so they could continue the battle procedure at the company and troop level. The squadron would launch in three hours, one hour before night covered most of the target areas, especially the primary one where Warrant Officer Kine was held. Though the Kryani might enjoy excellent night vision with Mark I eyeballs, the Marines' helmet visors gave their wearers the ability to see in absolute darkness and across a wider spectrum than the bare eye. It was an advantage Ghost Squadron used to good effect whenever possible.

**

Aleksa Kine's hyper-alert senses felt someone approach her cell before the door opened. The Kryani with the stained apron stepped in, hung a lit lantern from a wall hook, and pulled on the chains attached to Kine's wrist manacles, yanking her upright.

Once she hung by her arms, toes barely touching the cold floor, he briefly left to retrieve the same water container as before. He sprayed her heavily, washing away the grime, dried urine, and feces that stained her lower body after a full day and night unable to move away from the spot in which she sat.

When his water ran out, the Kryani vanished back into the corridor but left her cell door open. Approximately thirty minutes later, according to her internal clock, the great chieftain's beastmaster who'd bought her and the other rejects, entered with her jailer on his heels. He studied her from every angle in silence for an unnerving length of time. His tongue flicked out at intervals, touching various parts of her body. Kine wanted to scream at him, but without water in over a day, her throat was painfully dry.

The beastmaster then turned to the jailer and spoke. The latter gave a brief reply, then stepped aside so the visitor could leave. He lowered her to the floor and allowed her arms to drop. Then, with surprising swiftness, he pulled lengths of thin rope from his apron pocket and wrapped them around Kine's body, pinning her arms against her torso and binding her legs. After removing the metal shackles, the Kryani threw her over one shoulder with surprising strength, as if she was no more than a sack of potatoes.

He carried her to the large room where pots and cutting tools hung from the walls and ceiling beams and placed her on a metal table with a ten-centimeter-high lip running along its perimeter. He walked around the table several times, studying her with those soulless, bulbous eyes. Every so often, he would probe her limbs and joints by squeezing and poking at them, evaluating her anatomy.

At one point, he surprised her with a painful scratch on the upper arm that drew blood. His long tongue came out and licked the wound. Shivers of horror ran up her body, and Kine knew with certainty she was about to die.

But the jailer walked away after one last touch on Kine's neck, leaving her to stare at blackened ceiling beams bathed by the light of a dozen lanterns.

**

After giving the troopers a few last words of encouragement before they boarded *Mikado*'s armed shuttles, Decker and Paavola made their way to the CIC, where they joined Captain Virk and Major Bayliss, already seated at unoccupied consoles.

Petty Officer Jenks held the communications station, while the gunnery division's chief petty officer, a slender, short-haired woman in her forties, monitored the ship's combat systems in the absence of Lieutenant Adjeng, who led Condor Flight from the pilot seat in Erinye Company's lead shuttle.

"They're buttoned up," Virk reported without turning around. "Space doors are opening."

Decker dropped into the vacant command chair and looked around the CIC.

"Nice view. I can see why Sandor loves this seat."

"I'll borrow one from the Navy and install it in your office back home," Bayliss said.

"Unless the chair comes with a starship, don't bother."

Virk raised his right hand.

"They're launching. And right on the minute." A pause. "*Katisha* and *Pallantis* launched their flights."

Between them, *Mikado*'s shuttles and those of the two prizes required every single one of the Q-ship's qualified petty officers. More than that and Piech would have faced a choice between sending his remaining commissioned officers or leaving desperately needed shuttles idle because there was no one left able to take the controls. Decker made a mental note to see that a few of his sergeants obtained a secondary specialty as pilots, just in case, once they found a few spare weeks between missions.

"Excellent. Operation Magic Carpet is officially on."

"We aim to please," Piech's disembodied voice said. "And don't get attached to that chair, Zack. Once the operation is over, it's mine again."

"Fine by me. I don't want to become soft in the service anyhow." Decker winked at an amused Petty Officer Jenks.

He settled back and made himself comfortable. The mission was now in the hands of his company commanders and troop leaders. They had their orders, timetables, and individual plans, all derived from his scheme. The only way he could influence the coming succession of small-scale raids was if something went wrong and required his intervention.

— Twenty-Six —

An hour passed before her jailer with the stained leather apron returned. He opened the door leading to the courtyard, and a gust of damp air heavily redolent of decay filled the room.

After taking a few deep breaths, he walked over to Kine's table and squeezed her joints again, one after the other in quick succession. Then, he turned to a display of large cutting instruments hanging from hooks set in the stone wall.

Like an artist choosing his colors, the jailer hefted first one of the over-sized shears, then another, as if deciding which would be the most appropriate. But none of them seemed to please him, and he turned his attention on a set of ax-shaped cleavers hanging next to the shears. Kine, head to one side, watched him with terrified fascination, knowing the final minutes of her existence were nigh, and there was nothing she nor anyone else could do.

But then, a disturbingly familiar whine reached her ears through the open door. Shuttles. Several of them. Kine turned toward the sound and searched the early evening darkness for a sign that her impending doom wasn't triggering an auditory mirage while the madwoman living in her skull prayed to a long-forgotten deity, repeating half-remembered lines from the family book of hours without conscious volition.

The growing rush of thrusters firing to decelerate finally reached the Kryani's invisible ears, though he might not quite understand what he was hearing. He carefully rehung his chosen cleaver, walked to the door, and peered out. Moments later, the darkness beyond the rectangular opening brightened without warning, outlining Kine's jailer.

**

"Our target is on a lower level in that large structure, Captain." First Sergeant Hak, battlefield sensor in hand, pointed at the main building over Lieutenant Adjeng's head as the shuttle's descent slowed to a crawl before settling on an earthen parade ground. "Right behind where that lizard is staring at us as if we're apparitions."

Delgado nodded.

"Roger." He flicked his helmet radio to the company push. "One-one, this is One-Niner. Your objective is beyond the open door just below ground level."

"One-niner, this is one-one, confirmed. We're locked onto the tracker."

The aft ramps of Erinye Company's four shuttles dropped with dull thuds, and armored Marines emerged, plasma carbines at the ready. Alpha Troop — call sign one-one — thundered toward Kine's dumbstruck jailer. Meanwhile, Bravo and Charlie Troops — call signs one-two and one-three — deployed.

The latter established a perimeter around the shuttles while the former ran toward the barn-like structure where the target area's humans, save for Kine, were concentrated according to the last aerial sensor readouts taken moments earlier. Above them, two of *Katisha*'s cargo shuttles circled, waiting for the order to land and load the freed captives.

With the shuttles' thrusters falling silent, Curtis Delgado heard shouts in an alien tongue when he emerged from his craft and quickly spotted Kryani coming at the Marines. Their metallic harnesses and wicked, long-bladed spearheads glittered in the torchlight.

A howl, resembling that of a wounded predator, shattered the night, quickly followed by the first coughs of plasma carbines spitting death. A dozen of the charging Kryani guards dropped to the ground as if they'd hit an invisible wall, felled by Charlie Troop's Marines.

Kine's jailer, faced with large, hard-charging exoskeletal beings, turned tail and ran back into his workroom, past the prone Constabulary officer, and into the corridor where he vanished. Unable to comprehend what was happening, Kine stared at the open door only to see someone wearing familiar human combat armor come in, weapon at the ready.

"One-niner, this is one-one. We have her. She's trussed like a Christmas turkey and lying on what reminds me of a morgue table, but she's alive."

"I'm on my way," Delgado replied. He turned to First Sergeant Hak. "Stay here and keep an eye out for snags."

"Wilco."

The first snag rang out moments later as a Kryani, armed with one of the new Martini-Henry rifles, opened fire on the Marines. The slug sailed over their heads and ricocheted off the nearest outbuilding's stone wall with a whine. Three plasma carbines turned on the alien, killing him instantly.

Inside, Alpha Troop's leader opened his helmet visor and bent over Kine's head so she could see he was human.

"My name is Rolf Painter, Warrant Officer Kine. I'm a command sergeant in the 1st Special Forces Regiment. Your superiors asked us to find you and bring you home."

Incapable of speaking while she processed her sudden change of fortune, Kine nodded jerkily.

More Marines streamed into the room and fanned out, ready to repel any Kryani foolish enough to rush them.

"Stay still while I cut off your restraints."

Painter produced a sharp, black-hilted Pathfinder dagger and carefully cut each of the ropes until she was free. A second armored figure joined the sergeant and raised his visor.

"Warrant Officer Kine, I'm Captain Curtis Delgado. We'll take you out of here and get you aboard the Navy ship *Mikado* shortly, along with every other human on the planet we can find and load into our shuttles."

Kine nodded, but before Delgado could say anything else, a Marine emerged from the corridor, and upon spotting his company commander, said, in a strangled voice, "You'd best come see this, sir."

"I'll bring the warrant officer to my shuttle, Captain." Painter put his hands beneath Kine's back and knees and lifted her off the table in an effortless gesture.

More shots rang outside, and Delgado held up a restraining hand.

"Don't go out until Charlie Troop gives the go-ahead. It would be a bitch if we came all the way here only for her to take a twelve-millimeter slug in the chest."

"Roger that, sir."

While Painter gently helped Kine stand, Delgado joined the Marine with the nauseated expression on his face.

"What's up?"

"I think I know what was about to happen here with Warrant Officer Kine, sir. You won't believe this. I didn't at first either, but now I want to kill every damn lizard out there. We'll need night vision."

After both slammed their visors shut, he led his company commander past a heavy metal door and into what reminded Delgado of nothing so much as a primitive cold storage room. Though there was no lighting, Delgado saw everything as clear as day.

Sections of human bodies dangled from hooks, as if they were pieces of beef hung to dry age. Arms, legs, eviscerated torsos. And in one corner, vats with organs and decapitated heads.

"The God-damned lizards eat us, sir. They fucking eat humans for supper. That's what was about to happen with Warrant Officer Kine. I vote we flatten this whole rotten planet."

"It'll be the colonel's call," Delgado replied in a low tone as he fought against his rising revulsion and hatred. "But I'm in favor."

"What do we do?"

"Since I suspect the colonel will order a strike on this entire stinking palace, they'll receive as close to a decent burial as we can wish for under the circumstances. Let's record what we can and move out."

When they returned to what they now knew was a butcher's backroom, Painter and Kine were gone. A few Marines from Alpha Troop remained, waiting for Delgado.

"Rolf's in the shuttle with the Constabulary officer, sir," one of them said.

"Thanks. Off you go." Delgado gestured at the door. He switched his radio to the company push. "One-Niner-Charlie, this is One-Niner. Send sitrep."

Moments later, Hak's voice came through his earpieces.

"The tangos finally stopped with the bang sticks, but a few of Charlie's troopers have dents in their armor. Nothing we can't fix, though our guys will need a quick check by the medics. I figure we downed at least one hundred tangos, if not more. The rest are hiding. I've called the transport shuttles since Bravo has the rest of the captives ready to bring out of their barn."

Delgado, who couldn't wipe the image of the human abattoir from his mind's eye, rejoined his shuttle, eager to speak with Decker.

Adjeng glanced over his shoulder when the Marine made his way to the cockpit.

"That went well."

"Can you connect me with *Mikado*'s CIC?"

A curious expression crept across Adjeng's face at Delgado's unusual tone. He touched a control screen, then said, "Link your helmet to the shuttle's net and give them a shout."

"Zero, this is One-Niner."

A few seconds passed, then Captain Virk's voice came through his earpieces.

"This is Zero."

"We recovered Warrant Officer Kine and are about to load the remaining humans held inside Objective Gold One. The Kryani took over a hundred casualties and gave us a few dings with their Martini-Henrys. Right now, it's quiet because the enemy is hiding. I think they're waiting for us to leave. Is Niner listening?"

"Niner, here," Decker said. "Go."

"I'm not sure how to put this, but you'll see my sensor log recordings shortly. The Kryani — at least those around here — prefer to dry age their humans before eating them."

Silence greeted his declaration.

"Come again, One-Niner."

"We found a cold storage room with cut up human bodies hanging from butchers' hooks, like sides of beef. Organs and heads were in separate vats, probably pickling. Warrant Officer Kine was about to join them. If we'd landed ten minutes later, she would have been in pieces, eviscerated and bleeding out on a chopping table."

A string of invective escaped Decker's self-restraint.

"Okay. That does it. Once you're clear of the target, it becomes a large, smoking crater. We need to teach these damn barbarians that enslaving humans and making them their main course will result in massive punishment."

"Since I really want to unleash my company's namesakes, the Furies of antiquity, I wholeheartedly agree."

First Sergeant Hak, who'd come aboard the shuttle moments earlier, tapped Delgado on the shoulder and pointed out at a cluster of humans being herded toward two cargo shuttles settling at the center of the parade ground.

"We're within moments of sending up the first batch, then moving on to Objective Gold Two. Can I assume our rules of engagement will change from fire only when necessary for protection to kill on sight?"

"You can. Are you sending Warrant Officer Kine up with the cargo shuttles?"

"I wasn't planning on it, no. Considering what she just experienced, she'll be better off among us until we can fly her straight to *Mikado*."

Delgado glanced at Hak, who said, "Rolf dressed Kine in one of his shuttle's emergency suits and strapped her in beside the pilot. She'll be fine."

"I heard that. You can keep her with you."

"How are the others doing?"

"The same, except they haven't found abattoirs. Yet."

Command Sergeant Ejaz Bassam, who led Bravo Troop, trotted up the shuttle's aft ramp and gave Delgado thumbs up.

"They're loaded and about to lift. We're done here, sir."

Delgado raised a gauntleted hand to his helmet in salute by way of acknowledgment.

"Niner, the first batch is go. We're heading for Gold Two."

"Roger. Well done."

"One-Niner, out."

Delgado slowly exhaled as he fought adrenaline-fueled anger. His night was only beginning.

"Curtis?"

The Marine turned to Lieutenant Adjeng.

"Yes?"

"We heard about the lizards butchering humans for food. Would you mind if my fellow pilots and I carry out a strafing run over this place and give the lizards a twenty-millimeter plasma shower as a goodbye?"

"An excellent suggestion. We Marines shouldn't hog all the fun."

— Twenty-Seven —

"Colonel." Captain Virk raised his hand. "*Katisha* reports she's full. Diverting the next flights to *Pallantis.*"

"Thanks, Jory. That was quick."

"I know. Hopefully *Pallantis* won't fill up quite so fast. I'd rather not spend the next two weeks living in my tin suit."

Decker didn't take his eyes from the holographic tactical projection of Kryani's main continent. Over the last six hours, one red blotch after another turned either gold, silver, or blue as Ghost Squadron's companies raided their objectives and recovered human captives by the hundreds. The cargo shuttles belonging to both prize ships as well as *Mikado*'s administrative spacecraft would need complete overhauls once the squadron completed Operation Magic Carpet. They were doing more takeoffs and landings in one night than they did in an ordinary month of operations.

"Zero, this is Three-Niner." Decker glanced up when he heard Captain Lucius Farnes' voice come over the CIC speakers. "We found another abattoir at Objective Blue Five. Seven distinct sets of remains."

Decker clenched his jaw to keep from swearing. That was the third site discovered so far.

"Add it to the target list, Jory. And let Lucius know he can pound the objective at leisure on his way out."

"Yes, sir. Three-Niner, this is Zero," Virk replied. "Roger. Once you've evacuated the site, you may strafe at will."

"Acknowledged. Three-Niner, out."

The Saqqa Cartel and its backers would answer for this and find no forgiveness. Human trafficking was an old, old practice. But selling members of one's own species to non-humans who considered them a culinary delicacy when their other uses ran out?

Once the news spread on the Commonwealth's interstellar info nets and this outrage was linked to the name of a powerful political family from one of the Core Worlds, the worst political storm in generations would break loose in the frontier sectors. Especially after Centralist-inspired attempts in recent years to overthrow several of the most important Out World governments, those leading the fight to keep their sovereignty in the face of an increasingly authoritarian Earth.

Decker and his partner, Hera Talyn, were instrumental in stopping two of them at the last minute. One had been a military coup attempt by National Guard troops on Scandia and the other, a planned terrorist attack aimed at murdering not only senior members of the Cimmerian government but officials from every Rim Sector star system attending the annual sector conference.

Petty Officer Jenks' voice cut through his contemplation of the current mission's political fallout.

"Colonel, Lieutenant Toh is on the link for you."

Decker touched the controls on his borrowed command chair's arm.

"What's up?"

"Sir, remember when you warned us about problems with humans who worked as overseers during your briefing? I just experienced a group of rescuees attacking one of their fellows. We extracted him from the mob scene, but he's in bad shape. When I asked who else among them worked for the Kryani, no one stepped forward, but it didn't take long for denunciations to start. It looks as if the overseers are more fearful of what we'll do to them if they confess than they are of their fellow former captives."

"Not unexpected, I suppose. Tell you what, we'll concentrate the former overseers in *Mikado* after we recover everyone. Just keep yours segregated until then."

"Already done, sir. But you should know that my crew isn't feeling particularly charitable toward them."

"If justice needs dispensing, I'll see to it, Lieutenant. No vigilantism by our people."

"Yes, sir."

"Was there anything else?"

"No."

"Thanks for telling me. Decker, out." He turned to Bayliss. "Josh, call Lieutenant Dulay and make sure she weeds out former overseers from the general population as each shuttle comes in, then let *Mikado*'s bosun know, so he's ready when we bring people aboard."

"Will do."

Decker climbed to his feet and stretched. He would gladly trade the squadron and his lieutenant colonel's pips for a chance to be down there, fighting the good fight instead of moldering in a command post, no matter how fancy. But he also knew his place was here, making sure his company commanders and troop leaders received the support they needed to do their jobs. Besides, this sort of decentralized operation was a command sergeant's fight, with a few larger objectives to keep Ghost Squadron's captains busy.

"I'm getting myself a coffee. Josh, the chair is yours."

Major Bayliss snapped off a mock salute.

"I have the command post, *mon colonel.*"

Decker bumped into Sandor Piech when he entered the wardroom.

"You look tired, my friend," Piech said. "Not used to fretting while your troopers are in action?"

"Is that what I've been doing?" The Marine asked, heading for the ever-full coffee urn chugging away quietly on a sideboard. "Fretting? I thought I was twitchy. You Navy folks sure talk funny."

"We use a lot of fancy words, in contrast to your beloved Marine Corps, which relies on a condensed version of the dictionary. I've been following things from the bridge, but what's your gut feel on how this will end?"

Decker took a sip of coffee, then shrugged.

"My gut feeling is we'll recover everyone we can, kill a lot of lizards and high-tail it to Starbase 59 before we're drinking our own urine while slowly sucking every oxygen atom out of the ship's atmosphere."

"I was more thinking about the fallout when we make it home."

"That's a lot of levels above my pay grade, so I try not to worry. But the proverbial feces will strike the rotating implement. We already filled one ship with people who'll be happy when the newsies interview them, with two more shiploads coming, and no way of keeping anyone from revealing the deep, dark secrets of slavery on alien worlds. I fear that mythical civil war between the Core Worlds and the Out Worlds we keep whispering about will be one giant step closer to becoming a reality."

"Sadly, I think you're—"

The intercom cut off Piech's reply.

"Colonel Decker to the command post."

Decker drained his mug.

"The mission waits for no one. Talk to you later." He tapped the wardroom's intercom panel. "On my way."

When the CIC door swished open at his approach, Decker's eyes immediately went to the tactical projection, where a few more gold, silver, and blue dots had joined the others.

"Is there a problem?"

"F Troop ran into a potential blood bath at Objective Silver Four. Either the lizards run a better communications system than we thought, or they were already alert for another reason. But the moment our people landed, the bastards decapitated one of the captives in plain sight, then demonstrated the rest were living shields. Knudsvig faces a standoff. He can't shoot the lizards without harming humans and can't extract the humans without them dying. We're talking twenty-nine lives. Knudsvig is looking for a way to move his people into good firing positions, but he's short four guns to take all the lizards at once before they can slit throats. Wash is on his way with company HQ."

"Did I ever mention how much I hate bug hunts?" Bayliss asked no one in particular. "Can't talk to them, so you either make a clean kill shot or you walk away."

Twenty-nine lives hanging by a thread. Decker dropped into the command chair and rubbed his chin, mind spinning furiously while he searched for a solution.

"Zero, this is Two-Niner." Washburn Tesser's tired voice came over the CIC speakers. "Concerning the situation at Silver Four, the standoff is over. For an unknown reason, the tangos just massacred the twenty-nine remaining humans. Two-Three is mopping up the objective. There will be no survivors."

"Zero acknowledges."

Decker's fist slammed on the command chair's arm.

"Shit!"

"Concentrate on the ones we saved, Zack," Bayliss said in a low tone meant for Decker's ears only. "Rescue operations of this magnitude almost always end with a few civilian casualties."

"Add Silver Four to the target list, Jory."

"Already done, Colonel."

"You know Knudsvig will blame himself, right?" Bayliss asked in the same low tone.

"No doubt. I'll speak with him when he's back aboard."

"Let Paavola handle it. He has a good bedside manner with the noncoms. Reminds me a little of myself when I was a sergeant major and dealt with command sergeants who — how shall I put this politely — experienced certain problems, as you might remember. Except Paavola is more skilled than I was. If he'd been in my shoes back then, your life might have unfolded differently."

Decker gave his friend a sad look.

"Perhaps, but if you'd done a better job with me, we wouldn't be here now, rescuing a lot of innocents. So it's just as well."

"True."

"I wouldn't change a damn thing about my life, Josh. We're doing the Almighty's work, and that's what counts. Besides, I have Hera and my daughter is becoming a Marine officer. A man can't ask for better."

Bayliss clapped him on the shoulder.

"Atta boy, Zack. Now let's finish this show and go home."

— Twenty-Eight —

"How is she?" Decker asked when Warrant Officer Piotr Khadonov, physician's assistant and head of *Mikado*'s medical section, answered his call from the CIC. Khadonov made a so-so gesture.

"Dehydrated, Colonel, undernourished and perhaps suffering from a touch of post-traumatic stress. But unhurt and in most aspects, reasonably healthy. Compared to a fair number of people we're treating right now she's not coming off too badly."

Mikado's available spaces were rapidly filling with rescued captives, and more were on their way as Keres and Moirae companies took care of the last few targets.

"When can I speak with her?"

"Any time. I understand she'll be using Monique Dulay's berth. You can talk to her there. With the influx of patients, I need every square millimeter of space in the sickbay, so I'm releasing her now. One of the bosun's mates will take her to officer country."

Though Decker was impatient to meet Warrant Officer Aleksa Kine, he remained in the CIC until the last Ghost Squadron troopers were safely back in *Mikado* with the last human captives.

Once Moirae Company's last shuttle touched down, Decker slapped the command chair's arm.

"Ghost Squadron is declaring Operation Magic Carpet complete. I now return control to the senior naval officer."

"Sticking me with the former captives," Piech replied from *Mikado*'s bridge. "Fair enough. Let me sort out the final passenger balancing, and we can chat in my day cabin. Say in thirty minutes?"

"Thirty minutes it is."

Half an hour later, Decker and Piech settled across from each other on either side of the day cabin's desk, coffee in hand.

"Nice of you to return control," the latter said, "but we've not yet rained vengeance on Kryani. The target list is registered, but I still need your order to execute the fire plan."

Decker gave him a weary shrug.

"The order is given."

Piech touched the control surface embedded in his desk.

"Captain to CIC."

"CIC here," the gunnery chief petty officer replied.

"The Marines gave you a fire plan, Chief?"

"Yes, sir."

"Execute."

"Executing the fire plan, aye, sir."

"Captain, out." Piech settled back in his chair. "I don't know if you were keeping score, but while *Katisha* and *Pallantis* are just a bit beyond their carrying capacity, we're well over it. By almost twenty percent."

"If you need Ghost Squadron to land on Kryani and wait for retrieval…"

Piech raised a hand.

"Not so quick. This might be unethical in several ways, but Doc Khadonov made a suggestion which might allow *Mikado* to reach Starbase 59 without us choking on our waste."

"I'm listening."

"Recruit enough of our passengers for artificial hibernation. Doc Khadonov would administer an injection designed to slow human metabolisms in severely injured crew members when stasis chambers aren't available. Injecting the compound into healthy bodies isn't covered by the Armed Services Medical Orders and Protocols. But if he put, say, half of our passengers in artificial hibernation, my environmental systems will survive the trip, even if we don't push into the higher hyperspace bands so we can keep station with *Katisha* and *Pallantis*."

"That strikes me as an easy decision, Sandor. Explain the situation and see how many volunteer for the procedure. I think they might surprise you. And if an insufficient number raise their hands, con enough to make up the difference and don't fret."

Decker grinned at Piech.

"See. I can talk Navy. No one will cause a ruckus because you violated their right to consent if it brings everyone home healthy and intact. They've experienced the ugly side of life in this savage universe and will shut their yaps out of gratitude."

"Gratitude is vastly overrated. I've known plenty of folks for whom it stuck in their craw, especially when you save them from their own mistakes. That alone makes them crap on their saviors."

Decker shrugged.

"No sense in worrying. We'll ask for volunteers tomorrow and go from there."

"CIC to the Captain."

"Piech, here."

"First salvo away."

"Thank you." He turned to Decker. "Shall we watch righteous vengeance rain on the Kryani?"

"Sure."

Piech touched the controls embedded in his desk, and the main display in his day cabin came to life with the CIC's firing plot. Both officers watched in quiet fascination as *Mikado*'s launch tubes dropped high-velocity tungsten penetrator rods on each of the marked targets. They plunged through Kryani's atmosphere, gathering energy until they came to a sudden stop against the planet's hard crust. The resulting energy transfer created a string of smoking craters where industrial sites and slave pens once stood.

"CIC to the captain. Fire mission complete," the gunnery chief petty officer reported over the intercom after one full orbital pass.

"Scan for emissions inconsistent with preindustrial societies, in case we missed something the first time around, Chief. One full orbital pass."

"Aye, aye, sir. CIC, out."

Decker allowed himself a soft snort.

"You know certain political segments back home will scream blue bloody murder once they hear we literally bombed an alien species back to — well, not exactly the stone age, but close. Especially the cultural equivalency fringe."

"Fuck 'em," Piech replied in a cheerful tone. "We sent the Kryani back to where they should be — working hard at developing an enlightened civilization before they interact with the rest of the galaxy and risk pissing off a species less forgiving than ours."

The Marine let out a raspberry.

"An enlightened space-faring civilization such as ours? Funny. I remember a pair of civil wars that wiped out a fair percentage of our own species over matters of star system sovereignty. If I'd been a Shrehari observing us back then, I wouldn't have considered humanity ready to face the galaxy. Sometimes I'm not sure we are even now. As proof, I offer you the Hogue-backed Saqqa Cartel selling humans to barbaric aliens."

A thoughtful expression wiped away Piech's earlier air of satisfaction.

"I'll wager we've only pinched off a small part of the operation. Something equally evil will pop up to replace the lost cash flow."

"Not if we slice off the head of the serpent."

Piech scoffed.

"If it were possible, the Constabulary would have done so by now. Instead, one of their best undercover officers almost became lizard food after passing through the Hogue clan's New Oberon vacation property."

"Which no longer exists, nor will it ever be rebuilt. But who's speaking of doing so under laws crafted by the very people profiting from slavery and other vile activities, laws which allow them to operate with impunity? There's a reason the Core World-dominated Senate crafted rules which prevent the Armed Services from operating beyond the Commonwealth's sphere. But the balance of power in the Senate is shifting as both populations and anger grow on the Out Worlds."

Decker climbed to his feet.

"And that reminds me I should introduce myself to Warrant Officer Aleksa Kine, welcome her into our bosom, and gently tease out the details of her ordeal. The moment we're within reach of a subspace array, I need to send my mission report. Otherwise, Hera will become annoyed. And no one should suffer her wrath."

"Glad you're the one who's stuck dealing with the greater political picture. I prefer being a simple Navy officer doing his duty."

"I'm not quite sure you qualify as simple, but I'll ask around and see what the crew's general feelings are." Decker tossed off a mock salute. "Once Warrant Officer Kine settles in, may I suggest you invite both of us to dine with you? Perhaps not tonight, but tomorrow."

"My personal stores are no better than the wardroom's if your intention was noshing on higher-quality vittles."

"I was thinking we might help Kine by treating her as a valued colleague from the Constabulary side of our broader uniformed family."

Piech examined Decker for a few heartbeats, then nodded. "Sure. I understand. After what she's been through."

"You're a prince among spacers, Sandor."

**

"Come."

The door to Lieutenant Monique Dulay's quarters opened moments after Decker identified himself by name, rank, and unit. The Aleksa Kine before him seemed more emaciated, more haunted, and less confident than the picture he'd carried in his thoughts ever since Hera Talyn proposed the mission to recover her and showed him her official file portrait. She wore a borrowed black Marine utility uniform with a mercenary warrant officer's single bar at the collar.

"Pleased to meet you at last," he said, inclining his head in greeting.

She didn't immediately reply as her eyes searched his square, craggy face. When she finally spoke, it was with a raw, half-broken voice.

"I owe my life to your Marines, Colonel. They arrived moments before that damned lizard would have dismembered me. Thank you."

"The Kryani in question and every other of his kind in the palace paid for their barbarity. We bombarded the sites that held human slaves right after we finished evacuating our kind from the planet. We also destroyed anything they shouldn't have and wouldn't if it weren't for unscrupulous traders such as the Saqqa Cartel. They're back to a preindustrial level, and though I don't hold out much hope, perhaps they can climb out of obscurantism before they gain the technology to leave their star system unaided by other species."

Kine's humorless chuckle filled the small cabin.

"I hate to sound cynical, but part of me figures our bleeding hearts back home will die from apoplectic self-righteousness when they hear what the Commonwealth's glorious Armed Services did to a primitive people. Especially one exercising its cultural practices while aspiring to emulate us on the technological front."

"Like Commander Sandor Piech, *Mikado*'s captain, said just now when I made a similar remark, fuck 'em. Changes are on the horizon, big ones, and that horizon is closer than most people imagine. I spent a decade with Naval Intelligence working undercover operations against domestic enemies before taking command of 'A' Squadron,

1st Special Forces Regiment last year. Our Commonwealth is a lot more fragile than it seems. But, I'm not here for a political discussion. I wanted to introduce myself and make sure you were okay. Is there anything we can do for you?"

Kine tilted her head to one side. "I've not eaten a decent meal in weeks."

"If you want, we could visit the wardroom now and see what's on offer. I'm afraid that with the number of rescuees aboard, we will ration food during our trip home."

"You recovered every human on the planet?"

"Everyone whose life sign our sensors picked up. Well over a thousand. I can only guess the Saqqa Cartel's slave trade with the Kryani is recent. But if ever the Senate allows us to search every techno-barbarian world in this part of the galaxy for human slaves, we'll probably find more of them than a whole fleet of ships can carry in a single lift."

"I'd settle for one star system at a time." She climbed to her feet. "And I'd be grateful for a sandwich or even a bowl of soup."

— Twenty-Nine —

"I'll need to debrief you within the next day or so," Decker said after swallowing a bite from his sandwich.

As was usual in starships during combat operations, the wardroom offered a cold, self-service spread. The Marine suspected it would be one of his last non-reconstituted meals before Starbase 59. *Mikado*'s fresh food larder was already earmarked to help the most malnourished and ailing recover their strength.

A famished Kine waited until she'd inhaled her sandwich before nodding.

"That's what I figured. If you can give me a copy of the transcript afterward, I'll make sure my superiors see it."

"Of course, though I suspect my mission controller, to whom your superiors reached out, will do so as well. Anything that helps foster close cooperation between our services. We'll need each other's help more than ever in the coming years."

"Which is why the Fleet sent one of its famous black ops units to recover little old me."

"We prefer the term infamous, but yes. Not only because it was the right thing to do, but because of the cartel's involvement, and that of its politically connected backers. It wouldn't surprise me if you were the proverbial butterfly on New Oberon flapping its wings and causing a major storm over the fair city of Geneva."

Kine cocked a skeptical eyebrow.

"A Marine who knows chaos theory? I'm impressed." She nodded at the buffet. "Mind if I go for seconds?"

"You qualify as one of the malnourished and ailing rescuees with priority on our fresh food stocks, so eat your fill. And yes, I believe in the butterfly effect because I lived through its consequences so often, I became a convert. Your infiltrating the Saqqa Cartel's inner cadre might well cause a major realignment across the Commonwealth."

"My attempt at infiltrating." She put together another sandwich and took her seat across from Decker once more. "I didn't become a member of the inner cadre."

"The cartel has a fondness for recording everything. Obsessively. We saw a video of the loyalty test you refused."

"Oh." Kine took a bite and chewed on it, eyes losing their focus as she replayed the events of that day in her mind.

"Naval Intelligence is currently analyzing a few petabytes of data we recovered from the Hogue estate. I'm sure we'll be sharing with the Constabulary. And by the way, the Hogue estate is gone, along with Rabmag Rafalko and every other cartel goon working there. I hear the crater that replaced it is a rather peaceful spot. We extracted over four hundred captives beforehand. They should be home by now."

"Blessed are the warriors who protect the weak." Kine took a sip of her coffee. "It's a shame we cops can't simply barge into a place where crimes are being committed and shutter everything as permanently as you do."

"That's why the Fleet formed Ghost Squadron, though it will disavow knowledge of our existence. We take out the worst of the trash when political interference and corruption stymies your lot."

"Of which there is plenty." Kine shoved the last of her sandwich into her mouth and chased it with a gulp of coffee. "I'm beginning to feel civilized again. And please let whoever arranged for this uniform and the warrant officer's bar on its collar know I appreciate the effort. I doubt I'll suffer from post-traumatic stress, but every little thing that can stave off the possibility helps, I suppose."

"We take care of our own." When she opened her mouth, he raised a hand. "The Constabulary and the Fleet are two sides of the same coin. Your service was born from ours back in Grand Admiral Kowalski's day. We may have drifted apart in the last two or three decades, but we're coming together again."

"I won't argue the point. And I will be eternally in your debt." She held up her mug in salute.

"Swing by our home station, Fort Arnhem on Caledonia, one of these days and pick up the tab for a round at our watering hole, the Pegasus Club, and we'll call it even." He winked at Kine.

"If ever my job takes me to that part of the Commonwealth, I'll do my best for a stopover on Caledonia." She stood to refill her coffee. "Are the folks you rescued from the palace with me aboard this ship?"

"No. They're in *Katisha*, a cartel slaver we took in New Oberon orbit and renamed. It was there to pick up the folks we freed before flattening Hogue's estate. We also seized an illegal arms trader right here, in Kryani orbit, when we arrived, a ship by the name *Pallantis*. Why? Do you have any particular friends among them?"

Kine leaned against the sideboard and raised the mug to her lips before shaking her head.

"No. I wasn't there long enough to make friends. I was wondering about the overseer, Harko."

"He's in *Katisha*'s brig, for his safety. Every former overseer is in protective custody. We already saw attempts at revenge. We're transferring them to *Mikado* before heading for home." He glanced at the time. "That should already be done. What's the story with this Harko?"

Kine explained the events that led to her ending on the butcher's block.

"I'm convinced Harko knew the great chieftain and his retinue dined on humans who had no technical skills and otherwise failed to amuse them. How he kept his sanity is beyond me."

"And you want to know whether he's a run-of-the-mill sadist, a sociopath devoid of empathy or a victim of circumstances trying desperately to survive, right?"

She nodded.

"Pretty much. An undercover cop must be a devoted student of human psychology. It's the only way we both keep our cover and convince others we're not hiding something."

"As I mentioned, I was an undercover intelligence agent for a long time. Studying human nature became an obsession of mine as well."

"Which means you understand why I'm curious. I don't care what will happen to Harko and the other overseers, but it would add to my fund of knowledge if I could figure out what made them tick."

"Once the entire bunch is in *Mikado*'s brig, you can take whatever time you want. I can even lend you the tools of the interrogation trade. My partner and I were dab hands at making canaries sing during our undercover days, she more than me. Way more than me, scarily so. But I learned a lot from her."

"Is she still—"

"Alive? Yes, and doing well. Hera's a Navy captain on the cusp of getting her first star and command of intelligence's Special Operations Division. We still hang out together when I'm on Caledonia and not otherwise occupied."

Kine studied Decker for a few seconds while a faint smile relaxed her lean features.

"You're an interesting man, Colonel. And this Hera—"

"Talyn."

"This Captain Hera Talyn means a lot to you. As I said, I'm a student of human psychology. Your tone, your choice of words, the way your eyes lit up with admiration as you mentioned her interrogation skills. And you're not referring to her as a former partner. That tells me the word holds a different connotation these days."

Decker gave her an ironic round of applause.

"Well done. Yes, Hera and I have been an item for many years, and plan on retiring together, provided both of us make it that far. We're even looking at properties by Caledonia's Middle Sea. Nice subtropical climate. Not overly developed. If my daughter ever produces offspring, the grandkids can come and stay with us for a few months every year."

"Your daughter, but not Hera's. Interesting."

"A failed marriage long ago. My daughter's about to be commissioned as a Marine Corps intelligence officer." A wry smile twisted Decker's lips. "And you're a pretty good interrogator as well."

Kine took a theatrical bow.

"Why, thank you, Colonel. I'm both glad and a little irked you noticed."

"Glad because it proves I can tell when the tables are turned and irked because you weren't quite smooth enough with me?"

"Pretty much."

Both looked at each other in silence, then he asked, "What happens with you now? I mean professionally?"

Kine raised both shoulders in a helpless shrug.

"My undercover days are done. An officer whose cover failed the way mine did is considered compromised, both with the bad guys and psychologically. You've been there. Once the doubts about keeping an intact cover begin, they never go away. They'll probably transfer me to the Criminal Intelligence Division. People with my background usually are since we can tease out obscure but vital information from masses of data because we once walked on the dark side. Why do you ask?"

"As well as a student of the human psyche, I'm also a damned good judge of character. You won't enjoy riding a desk for the next ten years."

"I could always accept a commission as an inspector and run a Constabulary company on one of the colonies."

"Breaking up bar fights, chasing petty smugglers, and dealing with the odd livestock theft? You're not the type for that either."

She gave him an ironic smile.

"My, my. You're almost as good as I am at reading people. Impressive."

"Almost?" He snorted. "Perhaps."

"I sense you're about to offer me a job, Colonel."

"You sense correctly. There is a Constabulary liaison officer slot on my table of organization. Any rank between master sergeant and chief inspector. It's been vacant since day one because Special Operations Command insists on a vetting process that discourages anyone on your side from applying. Remember — a unit such as ours doesn't officially exist."

"And you're looking at me for the slot. We've known each other how long? Two hours at best, and you think I'd pass the vetting process?"

"We won't tell any of the other former captives that Fleet operatives rescued them. As far as they're concerned, we're mercenaries hired by unnamed interests for the job. But you know who and what we are, which means there's no point in making you jump through security hoops. I just need to tell Hera, who in turn will make the arrangements with the Constabulary and tell SOCOM HQ you're now a member of Ghost Squadron because of operational exigencies."

Kine sipped at her coffee again, though her gaze never left Decker's face.

"How do you know I won't turn around and betray your unit?"

"I know. When you said you would be eternally in our debt, you meant it, with no mental reservations whatsoever. I could use someone with your resilience and cunning and your unshakable loyalty to the Constabulary's values and ethos. How many undercover cops would have killed the poor sod at Hogue's estate under the logic that the needs of the many outweigh the needs of the one? Kill this guy who's a dead man walking anyway so you might save thousands at some point."

Kine didn't immediately reply, but he saw the answer in her eyes.

"Would you have killed that man?" She finally asked.

"When I was working as a field agent? I don't know. What I can tell you is that I wouldn't have put myself into a position where I faced that choice, because a cop's rules of engagement didn't constrain me."

"What does a Constabulary liaison officer in a Marine Corps Special Forces unit do?" She refilled her mug and sat across from him once more.

"Provide advice to the commanding officer on police matters. Talk to the local Constabulary unit if we need backup or for them to clear the field. Help with prisoner interrogation and prisoner processing. Act as frontwoman, in uniform if necessary, to distract people or give us added plausible deniability. That sort of thing."

She tilted her head to one side.

"What's the catch? There must be a catch. Otherwise, my peers would be lining up for such a job."

"You would be closing your cop's eyes now and then while we violate the law, which includes executing really bad guys who'd escape justice otherwise and continue victimizing innocents. You would need a basic Pathfinder qualification since we sometimes jump into a target from low orbit. But that's easily arranged. My second in command, Josh Bayliss, was the regimental sergeant major of the Pathfinder School before taking his commission and joining me. No one there would refuse his request they slide you in, even for a private course. You'd be living in or near Fort Arnhem on Caledonia, be on short notice for deployments, and rack up a lot of light-years crisscrossing the known galaxy aboard Q-ships such as *Mikado*. I don't need an answer now. So long as you decide before we dock at Starbase 59."

Kine held back her reply for a few heartbeats. Then, she nodded.

"Why not? I'll probably die from adrenaline withdrawal riding a desk in Criminal Intelligence. If this operation is an example of what you do for a living, it'll give me just enough of a hit, even if I don't bust through doors with your troopers."

Decker held out his hand.

"Welcome aboard, Warrant Officer."

As they shook, she asked, "It's that easy?"

"Yup. Hera will formalize it at the earliest opportunity. And now, how about I introduce you to Jory Virk, my operations officer, and Kaori Nomura, my intelligence noncom and let them debrief you?"

— Thirty —

"Do you think it was a good idea to offer her the Constabulary liaison job so quickly?" Major Bayliss asked once he, Decker, and Sergeant Major Paavola were alone in the small squadron office where they'd conducted the debriefing.

"You listened to her talk, Josh. That's not only one smart cop, but she has her head screwed on right. Good memory, able to deliver a concise, unemotional report, doesn't seem overly shaken by her experience. Besides, when was the last time I misjudged someone? Other than before I joined intelligence, I mean."

"None that I know of," Bayliss replied in a grudging tone. "And yes, she struck me as smart and capable. A survivor, just like you and Captain Talyn. She'll fit in with the rest of squadron HQ. I could tell she impressed Jory and Sergeant Nomura with her composure after what happened."

Paavola nodded.

"I'm with the colonel on this. If Kine's alternative is a soul-destroying desk job after a decade as an adrenaline junkie out in the field, we'd be wasting her God-given talents. It's not as if SOCOM's in a hurry to fill the liaison slot, and we could have used one on the last mission."

"You'll clear it through Captain Talyn?"

"Of course. Anyone who briefs the grand admiral regularly has the pull we need to make it official no matter what SOCOM HQ's security folks say about vetting or lack thereof, and Hera trusts my judgment implicitly."

"I just wanted to see if we were on the same wavelength. We don't usually recruit people into SOCOM in such a manner and certainly not within hours of being rescued from a horrible fate. However, as you said, she doesn't give off any signs of undue strain after what she's been through, which should make her a perfect fit. You discussed the fact we not only stretch the letter of the law but shatter it altogether at times?"

"Chapter and verse. I think her years undercover infiltrating the worst of the worst and watching them skate because of corruption in the system, plus her most recent experiences, will overcome any ingrained cop scruples if we're saving innocent lives."

Bayliss let out a soft snort.

"But we do more than save innocent lives, Zack. We're also the judge, jury, and executioner when nothing else will remove an evil stain from the galaxy. An upright cop of Kine's sort might see that as problematic. Then there's the small matter of our interfering with political movements deemed inimical to star system sovereignty and civil peace."

Decker raised a restraining hand.

"We'll deal with those situations when they occur. Kine will quickly understand why what we do is vital and inevitable. If she can't deal with it, I'm sure she'll find her way back to a Constabulary job and no hard feelings. But after what happened in recent weeks, I sense her view of the written law, and its uneven application to protect the corrupt and downright criminal from retribution might be shifting. I think I glimpsed a fire burning within her. One we would recognize."

"Understood. No need for further discussion, then. We agree. But Warrant Officer Kine will undergo the normal probationary period."

"Without question. And when we're home, please see if you can find space for her on a jump course. She may never need the qualification, but it would be best if she wore wings like the rest of us. One of the tribe, so to speak."

"Done." Bayliss smacked his hands on his knees and stood. "When are we holding the hot wash?"

"Since we've sorted everything out and are already on our way to the hyperlimit, any time is good."

"Just a reminder, we can't do it on the hangar deck because it's now a huge dormitory, and we can't fit the command ranks in the conference room."

"Then the company commanders will hold a hot wash at their level, and we'll bring them in with only their first sergeants." Decker glanced at his timepiece. "Let's do it in three hours."

"I'll let everyone know."

**

"Gentlemen, may I introduce our new Constabulary liaison officer, Warrant Officer Aleksa Kine." Decker gestured at her to enter *Mikado*'s conference room. "She was so impressed by her rescue that she accepted my job offer right away."

He introduced the company commanders and first sergeants one after the other. When Kine heard the name Curtis Delgado, a smile lit up her face.

"I believe Captain Delgado and I already met. He was wearing armor, and I wasn't wearing a damn thing."

Her quip drew amused chuckles.

"Don't worry," Delgado replied, grinning broadly. "You're not the first Constabulary officer I've seen in the altogether."

"I can believe it."

Decker clapped his hands.

"Right. Now that we're one big, happy family, sit so we can start."

But before he could say anything more, Lieutenant Commander Cotto's voice resonated throughout the ship.

"Prepare for transition to hyperspace in two minutes. For our passengers, that means sitting on the deck until you no longer feel the urge to puke. And please keep your food down. We barely have enough to keep everyone fed until we reach the nearest star base. That is all."

Paavola snorted with amusement.

"I never heard a warning phrased that way before. At least not on a Navy ship."

"Everyone did a complete company level hot wash, yes?" When Decker saw nods, he said, "Good. The contrary would have disappointed me. I suggest we wait until our stomachs settle before continuing."

As if on cue, a klaxon sounded three times, followed by Lieutenant Commander Cotto's voice.

"Jump in thirty seconds. I repeat, jump in thirty seconds. That is all."

"I hope the hangar deck guards are making sure our guests are prone," Paavola muttered. "Or I'll know the reason why."

Exactly thirty seconds later, the universe twisted, and more than one of the Marines in the conference room retched for a fraction of a second. Then, it stabilized, and the flashing psychedelic lights most humans saw when transitioning between normal space and hyperspace vanished.

Decker took a deep breath to shake away nausea.

"Well, that was as fun as always and reminds me why I'm not in the Navy. Everyone okay?"

When he heard no complaints, Decker said, "Curtis, the floor is yours. Runs us through Erinye Company's part of the mission."

Once they finished dissecting Operation Magic Carpet from first to last, Decker thanked everyone and declared the after-action review over.

"Another success which won't figure in the Marine Corps' history until long after we're dead. But the results are what counts. Major Bayliss, how are we set with the spirits ration?"

"Ready and waiting for distribution."

When Decker saw Kine give him a quizzical look, he said, "An old custom. When a starship's Marine unit returns to barracks after it carries out a shore action, each trooper is entitled to a dram of spirits. Whatever the ship carries. Rum, whiskey, vodka, or in times of need, less reputable distillations. Now that we finished our hot wash, Ghost Squadron is standing down save for the sentry posts guarding our passengers and the brig. Incidentally, we serve spirits in reverse order of rank. If the quartermaster sergeant runs out before those of us in this compartment receive a share, so be it."

"Interesting."

"Welcome to the Marine Corps' premier Special Forces unit, Warrant Officer Kine," Sergeant Major Paavola said. "We practice many strange rituals."

"I'll try not to run afoul of them, Sergeant Major, but I'll need a little help."

"Don't worry. We take care of each other."

**

Decker found *Mikado*'s captain nursing a cup of coffee in an otherwise deserted wardroom.

Piech looked up at the Marine and nodded in greeting.

"You're just the man I want to see, Zack. Grab a mug and join me."

"What gives?"

"Three-quarters of our passengers volunteered for the medically induced hibernation Doc Khadonov suggested. We don't carry enough doses for that many, but Doc figures he can knock about half of them out."

"Good news."

"Yeah. The take-up rate surprised me when I spoke with them earlier. Perhaps the volunteers figure it's a chance to rest and forget life for a bit after their nightmare on Kryani and at the cartel's hands."

"What can I do?"

"Have Ghost Squadron trade places with the volunteers. I don't want a few hundred civilians lying on the hangar deck, out cold until we're home. I need your bunks. Since two dozen of mine are in *Katisha* and *Pallantis*, we can squeeze you, your officers, and your command NCOs into crew quarters. Maybe even a few of the other sergeants. The rest can hot bunk it in various compartments, including my cargo holds, if you don't want them sleeping beside the rescuees. I figure there's enough space for at least a hundred to unroll their sleeping pouches at the same time. Probably more."

Decker nodded.

"Understood. When do you want us out?"

"As soon as possible. My chief engineer is already complaining about the strain on the environmental systems and it's only been what? Twelve hours?"

The Marine drained his coffee in a single gulp.

"Give me thirty minutes to clear the barracks."

"I'll let Doc know. He's choosing the fittest from among the volunteers."

"Does knocking back the strain of essentially doubling the number of human bodies aboard mean you won't push into the upper hyperspace bands once we're past the heliopause?"

"Yeah. We'll stick with our prizes."

"Good. I'd rather we don't take undue risks in these parts. Oh, and before I forget, could Lieutenant Corzon plot her course so we tack within range of a subspace array? I need to send my mission report and warn them we're bringing back over twelve hundred people who'll need interviews, processing, and repatriation. Starbase 59 won't thank us if we show up unannounced."

"We'll probably be told to land them on Santa Theresa directly. Starbase 59 isn't one of those behemoth orbitals which can take in over a thousand living bodies and not even burp. Besides, they're still building it, if I recall correctly. Mind you, landing and avoiding the star base altogether will help us keep up the pretense of being private sector, which should please SOCOM. Not that the local ground forces commanding officer will be any happier if we don't warn him or her ahead of time. Anyhow, so noted.

I'll make sure our navigation plan lets you tap into a subspace array."

"And I'll see that we vacate our bunks." Decker snapped off a mock salute and left Commander Piech to his ruminations.

— Thirty-One —

"Colonel!" Command Sergeant Rolf Painter intercepted Decker as he entered the Marine barracks. "Got a second?"

"Sure."

"My troop has guard duty at the moment and it seems there could be at least one ex-servicemember in the bunch. Maybe more. One of the women started chatting up Lance Corporal Dunn, commenting on how everything about the rescue, the ship, and the people felt familiar, as if we were retired from the Corps or the Navy. Dunn gave her the old 'no comment' routine, but she wasn't buying it. I just thought you might want to know, seeing as how she could poke a hole in the official story that we were never on Kryani or anywhere outside the Commonwealth."

"There's not much we can do if she tells the newsies Marines saved them and the Navy brought them home. Is she among the volunteers for medically induced hibernation?"

Painter shook his head.

"No. More's the pity."

"Ask the sergeant major to chat with this individual and find out about her background."

"Will do."

"Thanks."

**

The next morning, Sergeant Major Paavola greeted Decker at the door to the compartment he used as command post.

"How do you like those sleepers where our troopers used to rack out, sir? Spooky if you ask me. Can't see them breathe. They don't twitch. If I didn't know better, I'd say we were carrying a load of corpses."

"It feels strange, I agree." Decker entered the compartment and dropped into one of the chairs surrounding a bare table. "What's the word from the hangar deck?"

"Two things. First, I spoke with the hangar deck petty officer, and he's unlocked the shuttles so our people have a place to sit and chat where the civilians can't overhear them when they're not standing guard at the airlocks."

"Good thinking. And the other item?"

"I spoke with the woman who pestered Lance Corporal Dunn. It turns out she's a twenty-year army veteran. Retired as a command sergeant from the New Tasman Regiment."

"How did she end up on Kryani as a slave?"

"She was working private security on Arcadia when her employer met trouble with a powerful family. One night, intruders murdered the employer and most of her entourage. Our passenger was the sole survivor. They took her with them and shipped her out, probably via New Oberon. This happened approximately six months ago. Upon arrival, she passed herself off as a former combat engineer with expertise in weapons and explosives. She looks the part too. Tall, with a weightlifter's muscles." Paavola touched his right cheek. "Long scar from the corner of the eye to her jaw. Not overly noticeable. Just a thin white line. She was working in the head lizard's arsenal."

Paavola's description triggered a distant memory, especially the scar.

"Did this retired army noncom give a name?"

"Yeah. Miko Steiger. No way of checking if anything she said is real until we reach Santa Theresa." A frown creased Paavola's forehead when he noticed the expression on Decker's face. "Why do I sense she might be familiar to you, Colonel?"

"I remember a Miko Steiger, ex-army, working as private security who has a long white scar on her cheek and is built more or less like a female version of me, only prettier. I last saw her on Dordogne's civilian orbital station about six years ago. We worked together twice when I was running field ops for Naval Intelligence. She suspected who and what I was but never said so. We were pretty friendly."

Paavola gave him a knowing glance. "Is it time for a tearful reunion?"

Decker seemed at a loss.

"She covered my back in a few hairy situations, and I trusted her with my life at the time. But she's also rootless and I don't know what she's been into since we parted ways. Her story of working for someone who was murdered could mean she was involved with criminals. Not that I ever saw any sign of criminality on her part. But six years is long enough to pick up bad habits. Especially when honest work for freelance mercenaries is scarce.

"That's how we met, by the way. The first time she was buying weapons for the revolutionaries who eventually overthrew the Garonne government — with Hera and my help. The second time, she'd signed up as a soldier-for-hire with a shady organization that used the Confederacy of the Howling Stars as recruiters. I was looking for Hal Tarra, one of my oldest and best friends besides Josh. Remember him?"

"Vaguely. Our paths crossed, but we never served together. I heard he died not long after retiring."

A grimace briefly twisted Decker's features. "I was there when it happened. We almost escaped the shady organization together, but at the last minute, they caught up with us. Hal took a few rounds to protect me and died instantly. Miko Steiger was there as well and witnessed Hal's death."

Paavola winced in sympathy.

"Ouch. That is quite a history."

"What I don't understand is how she popped up in my path a third time. You know what they say about coincidences, right?"

"There's no such thing?"

"I was thinking about a famous quote from pre-diaspora times, but that works too." Decker exhaled slowly. "I just decided I won't indulge in a tearful reunion. For one thing, I'm still not beyond temptation, and for another, I can't risk plausible deniability, even if Miko is still trustworthy. Make sure the troops never mention my name when they're on guard duty."

"Roger that, sir. They're smart enough to keep *stumm* with names around civilians. Just stay away from the hangar deck until she's gone."

"If anything requires my presence there, Josh can take care of it. And if I need to climb aboard a shuttle, it'll be in armor, with visor shut. I guess I'd better tell Josh about this."

Paavola stood.

"How about I go find Major Bayliss for you?"

"Sure. Thanks."

With the sergeant major gone, Decker connected his command post display to the ship's net and called up a live video feed from the hangar deck. It was a lot less crowded now that half of the rescuees were in suspended animation next door from where he sat, and he found Miko quickly.

She appeared unaffected by the passing years and still wore that sardonic expression he remembered so well, but her eyes seemed eerily haunted by something. Her experiences on Kryani, perhaps?

He would include her name in his report, if only to surprise Hera. His partner never quite warmed to Steiger, although that could be because she never warmed to anyone but would pretend around people she respected.

"Sergeant Major Paavola said you wanted me?"

Decker looked down from the display as Major Bayliss entered. He pointed at Miko Steiger's image.

"I know her. Quite well, as a matter of fact. Or rather, I did." He repeated almost word for word what he'd told Paavola.

"Face it, Zack," Bayliss said when Decker fell silent. "You're a magnet for certain sorts of people. Such as warrior women. That's why you and Ingrid never stood a chance. She's the exact opposite of someone such as Captain Talyn, or your old friend on the hangar deck."

Decker grimaced at the name of his former spouse, who'd left him high and dry when she returned home to Scandia with their five-year-old daughter while he was away on a mission. Now the child who'd grown up without him was a twenty-seven-year-old about to receive her commission in the Commonwealth Marine Corps, following in dad's footsteps rather than mom's.

"And yet, my kid is becoming a warrior woman."

"That's because the genes she inherited from you took the upper hand when the plotters kidnapped her during the Scandia business."

"Getting rescued by her dad, his deadly partner, and Q.D. Vinn's H Troop probably helped too. Hera makes a great role model if you overlook the fact she's incapable of feeling empathy, or much of anything."

"Careful." Bayliss wagged a finger at him, smirking. "Though she's stuck behind a desk, I'll put my money on her instead of you every single time."

"Some friend you are. What do I do with this? My first instinct was ignoring her, make sure she never sees me or hears my name, and report her presence among the rescuees."

"Sure. But if Steiger was a fire team buddy, I question the idea of leaving her with the others. Plausible deniability is nice and well, but it'll get out soon enough that the Fleet sent a punitive expedition into techno-barb space. It doesn't matter one bit if a few of the rescuees can state without lying that they're sure we — the generic Armed Services we — carried out the mission. The damn politicos who'd rather hunt for our grand admiral's head without a shred of evidence, so they don't lose re-election funding from the lunatic and depraved fringe, will scream no matter what. Fuck 'em. A fire team buddy is just that. Someone who has your back."

"You're saying I should fish her out of the multitude, and then what?"

Bayliss gave him an exasperated glare.

"Treat this Steiger as you did Aleksa Kine. I don't mean offer her a job. If she was out of the service last time you saw her six years ago, her qualifications are expired anyway.

Give her the sense we take care of fellow Armed Services veterans, lend her something from the clothing stores and run her through a full debriefing. We might learn new things about the Saqqa Cartel. So what if she knows the 1st Special Forces Regiment raided an alien planet? Popular opinion, at least the minuscule slice that pays attention to anything beyond their belly buttons will yawn if she speaks with the newsies. Sure, activists providing cover for the cartels and their political enablers will scream, but who gives a shit?"

When he saw hesitation in his friend's eyes, Bayliss shrugged.

"Do what you think is best. It's not as if we're keeping the passengers penned in like animals. We can even debrief her without saying boo about our identity or commanding officer."

"She sits in front of Kaori, and she'll smell him out as a Marine Corps sergeant within seconds."

"We could ask our newest member for help. Kine doesn't scream cop, let alone military. I think this retired army command sergeant has useful information up here." Bayliss tapped the side of his head with an extended index finger. "And if we leave it in the hands of whoever HQ tasks with interviews on Santa Theresa, we might never find out what she knows."

Decker took a deep breath and released it.

"I should never argue with you when logic is on your side."

"That's what we deputy commanding officers do for a living. Make sure our COs make the right decisions at the right time. Shall I fetch her? As in now?"

Decker let out a disconsolate grunt.

"Okay. Let's give old Miko a surprise."

Once Bayliss left, Decker turned to the display again and zeroed in on Steiger. He watched as his friend approached her, said a few words, then led her past the guard post and through the airlock. A minute passed, then he heard voices in the passageway.

"Our CO is in the command post, right through that door, Sera Steiger."

"Sera Steiger was my mother. I answer to Steiger, Miko, or hey you. Uncap a beer bulb within hearing, and I'll answer to that as well."

She stepped through the opening and halted abruptly, eyes widening in shock.

"Of all the starships in the known galaxy, I had to step aboard yours. Figures it was you who carried out that remarkable rescue. It reeked of your old style. How's business, Big Boy?"

— Thirty-Two —

"Hello, Miko. How about, of all the alien slave pens in the Shield Cluster, I had to liberate yours?" Decker nodded at a chair across from him. "Sit."

"What? No hugs and kisses? I'm crushed. Did you finally marry your assassin friend and leave your old ways behind?" She dropped into the seat and grinned at him. "You're still my type. If you want to get frisky..."

"No, we're not married, but we might as well be. And there's no friskiness in this ship. Not with over six hundred rescuees, three hundred and fifty of my troopers, and over two hundred crew."

Steiger let out a low whistle.

"Wow. That is seriously overloaded, even if half of us are snoring through this voyage of the formerly damned. What gives? Are you in the 1st Special Forces Regiment now? The one that runs the secret squirrel ops?"

"I command the regiment's 'A' Squadron. We handle the blackest of the black."

"Based on what I saw, you lead one hell of a good unit, Zack. Congratulations. Since you and the ship's crew are pretending to be private sector, may I infer this is also a black op because you don't have Senate permission to leave the Commonwealth sphere?"

Decker exchanged a glance with Bayliss, who gave him his best 'I told you so' shrug.

"Sergeant Steiger wasn't born yesterday."

She looked at Bayliss over her shoulder.

"Nope. And not the day before either. I can recognize real pros when I see them." Steiger turned back to Decker. "And since it took you so long before inviting an old comrade for a cup of coffee, may I also infer you didn't know I was among the multitudes until I spoke with one of your men?"

He nodded. "That's pretty much it."

A sly smile spread across her face.

"And I'll bet you almost left me there to keep your cover intact. What do you call it again? Plausible deniability? Because this rescue will make the news?"

Decker pointed at Josh.

"I discussed it with Major Bayliss, who is my second in command."

"Does that mean you're a lieutenant colonel? Congratulations. Well deserved."

"Thanks. Josh convinced me it would be better if we fished you out of the hangar for a thorough interview. An old soldier and wandering mercenary would probably notice more throughout her captivity than a career civilian."

"I figured that's what the invitation was about. Ask away. There will be no secrets between us because I owe you my life and will probably never repay that debt in full."

"My people will put you through a proper debriefing later but satisfy my curiosity. How did you end up as a slave on Kryani?"

"Could I beg for a cup of coffee while I speak?" Steiger asked in a plaintive voice.

"Sure."

Without saying a word, Bayliss filled a mug from the urn he'd installed in the command post compartment and handed it to Steiger. She took a greedy sip before sighing.

"What a delightful nectar! You are truly officers and gentlemen." Steiger closed her eyes for a moment, as if wallowing in the coffee's aroma. "So. How did I end up on an alien shit hole far from the nearest human star system? It started on Arcadia, where I was working as a personal security contractor."

When she saw Decker's expression at hearing the planet's name, Steiger gave him a suspicious look.

"What?"

"Earlier today, I was discussing the nature of coincidences with my sergeant major. He believes they don't exist. But please go on. I'll tell you why Arcadia means something to me later. What were you doing?"

"I hired on as a bodyguard for a rich Arcadian businesswoman who dabbled in star system politics, one Aldene Rusten." She paused, then said, "I guess her name means nothing to you."

"No. How did you find the job?"

"Through a private security employment agency called UniSec. I've been on their books for years, and Sera Rusten wanted ex-military women as bodyguards. She was feuding with the family who seems to run Arcadia, or at least thinks it does. Ever heard of the name Hogue?"

Decker nodded.

"And that's where the non-coincidence comes in. As I mentioned, we'll discuss it when you've said your piece."

"Anyway, one night, just around three in the morning, two dozen masked gangsters invaded the Rusten estate, out in the countryside south of the star system capital. An insider helped them, someone who made sure none of the alarms and security measures came online. As far as I could tell, they killed the property's guard detail, eight rent-a-cops, out of hand. There were three of us working close protection on Sera Rusten, one awake and near her at all times. I wasn't on shift and woke to stare into the barrel of a large-bore blaster. Tessa, who was on night duty, took a round through the heart before she even drew her gun. Hali, the third bodyguard, was spending the night in town. Or so we thought."

"The insider?"

"Yep. I watched the goons execute Aldene Rusten, her mother, two of her children, and an ailing uncle. And when I say execute, they did it cartel-style. They shackled me and bundled me off as if I was a sack of dirty linen. I couldn't understand why I wasn't lying on the marble floor in a puddle of my blood, like the Rustens, for the longest time.

But now I figure being condemned to spend the rest of my life as a slave on an alien world was Hali's revenge. We didn't exactly agree on much. She was one of UniSec's bad bargains, and I let her know what I thought."

"Then this Hali was cartel or at least taking its money if she kept them from shooting you."

"Probably. And I'm convinced the Hogue family arranged the murders. Aldene Rusten wanted to break their stranglehold on Arcadia politics. She was what you might call an anti-corruption crusader. Anyway, I took two long starship rides with a break in a stockade on a frontier planet between them. They kept me in a drug haze from start to finish."

"We raided and destroyed that stockade before coming to Kryani. It was on New Oberon, hidden in a country estate owned by Allard Hogue and operated by the Saqqa Cartel. The Hogues still consider New Oberon part of their fief even though the star system has been under direct federal control for years. And yes, you guessed it, they utterly corrupted the colonial administration appointed by Earth, police included."

Steiger scoffed.

"Figures. From what I saw of Sera Rusten's work, it'll take three lifetimes to clean up Arcadia. If you ever visited the Hogue compound, you'll understand why. The amount of money involved—"

"You were in there?"

"Several times. Sera Rusten enjoyed bearding Elize Hogue in her den. She'll need terminating first, followed by every last member of that evil clan." A frown creased her forehead. "And how did a squadron from the 1st Special Forces Regiment end up raiding Kryani, anyway? I didn't know the Marine Corps was at war with the cartels."

Decker gave her a cold smile.

"No one from the Marine Corps ever came near Kryani. This mission never happened. A private military consortium arranged for the rescue, and that's it."

She stared at him for a few seconds, then inclined her head.

"Understood. The why is none of my business, and I will be forever grateful that kind-hearted mercenaries rescued me and the others."

"Glad you see it my way, Miko. I told you as much as I did for old times' sake. I would be chagrined if I couldn't trust your discretion anymore. And the Hogues? I'm sure they'll pay for their misdeeds sooner than you think. Even the dumbest newsie will trace this human trafficking operation back to them, and there's no recovery from that."

"Really?" She cocked an eyebrow at him. "Rich as they are, the Hogues can buy off the entire damned Senate and see that the senator in the family is elected Secretary-General."

"Not this time."

Steiger studied him with an air of intense curiosity.

"You seem sure of that, Zack. But I probably shouldn't ask, right?"

"Right."

"Well, if there's anything I can do to help, ask me. Aldene Rusten was a good egg, even if she came from the same social class as the Hogues. She didn't deserve to die, and neither did the rest of her family."

"For now, you can tell your story in excruciating detail to my operations officer and intelligence sergeant."

Bayliss made a gesture to attract his attention, then mouthed 'Kine.'

"And my Constabulary liaison officer, who also wasn't anywhere near Kryani."

"As long as that coffee urn keeps dispensing the good stuff, I'll sing like a little birdie." She emptied her mug. "And after that, I suppose you're putting me back in the general population?"

"Considering most of my people are sleeping in the same conditions as the rescuees and we're eating the same rations, does it matter?"

"I was a member of the family for twenty years, Zack," she replied in a soft tone. "Spending the trip among my kind, even if they're from the jarhead branch, will be a balm to my tortured soul. Life on Kryani wasn't exactly fun or easy. And the food. Yuck. Speaking of which, if I stayed with your unit, we could skip down memory lane while eating those rations you mentioned."

"Calling us jarheads isn't helping your cause, pongo."

She put on the sardonic grin Decker remembered well.

"But think about it, between us we can diss the squids."

Decker looked up at Bayliss, whose eyes told him it was his decision.

"I'm sure we can find a bit of empty deck for your bedroll, Sergeant Steiger. Behave and don't try to make my folks tell you stuff they shouldn't."

Steiger placed her right hand over her heart.

"Upon my honor, Colonel, sir."

"Because we fought together, and that means everything to you?"

The grin widened.

"I don't think 'fought' is the word you want."

Decker turned a mock-serious glare on her.

"Yes, it is. Josh, could you please call for Jory, Warrant Officer Kine, and Sergeant Nomura? We should get the formal debriefing out of the way before Command Sergeant Steiger, Commonwealth Army, retired, turns overly nostalgic on us. Some memories are best left undisturbed."

— Thirty-Three —

"Colonel Decker's findings are beyond explosive." Admiral Kruczek sat back in his chair with a thoughtful expression on his hawk-like face when Hera Talyn finished summarizing the encrypted mission report they'd received over the subspace net less than two hours earlier. "And you've met this retired army command sergeant — Miko Steiger, was it?"

"Yes, sir. She struck me as reliable."

"But you're not fond of her. I can sense it."

Talyn knew better than to dissemble in front of the Chief of Naval Intelligence. Kruczek didn't earn his four stars through political patronage, and he was nobody's fool.

"I'm not a fan of her personality, sir. But that's no reflection on Steiger's trustworthiness. She was instrumental in helping the Garonne uprising succeed. What she told Colonel Decker dovetails with our investigation into the Hogue family and its connection to the Saqqa Cartel. As does Warrant Officer Kine's testimony."

"Ah, yes. Warrant Officer Kine. And you agree with Colonel Decker appointing her as Constabulary liaison to Ghost Squadron?"

Talyn glanced at Rear Admiral Ulrich, sitting next to her. "I do."

"As do I," the latter said. "We trust Zack's judgment in such matters. If he thinks she'll make the perfect liaison, then so be it. After we saved her from a horrible fate, Kine's superiors in the Constabulary will be grateful and allow her secondment to SOCOM for the next few years. Her usefulness as an undercover officer is over anyhow."

"A horrible fate indeed. But back to the Kryani. News they consider human flesh a delicacy and enslave human know-how to bootstrap their barbarous race into a space-faring society will not go over well with the citizens of the outer star systems. Especially with prominent Core Worlders involved. There will be demands that heads roll. Perhaps figuratively at first, but we know from history how fast it turns literal given the right conditions and enough provocation."

"Indeed, sir. Which is why I propose we stay ahead of the situation and make the heads roll first. Literally."

Kruczek's gaze went from Talyn to Ulrich and back.

"I'm listening."

"We're still analyzing the data Ghost Squadron seized on New Oberon. But we can already track the Saqqa Cartel's various operations and link them to the Hogue family, whose bank accounts — hundreds of them — see massive amounts of money flowing in and out. They filter much of it through so many shell companies any normal audit loses the trace. A good thing our analysts aren't normal auditors. The only problem with this evidence is how we obtained it. Inadmissible in court doesn't even begin to cover the problems federal prosecutors would have in building a case if we could even find federal prosecutors sufficiently brave for a frontal assault on the Hogues and their cartel lackeys. In other words, a formal process aimed at indicting and trying the principals involved is out of the question."

Kruczek nodded. "Hardly a surprise. Little of what we do, especially in your division, can withstand scrutiny by our legal system. Are you suggesting we take matters into our own hands? I know we crossed that Rubicon when you and Colonel Decker set off the MHX-19 bomb on Amali Island during your last mission as a team, but we enjoyed a great deal of plausible deniability back then. With what happened on New Oberon and the coming explosion of outrage once *Mikado* and her prizes land the rescuees on Santa Theresa, it'll be an open secret we, the Fleet, were involved. All eyes will be on us and many accusing fingers will point at Grand Admiral Larsson."

"Without a doubt, sir," Talyn replied. "But the Saqqa Cartel and the others with whom it sometimes cooperates and sometimes competes must still be terminated. Otherwise, they present a growing and uncontrollable threat to political stability. If an old family such as the Hogues, who've been sending senators for Arcadia to Earth since well before last century's Shrehari War, can run a criminal organization, then I suggest we're only seeing the tip of the iceberg. Step one should, therefore, be to act on the information we obtained and decapitate Saqqa by removing its senior leadership, now that we know who and where they are."

"With Ghost Squadron?"

Talyn shook her head.

"Not for that part of the operation. I'll use our division's field assets and, if need be, call on the 1st Special Forces Regiment for backup. I prepared other plans for Ghost Squadron once they deliver the rescuees to Santa Theresa."

"I approve the removal of the Saqqa leadership, as a black op. No links with the Fleet."

"Of course, sir."

"And your plans for Decker's unit?"

"We'd hoped Graciela Hogue would disavow her cousin Allard after news came out linking him to cartel activities on New Oberon. But it seems the family has closed ranks instead. Allard was last seen enjoying life inside the Hogue compound on Arcadia. The general public will perceive that as an admission the entire clan was involved and doesn't give a damn who knows."

"Part of the growing culture of impunity among Core World elites," Rear Admiral Ulrich said. "We're hearing a lot about it these days, with justification. And since Senator Hogue is one of the Centralist faction's leading lights while the human trafficking victims are probably Out Worlders by a wide margin, you can imagine how it'll play out in the Senate. Which is why we cannot simply take out the Saqqa

Cartel and leave it at that. We must deal with its enablers as well."

Kruczek made a gesture of agreement.

"Certainly, but perhaps the grand admiral would prefer advising the Secretary-General he put pressure on Graciela rather than allow a direct action."

"The Secretary-General has already done so," Talyn replied in a flat voice. "To no avail."

"Should I ask how you know that? Never mind. What is your proposal?" When Talyn didn't reply, Kruczek sighed. "I see. Don't you think Graciela Hogue's assassination could precipitate the very crisis we're trying to avoid?"

"We would aim our action at the family matriarch, Elize Hogue, and at Allard Hogue. They are the ones who run the cartel through several cut-outs and have the lives of countless humans on their conscience. Graciela, who is on Earth and won't visit Arcadia while the Senate is in session, will escape personal retribution, though I daresay with Elize Hogue dead, Arcadia should experience an extensive political realignment which will end the senator's career. And since we traced the family money through those shell companies, we'll make sure she spends her retirement in penury and friendless, which shouldn't be hard once we anonymously leak juicy tidbits."

Admiral Kruczek placed his elbows on the desktop and joined his fingertips while a thoughtful expression appeared on his face.

"I approve the plan. And I won't inform Grand Admiral Larsson, so he can deny our involvement in Elize Hogue's death without lying. Is this what you intend for Ghost Squadron?"

A humorless smile tugged at Talyn's thin lips.

"I can't think of anyone better."

"Neither can I. And you're sure Elize and her grandson are the real masterminds behind Saqqa?"

"Based on the evidence we found, a minor branch of the Hogue clan formed it at Elize's orders, possibly so she could recover the family's squandered fortune. Elize's late husband was both unlucky in business and at the gaming tables. When he died, she assumed absolute control over the family's affairs and became the undisputed kingmaker on Arcadia. As the old saying goes, it's not the people who vote that count but the people who count the votes, and Elize owns the latter lock, stock, and barrel."

"She sounds like a real piece of work."

Talyn's smile hardened.

"When I examined every bit of information we dug up on Elize Hogue, I couldn't help but conclude she displayed the signs of being a highly functioning psychopath. And I should know better than anyone what those signs are."

"When will this unfold?"

"Zack sent his report via a subspace array while *Mikado* and her prizes were tacking between jumps, so they still face a bit of travel before reaching Santa Theresa. Add two or three days spent landing the rescuees, turning the prize ships over to the local system commander, taking on supplies and spare parts. They'll be cleaned out of the former by the time they arrive there, and *Mikado*'s environmental systems will need an overhaul. Then, there's the trip inward to Arcadia. Call it three, maybe four weeks before they strike. I'll put people in place to take out the various cartel branch offices in the meantime, so we can act against them once Zack deals with Elize."

"And what arrangements are in place for the rescuees on Santa Theresa?"

"We warned Rear Admiral Jubal, the system commander, and Lieutenant Colonel Klaes, the Marine garrison CO. They'll process the rescuees on the ground and debrief them while Fleet Operations arranges for transportation." Talyn seemed to hesitate. "There's one last item, sir. Command Sergeant Miko Steiger, Commonwealth Army, retired. Zack wants her as a civilian consultant for the mission. Steiger knows the lay of the land on Arcadia, including the Hogue family compound since she accompanied her late employer there frequently."

"A civilian who'll witness troopers from the Marine Corps' 1st Special Forces Regiment terminating Commonwealth citizens, prominent ones at that, on a sovereign Commonwealth planet? I'm not sure it's a good idea, even if she was helpful in the past and is a friend of Colonel Decker's."

"There's a way around that, sir."

One of Kruczek's bushy eyebrows twitched.

"Do tell."

"Steiger is still on the inactive reserve list, though her qualifications have expired. We could ask for a waiver on the qualifications from the Army Chief of Staff and recall

Steiger to active duty with SOCOM. That would put her under the Code of Service Discipline and make sure anything she witnesses is covered by operational security regulations. I ran a background check on Steiger and there's no record of her doing anything that would prevent the reactivation of her security clearance."

"And afterward? What if Steiger decides she enjoys being back in a regular uniform?"

"That would depend on the army. Or we could keep her ourselves. I can always use more field agents. After seeing how she handled herself during the Garonne uprising, I think Steiger would graduate from Camp X without problems."

Kruczek tapped his fingertips together a few times, then nodded.

"If you can arrange everything before *Mikado* leaves Santa Theresa, and if Steiger agrees to a recall, she can go with Ghost Squadron. Otherwise, no."

"Yes, sir. Thank you. That was everything. Did you wish a written briefing for the grand admiral on this matter?"

"No. Let's give him the ability to disavow our actions with convincing sincerity."

— Thirty-Four —

"So, that's it?" Steiger asked after Zack laid out her options. They'd received Talyn's message when *Mikado* dropped out of hyperspace at the Santa Theresa star system's heliopause and queried its subspace relay. "I either accept a recall to active duty and go with you on the next leg of your mission, which is obviously Arcadia, because why else reenlist me for the duration, or you unload me along with the rest of the former captives. And you can't say what you're about to do next."

"That's it. I can't take a civilian where *Mikado* is heading after we land our passengers. But I can take an army command sergeant subject to the Code of Service Discipline and the operational security regulations."

"What would I be doing? Let me guess. You can't say. Meaning the deal is, put my uniform on again, or whatever you secret squirrels wear when you're being sneaky, and I'll find out what I signed up for?"

Decker nodded.

"Yup. The army is giving you a waiver on the expiration of your qualifications, and you regain the seniority in rank you held on the day you retired. But if you say yes, your soul is mine, as are the souls of everyone else in Ghost Squadron, including our Constabulary liaison officer."

"A very nice person for a cop. She knows a lot about life on Kryani. Anything you'd care to mention about her?"

"No. Sign up, and you'll find out. Or not."

"Did I ever tell you I prefer the old Zack? The super spy who threw caution to the wind whenever he felt the urge? This one, the commanding officer of a Special Forces unit, lacks that zest, that *joie de vivre.*"

"We change with time and responsibilities, Miko. Now, what is it? Are you in or are you out?"

She shrugged. "I assume my oath is still valid?"

"It is."

"What do I have to lose? After letting the cartel murder my principal and her family, I won't find any close protection contracts ever again. At least not legal ones, and I'd rather stay on the side of light. It's a given UniSec already struck me off the roster. When and where do I sign up, Colonel, sir?"

"When is now. Where is here." He held out a slim tablet. "You know the drill. Read the recall to active duty contract and thumbprint it. Then, read the operational security regulations and thumbprint them. Once that's done, if you say a word about our mission to anyone, I will make sure you spend what's left of your life in a stockade on Parth. This is no joke, Miko."

Steiger winced theatrically at hearing the name of the Commonwealth's infamous prison planet before meeting Decker's eyes and deciding he was dead serious.

"I will take your secrets to the grave, fear not. I know how it works, and I understand black ops units do things for the good of the Commonwealth that can never be revealed. What happens with me after the mission?"

"Let's cross that bridge when we reach it, okay? Contract and regulations first."

She took the tablet, carefully read each word, and silently thumb-printed the documents.

"Welcome back to the army, Command Sergeant Steiger. You're now attached to Ghost Squadron's HQ Troop and will work for Captain Jory Virk in whatever capacity he decides until we reach our target and need your special insight."

"I think I can guess what that target is."

"No doubt. But you'll wait until I inform the squadron at large before speculating openly, and that won't be until we offload our guests."

She nodded once.

"Understood. The bulkheads have ears."

"Special Forces units exist in a very different universe from the rest of the Armed Services when it comes to hiding or divulging information. We do a lot of the former and damn little of the latter."

"Understood, sir."

Decker let both hands drop to strike the tabletop. A meaty smack filled the command post.

"That was it. I'm sure you've met Cyril Burkitt, the squadron quartermaster sergeant by now."

"Yes. Nice guy."

"Speak with him about getting outfitted from *Mikado*'s stores. As you can see, we're wearing mercenary chic, so don't go looking for an army uniform. Anything we can't give you now, Cyril will beg, borrow or steal from Starbase 59 or the Santa Theresa Marine garrison. He has to equip Warrant Officer Kine as well."

"Oh?" A suspicious gleam appeared in her eyes. "Should I not ask why your — pardon, our Constabulary liaison didn't come on this mission with her gear?"

"She was a slave on Kryani and our primary reason to raid the place. We merely decided we'd bring every human home, not just the one for whom we were looking."

Steiger snorted.

"Figures. Her questions about my time there were way too pointed." She stood. "*Con su permiso, mi teniente coronel?*"

Decker frowned at her. "How many languages do you speak?"

"Human or in total?" When Decker gave Steiger an irritated look, she hastily said, "Ten human languages, Shrehari, Itrulan, Arkanna, and for my sins a smattering of Kryani."

"What human languages beside Anglic?"

"Mandarin, Spanish, French, German, Arabic, Hindi, Russian, Italian, and some Swahili."

"How good are your alien languages?"

"My Shrehari and Arkanna are pretty good, though I bet my accent grates on their ears. The Itrulan and Kryani, less so, but I get by. And as you might recall, I can understand a bit of Darsivian."

"Why am I finding out now, Miko? We worked together twice before."

She put on a contrite expression.

"It never came up in conversation."

"Do you know how useful a linguist is for us?"

A mischievous smile pulled up the corners of her lips.

"Especially a cunning one?"

Decker groaned as he shook his head.

"No. Don't. Please, don't. Between the lot of us, Ghost Squadron can cover the major human languages, but that doesn't help me if, for example, I need a Russian speaker, and the only one in the outfit is a troop leader who I can't yank into the command post during an operation. As for alien tongues, nada. Let's finish this mission, and if we're both still alive and haven't been cashiered, we can talk about your future."

"Does that happen a lot in this line of business? I mean getting cashiered?"

"Only if we divulge information that should stay hidden until the end of time."

**

"I'm surprised Steiger is back in uniform that fast," Bayliss said around a mouthful of reconstituted food. Both he and Decker were sharing a table in the wardroom.

"Hera's doing. She developed one hell of a good network inside Fleet HQ."

"Probably because she knows where every skeleton-bearing closet is by now."

"Could be. Especially after the nonsense we went through cleansing HQ of the Black Sword conspiracy." Decker shoved another bite into his mouth and chewed thoughtfully before swallowing. "Man, will I be happy when we offload the passengers and refill our pantry. This stuff may be nourishing, but it gets old after a while. Anyway, back to Hera. I figure a captain already assured of her promotion to commodore and who briefs Grand Admiral Larsson at least once a month can get anything she wants for the missions she controls. The people at HQ know better than refusing her requests if saying yes is possible."

Bayliss grinned at Decker.

"So basically, she scares people into obedience with connections nowadays instead of using her stiletto."

"Wait until she takes over from Admiral Ulrich. You ain't seen nothing yet."

"How come Captain Talyn isn't skipping commodore and going straight to rear admiral?"

"Fleet HQ politics. If she doesn't screw up, I figure that second star will come in as little as twelve months after the first. And then I'll never catch up with her. I bet she'll sit in Admiral Kruczek's chair one day." Decker drained his water glass and grimaced. "A good thing we're almost there. *Mikado*'s recycling filters are losing the battle."

"We can break out our field purifiers if it gets too bad." Bayliss emptied his glass and made a face. "I think the battle is almost over. But let's talk about more important stuff. So Steiger is a linguist. Interesting. For us, I mean. Will you keep her after we're done?"

"Depends on how she performs and what she wants. As I told her, let's complete the next part of our mission first."

Bayliss, who'd read Hera Talyn's message, nodded in agreement.

"Yep, seeing as how it could be dicier than Kryani. Too bad we didn't think of bringing our light armor. That could easily pass for civilian gear used by mercs and cartel goons. Sergeant Burkitt will see if he can scrounge a few sets on Starbase 59 and Santa Theresa, but we'll never find enough for everyone."

"So long as we can equip the door knockers, I'll be happy." Decker pushed away his empty plate and sat back just as Lieutenant Commander Cotto's voice boomed from hidden speakers, warning them *Mikado* would come out of FTL at the Santa Theresa hyperlimit in two minutes.

"That means Doc Khadonov is about to revive the sleepers," Bayliss said. "I better make sure our people are where they should be once we're sublight."

**

Decker and Piech watched from the hangar control room as the last batch of rescuees climbed aboard *Mikado's* shuttles.

"I'm glad that's over," the latter said in a tone of deep relief. "My chief engineer is crying into his tea over the damage to his beloved ship."

"What do you mean damage?" Decker asked with alarm. "We're expected in a star system far, far away."

"Consumable parts only, the Almighty be praised, nothing that requires a stay in the nearest dry dock. Starbase 59 has replacements waiting for us, so it'll only be thirty-six to forty-eight hours until our on-board water no longer has that wonderful ammonia tang."

"Glad it's not just me complaining."

"Be happy you didn't make coffee with that last batch."

Decker turned narrowed eyes on Piech.

"My last coffee was five days ago when the water still tasted reasonably good. Did you hoard?"

"Of course. Being a starship captain has its privileges."

The Marine glared at his friend.

"I'm the mission commander."

"And not the starship captain. But relax. My logistics officer is already lining up our replenishment from Starbase 59's stores, including coffee, tea, fresh food, and anything else your heart desires. The moment our shuttles are back, we're docking."

"And your prizes?"

"Docking as well. We're turning them over to the system commander, which means I get Torrance Toh, Monique

Dulay, and two dozen crew members back. And in due course, we will find a little extra in our pay when the Fleet either sells *Katisha* and *Pallantis* or takes them into service. As will you and your Marines."

"How generous."

"Your share will be the same as mine, as per the rules. Serving aboard a Q-ship when it captures criminal scum helps top up the old retirement fund."

"I'll make a note." Decker nodded at the armored window separating them from the hangar. "And with the space doors closed on that last batch of passengers, we can finally reoccupy our barracks. Since we'll be docking with the star base, I won't discuss the next leg of our mission yet, except that we're going on a long trip into the Commonwealth core before heading home to Caledonia. Your logistics officer should load *Mikado* with consumables accordingly. We'll be crossing interstellar space for a few weeks."

"No worries. I already told her she should bring us back to a full load of everything we need, including replacements for the environmental filters, in case you're taking us on another rescue."

Decker shook his head. "It won't be a rescue this time. Did you ever hear a pre-diaspora piece of music called *The Battle Hymn of the Republic*?"

"No, but I'm not a student of history like you."

"One of its lines is *He hath loosed the fateful lightning of His terrible swift sword*."

"And Ghost Squadron is that terrible swift sword," Piech said after a pregnant pause.

"It is."

— Thirty-Five —

"And that is the next phase of our mission." Decker let his eyes roam over the assembled Ghost Squadron officers and command noncoms and *Mikado*'s department heads after explaining their orders on the hangar deck, the only place large enough for everyone. The Q-ship, now fully replenished and its filtration systems once again producing tasteless and odorless water, was nearing Santa Theresa's hyperlimit on the first leg of the journey inward to Arcadia.

"I'll entertain questions, although details on the how will have to wait until we get there. Fortunately, Sergeant Steiger has been inside the objective, which is why she's back on active duty and coming with us. But keep in mind, what will happen never did. *Mikado* never entered the Arcadia star system, and Ghost Squadron definitely never set foot on Arcadian soil."

"Just another day in SOCOM," Lieutenant Commander Cotto said in a stage whisper. "We don't exist, we see nothing, hear nothing, and do nothing. We're the military version of the three wise monkeys."

"Exactly. Same shit, different star system. Needless to say, the plausible deniability factor will be pegged at eleven on this one. *Mikado* will enter the star system as her merchant alter ego and Ghost Squadron will do its best to make everyone believe a rival cartel is looking for a bigger market share. The people who matter, meaning those for whom the message we're sending means something, will know the Fleet did it. But they won't find proof. Just a warning they should cease and desist."

"If I may, Colonel, most will ignore the warning," Warrant Officer Kine said. "Criminal minds are full of undecipherable kinks. But they share one thing in common — a deeply held belief that the long arm of the law, or in our case the deadly arm of the Fleet, will not and cannot reach them. Those who enjoy political top cover or offer it are especially prone to that sort of thinking, and not without reason."

Decker inclined his head.

"I will defer to your greater knowledge of the criminal psyche. But what you said reminds me of the last eight lines from a poem by a pre-diaspora writer named Rudyard Kipling, whose writings were full of wisdom. *The Gods of the Copybook Headings* was probably his wisest work of all."

He took a deep breath before declaiming,

"As it will be in the future, it was at the birth of Man
There are only four things certain since Social Progress began.

That the Dog returns to his Vomit and the Sow returns to her Mire,
And the burnt Fool's bandaged finger goes wabbling back to the Fire;
And that after this is accomplished, and the brave new world begins
When all men are paid for existing and no man must pay for his sins,
As surely as Water will wet us, as surely as Fire will burn,
The Gods of the Copybook Headings with terror and slaughter return!"

Kine stared at Decker with astonishment when he fell silent.

Bayliss nudged her and said, "Our colonel's second love is pre-diaspora history and he enjoys sharing it with us. Boy, does he ever enjoy sharing. Pretend you enjoy it."

Decker glowered at his second in command as the officers and noncoms chuckled.

"Philistine. History is the greatest teacher of all. And if you haven't figured it out yet, we are the direct action arm of those Gods of the Copybook Headings. In any case, removing the immediate threat will suffice even if it doesn't fully or even partially deter others from doing the same. At least the Hogue family and its tame cartel won't screw honest citizens over anymore."

"Agreed, sir," Kine replied. "Sorry for the interruption."

"Interrupt if you can impart something useful. We don't stand on ceremony when I issue warning orders. In any case, the mission won't be a sledgehammer thump and I might only deploy part of the squadron since my inclination is for a very narrow, surgical strike. Sergeant Burkitt scrounged forty sets of light armor from Santa Theresa, enough for a troop and a half. They'll equip whoever ends up taking point when we penetrate the objective. Follow-on forces will fight in battledress with helmets, but if we do this right, there shouldn't be much of a fight, if any."

"How will you decide which company or companies carry out the mission, Colonel?" Captain Delgado asked.

"I'll give you a choice between poker, with Major Bayliss as the dealer, or a shooting competition in the simulator, your best marksmen against each other."

Commander Piech cleared his throat.

"We do not allow gambling on Navy starships, as you well know. It's not a valid option."

Decker grinned at him.

"At Ground Forces Staff College, they call that a throwaway, Sandor. You can't present just one course of action, even if there is just a single practical choice. The shooting competition it is. Tell you what, during our trip, we'll transform the hangar deck into a simulation tank, and everyone will practice at least an hour a day, squadron HQ included." He glanced at Kine and Steiger, standing with Captain Virk off to one side. "Especially the squadron's newest members."

**

"Our superiors don't fuck around with half-measures, do they?" Command Sergeant Miko Steiger said in a low voice as she followed Decker to the Marine barracks. "Taking out one of Arcadia's most prominent families as if we're judge, jury, and the executioner, while others of our sort us hunt the cartel leadership and do the same unto them? Wow. Now I understand the speech you gave me the other day when you asked if I wanted back in."

"Welcome to Special Operations. We never do a little injury. If a job is worth doing, we put in a hundred percent effort. Otherwise, we walk away, no harm, no foul. Are you getting second thoughts?"

Steiger scoffed.

"Not for a nanosecond. I was one of the trafficked, remember? And I don't care about the future of the Hogue clan. I'm merely absorbing the fact that our glorious Armed Services can do things that need doing despite political and legal constraints."

"It's been long in coming but recent in execution. Remember the Garonne job?"

"Sure. That was fun. Some of the best parts happened not long after we met."

"Garonne was us expelling the Celeste-appointed colonial government and giving the locals freedom to choose their future. Us. The Fleet."

"I figured that at the time. But still."

"If you want a pound of flesh for what they did, this mission will give you a chance, even if you're not among the trigger pullers. Just help us into the Hogue estate so we can shoot Elize and Allard Hogue, and you'll do more for the

Commonwealth's political and social stability than ten Marine regiments put together."

"Is it wrong that I smile when you say the words, shoot Elize Hogue? She is pure evil."

**

"No messages for us," Petty Officer Jenks reported after querying the Arcadia system's subspace relay shortly after *Mikado* dropped out of FTL at the heliopause.

Decker exhaled with theatrical vigor.

"Thank the Almighty. Receiving an abort at this stage would do wonders to lower our morale."

"Do aborts happen often?" Piech asked, glancing over his shoulder at the Marine.

"Occasionally. Conditions can change while we're burning up the light-years in hyperspace. Ghost Squadron hasn't received an abort since its formation, but Hera and I occasionally got them when we were operating undercover, mostly because a target vanished or, as in one case, offed herself by flying while stupid. No great loss to humanity."

"I don't doubt it. Thirty minutes, and we're jumping inward. It'll take fourteen hours to reach Arcadia's hyperlimit. Once we're there, I'll give you control of the mission again. And don't worry, we already resemble an unremarkable and inoffensive tramp freighter. Traffic control will give *Mikado* a parking orbit and promptly ignore us."

"So long as they also ignore our shuttles."

Piech's expression told Decker not to worry.

"A Core World such as Arcadia sees so much orbital traffic, they won't give much of a damn so long as my people follow established flight paths. Once they're on the deck and vanish from sensors…" He left the rest of his reassurance unvoiced.

Decker grunted in acknowledgment.

"I suppose."

"Don't tell me an old pro such as yourself is getting nervous in the service. From what I hear, you did this sort of thing before with only the delightful Captain Talyn watching your back."

"Different missions, different objectives, different situations. Arcadia has a serious National Guard with enough full-timers who can react quickly. And since the objective is near the capital, where an entire active service brigade group is garrisoned, the stakes are higher. It wouldn't surprise me if Elize Hogue could reach out and give the Guard's chief of staff orders without going through the Arcadia Defense Secretary. Getting into a fight with Arcadian troops will not end well for them, us, and the political situation."

Piech nodded once.

"Seen. What's the possibility Hogue has a battalion of troops guarding her estate after what we did to the family's country manor on New Oberon?"

"Doubtful. If she has anything, it'll be a private security detail. Elize operates behind the scenes, where her lack of morals remains hidden from ordinary citizens, and that means no government-sponsored protection. It's even possible the cartel is guarding her. If you put violent goons who swore a blood oath on the payroll, you might as well use them for legal purposes. But apparently Elize keeps cartel people well away from Arcadia and lets several layers of management run by members of her extended clan do the dirty work."

"Blood oath? A bit dramatic."

"But true in many ways. Once you join a cartel's inner circle, it's for life. Try leaving and that life becomes awfully short, with an extremely brutal end."

"Charming. How do you know these things?"

"Hera's orders included a complete briefing package covering everything the intelligence analysts discovered about criminal cartels, and Saqqa in particular, after digging through the data we seized on New Oberon. You can read it if you want. It's in the mission repository."

Piech smirked.

"If ever I suffer from insomnia, sure."

"As a cure for insomnia, it's a bust, buddy. A lot of the stuff in that package will curdle your blood. These are supremely nasty people. As in shoot on sight nasty."

"Hence your orders."

"Decapitate the snake called Elize Hogue."

— Thirty-Six —

"Seems a much nicer place than the planet of the man-eating lizards," Decker remarked as he studied Arcadia's image on the command post's main display. "Too bad it's infested with even nastier critters."

The image jumped as *Mikado*'s sensors zeroed in on the sprawling capital, Tripoli, before shifting north.

"Those are the coordinates you gave us, Colonel," Lieutenant Adjeng said from the CIC. "About fifty klicks beyond the city limits."

A red dot labeled 'Hogue' appeared.

"I'm taking detailed readings and feeding them to your database."

"Thanks."

Two of the secondary screens lit up at Captain Virk's touch, orbital views of the sprawling estate, with incredibly sharp details that grew exponentially as the operations officer increased magnification. One was a direct visual feed, the other an infrared scan.

"And the tactical AI is off to the races," he said.

Decker glanced at Miko Steiger, who was sitting quietly in one corner.

"Recognize the Hogue spread?"

"Sure. You want me to mark what I know?"

"Absolutely. Step right up and leave your fingerprints on my display." Jory Virk made a come here gesture.

Within a few minutes, most of the buildings sprouted labels identifying their function. After an hour poring over large-scale renditions of the estate, Steiger had identified a long list of security features she recalled from her visits — sensors, video pickups, automatic shutters, and doors. And what looked to Decker's eyes like prepared fields of fire around the perimeter.

"That's a decent setup for a civilian place. I can't help thinking a kinetic strike from orbit would be simpler," Virk remarked. "I'm willing to put money on remote weapon stations covering every approach, sir. Those fields of fire look too well planned out."

Virk pointed at several spots.

"Perhaps they were installed after we did the New Oberon job, considering Sergeant Steiger noticed nothing of the sort back when she worked close protection. If this Elize Hogue has so much pull on Arcadia, the authorities won't dare object, let alone point out that military-grade RWS arrays aren't legal on private property."

"What are we staring at?" Josh Bayliss' voice boomed through the compartment door.

Decker waved at an empty chair.

"Grab a seat if you can spare a few minutes. We're looking at the modern equivalent of a robber baron castle. Jory, Miko, why don't you run Josh through our findings."

Bayliss listened intently as he studied the images. When Virk fell silent, he leaned back and grunted.

"I agree about the possible RWS. The target has too many similarities with our prepared defensive positions for it to be a coincidence. At least it clearly shows the inhabitants suffer from a guilty conscience. Honest people don't turn their properties into fortified camps on the Core Worlds. They use normal security measures. Manors covered by large caliber guns are a frontier phenomenon. But I can tell you two things right off. One, we'll need a Growler overflight at low altitude and pound the place with its sensors. And two, we won't need the light armor sets Burkitt scrounged on Santa Theresa. It'll either be full armor or nothing. A shame we can't just launch a penetrator rod and go home. Chances are there will be unconnected people living there who we can't just consign to eternity along with the guilty — domestic staff, contractors, rent-a-cops, children, etcetera."

Decker nodded.

"Pretty much. But there's a bigger consideration. The Arcadia authorities must find Elize Hogue's body and that of her grandson Allard, so word gets out their sort is no longer immune from retribution. Should the Out World faction not see justice done for the Saqqa Cartel outrage, even if it's our type of summary justice, then there's no point in carrying out the operation. We're doing this to stave off a crisis and not simply as punishment. But yeah, I agree with your two points. Jory, please talk to Monique Dulay and see about launching *Mikado*'s Growler when it's the middle of the night over the target area."

"Will do, Colonel." He glanced at a small status readout. "The CIC has fed us life sign scans of the target."

"Bring it up."

The infrared aerial view vanished, replaced by a fresh image upon which the sensor tech had superimposed life sign readings. Decker made a quick count of the bright blobs.

"At least fifty, but three-quarters of those could be security. If Hogue is running her operation from the estate, she'll rely mostly on service droids and keep staff to a minimum." He glanced at Steiger. "What do you think, having been there?"

"Seems about right on both counts. Elize isn't fond of outsiders, and she's not the trusting sort. Domestics talk, machines don't. I didn't see any security staff inside the manor either. My sense is she relies on the outer perimeter for protection. None but those invited ever make it inside the gates."

"Too bad we didn't bring our chutes," Bayliss said. "Vertical envelopment is always best for this type of raid."

"That close to Tripoli and the star system's biggest and busiest spaceport?" Virk made a face. "The traffic control sensor net would pick us up and wonder why three hundred Pathfinders were coming down on a nice, moonless night. At least shuttles won't excite as much curiosity, especially if we go further north then fly nap of the earth for eight or nine hundred kilometers."

"True, but it's a shame. Ghost Squadron has yet to do a combat drop."

Decker thumped Bayliss on the shoulder with his fist.

"We're Special Forces, not Pathfinders, even though every one of us passed through the School and served in Pathfinder units. Jumping out of perfectly good shuttles is one of our tools, not an act of devotion."

"That's heresy! And any self-respecting amateur historian such as you should know what they did to heretics back in the day."

"They promoted them?"

**

"So." Decker studied the nighttime Growler data. "I think we can safely assume the concentration of life signs is the security detail's quarters."

"And the electronic emission signatures are definitely from power cables leading to perimeter defenses." Virk touched the screen in several spots. "If we assume the termini beyond the perimeter are sensors, then the ones slightly back from the perimeter probably connect to remote weapon stations. We should assume those systems can cover a one hundred and eighty-degree vertical arc and three hundred and sixty horizontally."

"Make them and the sensors priority targets for our shuttles just before we land," Sergeant Major Paavola suggested. "We'll be on the ground and cleaning up filth before they wake and realize what happened. Since we know where the security post is, we'll make it a priority target as well."

Miko Steiger shook her head. "The last time I was there, Elize's guards came from one of Arcadia's biggest rent-a-cop businesses, one owned by the Hogues, mind you, but it means they wouldn't be legitimate targets. Of course, cartel goons could have replaced them."

"Rent-a-cops come and go, and wear company uniforms, right?" Bayliss asked. "With the resolution we're getting, we should be able to see the guards' uniforms."

"On my last visit, they wore royal blue jackets and gray trousers. Rather distinctive."

Virk nodded.

"Thanks, Sergeant. I've added that info to the AI's BOLO list. We should also make sure we can see both Elize and Allard on the grounds, even though Captain Talyn's briefing package said Allard's been hiding there since his return home and Elize rarely leaves the place."

"Might as well." Decker rubbed his chin while studying the display, eyes narrowed. "How long would it take for a quick reaction force from the Tripoli brigade's aviation company to get organized and reach the estate?"

"Fifty klicks?" Virk gave it some thought. "If they're flying something like our Warthog gunships, I'd say ten, perhaps fifteen minutes in the air. Provided there's a flight warmed up and ready, with wide-awake crews, perhaps another ten to brief and load. I doubt they keep aircraft on standby if there's no immediate threat, meaning any QRF will probably come overland. That's about thirty minutes of travel time over clear roads, less if they use aircars. We'll be in and out before anyone gets there."

"Let's hope the Arcadia National Guard isn't faster and better organized than most."

"Okay." Decker turned and faced his planners. "My intentions are as follows. We will land a single company, in full armor at oh-three-hundred hours local time on the day after I decide we've observed the target long enough to be sure of our assumptions. I will go with the strike force because taking care of Elize and Allard is my responsibility as CO. We will destroy the sensor and RWS array just before landing, and the security post if we're sure they're cartel and not civilians."

"Which company?" Bayliss asked.

"Who won the overall skill at arms competition?"

"Erinye Company. By a hair."

"Then theirs will be the honor. Let's make sure *Mikado*'s sensors scan the objectives every time our orbit takes us within sight and feed the results into the tactical AI for comparison to earlier scans. Jory, work with Lieutenant Adjeng and figure out the optimal flight path for his shuttles, so we stay off the spaceport's screens. I want *Mikado* overhead from shortly before we strike until we're clear, so plan the launch accordingly. If the Tripoli brigade activates its QRF, I need to know right away. Did I forget anything? No? Thank you, everyone."

— Thirty-Seven —

"I think we won't discover anything more at this point." Decker climbed to his feet after going through the tactical AI's summary two days later, just as the sun was setting over the Hogue estate. "We're hitting the place in nine hours, Jory. It's time we issued orders."

"Agreed, sir. At least we saw evidence of those uniforms Sergeant Steiger mentioned. And both Hogues taking a stroll around their private park."

"They could still be cartel in fancy duds," Major Bayliss said. "But I guess how they react when a company of armored mercenaries lands on their heads will tell us. Rent-a-cops will either run or surrender if they don't hide in place. Cartel thugs will fight back. The rules of engagement should mention that distinction, so we don't end up killing folks who'd rather go home than die for their employer. But if they're stupid and shoot at us, then so be it."

"Noted, sir."

"One more thing." Bayliss pointed a finger at Decker. "You will stay aboard the shuttle while Curtis and his men secure the place."

Decker put his hand over his heart.

"Promised. Not that the shuttle will offer any added safety if we miss a large caliber RWS."

"We won't," Virk said.

"Since the Navy is piloting those shuttles, we aren't able to hit or miss anything, Jory. And on that note, I'll warn Captain Piech that we're launching." Decker saw Steiger open her mouth. "And no, you can't come. I want as few witnesses as possible. You can't testify to something you didn't see."

Her mouth closed again, and she gave him a nod of acknowledgment.

"That also means no monitoring the mission while it unfolds, either. Once we leave the ship, we're under total communications blackout until our return, unless *Mikado* spots a quick reaction force leaving the Tripoli brigade's base. That way, there's no risk of something getting inadvertently logged by our tactical AI or the ship."

**

Six hours later, Sandor Piech entered *Mikado*'s hangar deck and walked over to where Erinye Company stood in three ranks while his four pilots and, for this mission, co-pilots who would control the shuttles' weaponry, were preparing their craft. Decker, armored like his troopers, stood on one side, chatting with Major Bayliss and Sergeant Major Paavola.

"Everything is quiet on the surface," Piech said when he was within earshot. "And Arcadia Traffic Control is still ignoring us. I'll tell them about the shuttles after you launch. Considering the amount of surface to orbit traffic, even in the middle of the Tripoli spaceport's night, there's no choice. But since your supposed destination is a private strip in the middle of nowhere, they'll ignore the flight once it drops below a thousand meters. Just make sure it looks as if you're lifting off from that same strip on the return leg."

Decker gave Piech an amused look.

"You sound more nervous than I feel about the operation. I'm sure Lieutenant Adjeng will execute a perfect flight plan. Besides, isn't there a thunderstorm brewing over the area? That should distract the Tripoli spaceport controllers."

"Nervous? Not particularly. But I'd rather we took pains to guarantee no one can point at us and say they spotted our shuttles near a certain location where prominent citizens lost their lives."

"We'll be as discrete as possible." Decker spotted Adjeng waving at him out of the corner of his eyes. "I guess we're ready."

"Good luck."

Decker winked at him.

"Thanks, Sandor. But you don't need luck if you're good."

**

Decker, sitting in the jump seat behind Lieutenant Adjeng and his number two, watched with fascination as they approached a carpet of dark clouds lit at random intervals by lightning. The sight was both eerie and awe-inspiring. He'd been in a shuttle struck by lightning years ago and didn't notice until they landed and saw a black dent in its hull, so he wasn't worried when they finally plunged into the heart of the storm.

But the buffeting of the wind still took him by surprise. The shuttle yawed several times as it passed through pockets of turbulence. They finally emerged less than three thousand meters above ground level and cut through torrential rain on their way to the private strip approximately five hundred kilometers east of the Hogue estate, in a part of the countryside so remote it was still dominated by native vegetation even centuries after the first humans settled on Arcadia.

A lightning bolt lit up the forest a few minutes later, proving they now flew nap of the earth on their last leg to the target. The change in their flight profile was so smooth Decker didn't feel a thing.

He glanced at the pilot's primary display, and a timer now filled the lower right corner, ticking off the hours, minutes, and seconds until they landed. Like the old trooper he was, Decker composed himself and fell into a light sleep since the most turbulent part of the trip was behind them. He woke with a start when his internal clock told him they were less than fifteen minutes out.

Decker noticed the co-pilot had switched on the shuttle's weapon suite and targeting sensors and was silently running through his checklist one last time. Outside, the rain still fell in sheets while lightening occasionally kissed the horizon as the storm moved further west. Since they didn't dare use the radios, he couldn't check on the other shuttles, but they appeared as small icons on the primary display, one to either side of his and the fourth behind them.

When the timer hit five minutes, Lieutenant Adjeng touched a control, and the lights in both the cockpit and aft compartment turned red, the color of night operations. Though the Marines wore helmet visors with integrated night vision, the equipment could malfunction, or they might need to raise their visors. The change also warned everyone they were almost at the objective.

Adjeng pointed toward the front window.

"That faint light is it, Colonel. We'll climb a hundred meters now so we can engage the sensor and RWS array."

Decker felt the shuttle rise as his view of the Hogue estate shifted.

"Acquiring targets," the petty officer at the gunnery console said. "And locked."

The forest petered out and dark, regular shapes appeared at the heart of a manicured park dimly lit by garden path lights and very little else.

"Executing attack plan alpha in three, two, one, firing..."

Simultaneous streams of plasma erupted from the shuttles and methodically ravaged suspected sensor and remote weapon station emplacements per their programming while the spacecraft came to a hover in preparation for landing.

The violent salvo was over almost as quickly as it started, and within seconds, Decker felt them settle on Elize Hogue's carefully tended lawn. He unfastened his seat restraints and stood so he could watch the aft ramp drop, releasing his Marines into the rain-lashed night.

They raced out in silence, one troop to take the security guard barracks, one troop to take the guard post, and the final troop, along with Erinye Company HQ, to seize the main house. Decker kept expecting an alarm siren, but he heard nothing more than the pop of explosive charges opening locked doors.

Unable to contain his curiosity any longer, he exited the shuttle's aft compartment and stood on the very edge of its ramp. Technically, he was still aboard as per the promise made to Josh Bayliss, but he could finally see. And what he saw were several electric fires along the estate's perimeter, and the fast-moving shadows of armored Marines securing their target.

But because of the total radio silence he'd imposed, Decker couldn't even ask about their progress and was stuck waiting until a runner came to report. But he heard no shouts, no screams, and no shots fired.

First Sergeant Hak finally jogged up to the shuttle, raised his helmet visor, and said, "Guard post and barracks are secure, we immobilized the people inside. They were rent-a-cops and gave up without a fight. We secured the two primary individuals and a third one in the living room of the main house. If you'll follow me."

"Coming."

Hak led him through the manor's open door and into a marble-clad foyer. Niches filled with statues, busts, and carvings, many of them no doubt antiques from Earth pierced its walls. A trooper, waiting at the far end, pointed toward an open door.

Decker passed through the opening and found himself in a salon not much smaller than a sloop's hangar deck. Two women and one man wearing nightclothes, shackled at the ankles and wrists, sat on a white leather sofa, cringing under the watchful eyes of armed and armored Marines who resembled exoskeletal alien beings. He stopped in front of the prisoners, raised his helmet visor, and gazed down.

The eldest of the three, a woman whose stringy gray hair framed a thin, wrinkled face, glared at him with eyes devoid of any human feeling.

"What in the name of every deity invented by our species is the meaning of this?"

"Elize Hogue, I presume?" Decker asked in a tone of utter disinterest.

"Indeed. And if you are Fleet as I suspect, you should know your career is over. This is an outrage, and I will make sure you end up on Parth's Desolation Island for the rest of your miserable life."

Decker snorted derisively.

"Been there, done that. Not the best place to rest your bones, but the folks are more honest than anyone in your clan, Sera Hogue, let alone its ugly offshoot, the Saqqa Cartel. But you're beyond making sure of anything."

"I beg your pardon."

Decker ignored her and turned to the second woman.

"Senator Hogue, you're not supposed to be here, but fate plays strange tricks on mere humans. If only you'd disavowed your idiot of a cousin Allard," he glared at the man, "we wouldn't be here. But you placed tribal loyalty over the good of the Commonwealth. And now Arcadia will need to choose another as one of its two representatives in the Senate. But it won't be a Hogue, because your dynasty ends tonight. It fucked with the wrong people."

He gestured at Curtis Delgado, who'd been watching in silence from the sidelines, along with Hak and a half-dozen troopers.

"Take her away and give her knockout juice. Make sure she's comfortable and unrestrained. Someone needs to call the morgue in the morning, and since the security detail is unavoidably detained..."

Two Marines lifted the stunned senator as if she weighed nothing and quickly carried her out. When the sound of their footsteps died away, Decker smiled at Elize Hogue.

"My name is Zachary Thomas Decker, and you're correct. We are Fleet. I am a lieutenant colonel in the Commonwealth Marine Corps and command 'A' Squadron, 1st Special Forces Regiment. I was appointed as your judge, jury, and executioner for crimes against humanity."

"What?" Elize Hogue's voice rose to a piercing screech. "You can't be serious. Do you mean to kill us?"

"The proper term is execution. You see, the Saqqa Cartel, which your clan formed to refloat its fortunes, drifted into the lucrative and oh so despicably evil slave trade. My unit rescued almost five hundred from your New Oberon estate, and over twelve hundred from an alien world called Kryani. Funny thing about those Kryani. They developed a taste for human flesh and ate many of those sold to them by your people. It means you, your grandson Allard, and that minor branch of the family running the Saqqa Cartel are guilty of crimes for which the only punishment is death. Since our legal system is corrupt enough that it would make sure you never receive the punishment you deserve, I'm here as a proxy and will carry out the proper sentence. Be grateful your granddaughter, the senator, will live because she is not on my list."

Decker pulled the massive Shrehari blaster from its holster.

"And that cartel you created, Sera Elize? It will die shortly after I send you to hell. Others like me are standing by across the Commonwealth waiting for my word. They will terminate Saqqa's senior leadership. Then, we'll round up the rest and dump them on Parth. But take heart. Eliminating your diseased clan should keep the Commonwealth from fracturing just now. I don't know if your granddaughter the senator bothered to say so, but the cold civil war between the Out Worlds and the Core World Centralists could easily ignite if the former don't see justice meted out to those who pillage Out World colonies and starships for the slave trade. And once word spreads about humans roasted over open flames as delicacies for alien techno-barbs? Well, I'm sure you understand the implications. Two of my people almost met that very fate, so it is rather personal."

The last statement was a minor exaggeration, but Decker saw a reaction in the eyes of both.

"And you'll shoot us with your gun?" Elize asked, trying for a contemptuous tone that did not mask her growing terror.

"Yes. There is an old expression first uttered by a wise man called Edmund Burke. He famously said the only thing necessary for the triumph of evil is for good men to do nothing. You are evil, and since I consider myself a good man, I must do something. That something is to make sure you never send another human into alien bondage, let alone an alien larder, and send a message to others of your ilk. The days of abusing Commonwealth citizens with impunity because of your wealth and power are over. This garbage either stops now, or the Commonwealth will fracture and descend into civil strife which could make the last Migration War look like fisticuffs between toddlers."

Elize tried on a sneer that barely registered with Decker.

"You can't simply waltz in here and threaten to kill us."

"Just watch me."

"Do you know who I am?"

"An evil old hag whose best before date was last century." Decker raised his gun and aimed it at Allard Hogue. "You are guilty of human trafficking, in particular enslaving humans and selling them to non-human barbarians. The sentence is death, to be carried out at once."

Allard stared at Decker with the eyes of a stunned deer, as if unable to process his words.

"No," he stammered. "Please. I have money. I can pay you anything you want. It's grandma's fault, anyway. She forced me to—"

The blaster coughed, and a dark hole appeared in Allard's chest, where his heart was beating a fraction of a second earlier. He slumped forward, dead. Decker turned his weapon on Elize.

"You are guilty of operating a cartel involved in the slave trade, among other capital crimes. The sentence is death, to be carried out at once."

"Get bent, asshole," she hissed while feebly struggling against her restraints.

A flash briefly lit up the room's west-facing windows. Moments later, the dull roar of thunder reached Decker's ears.

"Say hi to the devil for me when you enter hell. I'm his favorite purveyor of rancid souls." The blaster coughed, and a dark hole appeared in Elize's chest. She slumped over, as dead as her grandson.

Decker holstered his weapon.

"Let's live up to our nickname and ghost out of here, Curtis."

"Yes, sir."

— Thirty-Eight —

Admiral Kruczek waved Rear Admiral Kos Ulrich and Captain Hera Talyn into his office and pointed at the chairs in front of his desk.

"So?"

"Mission accomplished, sir," Talyn replied. "*Mikado* transmitted the code word via Arcadia's subspace relay just before going FTL at the heliopause. But there's a twist, and we won't know the how or why until Ghost Squadron is back. News came from Arcadia that Senator Graciela Hogue claims armed and armored troops invaded the family's estate, then murdered Elize and Allard Hogue."

A look of dismay crossed Kruczek's face.

"Damn."

"She, her cousin, and grandma Elize were roused from their sleep at three in the morning by loud explosions, then dragged out of their rooms by men who didn't speak and wore no insignia. They were bound and dumped on the living room sofa. One attacker, the only one whose face they saw, entered and made threats. She was then taken from the room and drugged. When she woke up, her restraints were gone, the men had left, but Elize and Allard Hogue lay on the living room floor, shot through the heart. The estate's security detail was shackled but otherwise unharmed. Graciela claims undercover Fleet operatives are responsible. Thankfully, she could not offer a clear description of the man whose face she saw, which I assume was Colonel Decker."

"Not good. Decker should have killed her as well."

Ulrich made a face.

"Perhaps. Yet Graciela wasn't on the list we gave him, and Decker is scrupulous about such matters. But we can turn this to our advantage by leaking evidence that hints at a gang-related execution. Few if any of those in powerful positions will believe it, but the fiction can help deflect any politically motivated attacks on Grand Admiral Larsson."

Kruczek thought about the proposal for a few seconds, then shook his head.

"No. Let's not do that. I would rather people believe we're responsible, so the message isn't lost on those who share the Hogue clan's disregard for the law and the citizens of the Commonwealth. Besides, belief the Fleet was involved will bring a certain sense of justice being served to those in the outer star systems whose outrage is already stirring to life based on the stories of the rescuees. Best we say nothing, silence rather than denial. Let everyone fill that silence with their own beliefs. It will do better for our cause than misdirection. And draining away the Hogue's ill-gained wealth will eliminate the rest of the family from the equation."

"In that case, a few directed leaks would be better, sir," Ulrich said. "Just enough to hint we did it."

Kruczek gave the proposition a few moments of thought, then nodded.

"A few, to trusted outlets. And only hints."

"Yes, sir." Ulrich gestured at Talyn. "Go on with the rest of the report, Hera."

"After receiving Colonel Decker's message, I activated the teams aimed at the Saqqa Cartel's senior leadership. There will be more reports of mysterious deaths and outright assassinations over the next week or two, many involving prominent members of their respective communities."

"So be it. I want to speak with Colonel Decker in person when he returns."

"I'll bring him up from Fort Arnhem once Ghost Squadron lands."

A smile briefly lit up Kruczek's ascetic features.

"Perhaps I might visit Fort Arnhem and meet Colonel Decker in his natural habitat."

"I'm sure entertaining you as his guest in the Pegasus Club would please him."

"You're a member as well, correct?"

"Life member, sir. Those of us who jump out of perfectly functioning shuttles from low orbit to earn our wings consider it one of our spiritual homes."

"So I understand. I never could figure out the attraction myself."

Talyn gave him an amused look. "Me neither. But here I am, with enough combat jump stars to make the average jarhead envious."

**

"There she is." Decker's voice boomed across Fort Arnhem's parade ground the moment he spied Captain Talyn standing to one side, watching Ghost Squadron disembark from *Mikado*'s shuttles. He closed the distance between them with big, energetic steps, bags in hand, weapon slung over one armored shoulder.

"I'm not hugging you while you're in that tin suit," Talyn said when he stood in front of her, grinning with pleasure.

"Then walk with me to the office so I can climb out of it and greet you properly."

"I want to meet the one who triggered this — Aleksa Kine. You can't imagine the storm brewing on Earth and in every Commonwealth star system because of her rescue." Talyn fell into step beside him as they headed for the three-story block housing the 1st Special Forces Regiment offices.

"You will, but later. The first order of business for my new Constabulary liaison is getting her own suite in the officers' apartment block and a full issue of clothing. She's been wearing borrowed duds since Kryani. Tell me about the storm engulfing our little piece of the galaxy."

"I should say storms, plural. There's the uproar about the Commonwealth government not stamping out the slave trade and letting humans languish on alien worlds because the Senate forbade the Armed Services from carrying out operations beyond the Commonwealth sphere. The official story is a private military corporation made the rescues on New Oberon and Kryani because the Navy and Marine Corps aren't allowed to do so. But we quietly leaked the truth to a few of the more useful newsies — that the Navy and Marine Corps did it under the guise of a PMC to circumvent the Senate. You can imagine the reaction. For Out Worlders, you're heroes whose names will never be known. To the Centralists, you're rogue operatives who should be hunted down, court-martialled, and imprisoned."

Decker let out an amused snort.

"Good luck to the Centralists."

"The Senate was already in an uproar before you reached Arcadia, with Centralists demanding Grand Admiral Larsson be summarily dismissed from his functions, along with the Commandant of the Marine Corps and the Chief of Naval Operations. The SecGen is caught in the middle of this and seems to have lost control."

"Couldn't happen to a nicer guy."

They entered through a side door marked *A Squadron* and walked down a silent hallway until they reached Decker's office. There, he unloaded his carbine and blaster and stowed both weapons in a case with a biometric lock.

"Oh, it gets better." Talyn dropped into the chair behind Decker's desk while he methodically began removing and stowing each part of his armored battle suit. "Then Graciela Hogue woke up to find her cousin and grandmother both with charred holes where their tiny, shriveled hearts used to be. That's when the next tempest started with accusations Fleet assassins murdered two of Arcadia's most prominent citizens, who were not connected to the terrible business on New Oberon and the slave trade.

"Of course, the more she insisted, the less believable she was, but the Centralist faction in the Senate formed ranks behind her, and the calls to dismiss Larsson and half the flag officers under him became painfully strident. If their accusations against Larsson hadn't been made in the Senate chamber, they would be deemed grossly libelous. The Out World faction proposed a vote of thanks to the unknown people who rescued so many victims of human trafficking. The Centralists quashed the proposal since they can still muster two more senators than the Out Worlds."

"Not for long. I can think of at least two colonies who qualify for full star system sovereignty."

"Which the Centralists will bitterly contest for obvious reasons. The Out Worlders then put forward a motion demanding the Constabulary's Professional Compliance Bureau investigates Centralist connections to criminal cartels, beginning with the honorable senators from Arcadia. The motion was, of course, voted down as well. The Out World senators then walked out *en masse*, vowing they would shutter the Senate until Commonwealth citizens obtained answers."

"Meaning the federal government is essentially dysfunctional at the moment."

"And will stay so for a while."

With the last of his armor stowed, Decker held out his arms.

"Come here, you wonderful future flag officer."

She stood and approached him with exaggerated caution, sniffing the air.

"Hey, I showered this morning and didn't sweat during the trip from *Mikado*."

"Sure. That's what they all say." Talyn wrapped her arms around his neck while he squeezed her. "Welcome home, Big Boy. I'm staying here for at least two nights so that we can go over the mission in detail."

"Party time!" Decker kissed Talyn.

"But not just yet. And Admiral Kruczek wants to speak with you in person. He's flying here this afternoon and will stay for supper with us in the Pegasus."

"Why does he want to speak with me in person?" Decker released her and leaned against his desk.

Talyn walked to the office door and pulled it shut.

"When I said Aleksa Kine triggered this, I wasn't just referring to the Senate's civil war between factions and the uproar in every outer star system. We've known for years that the current political arrangements won't survive much longer. The dynamics that caused the last Migration War never went away. The growing chasm between those who favor greater control from Earth and those who refuse to surrender a single atom of star system sovereignty is making that more and more clear each passing day. Until you came back from Kryani, that chasm was still papered over to some extent, hidden from the average citizen's view. No more.

And our politicians, as they usually do, are using the growing outrage for their purposes.

"Rumors that a leading Core World senator's family sold humans to the Kryani and the Almighty only knows how many other alien species, is only making things more volatile. Demands that the Navy sends out expeditionary forces to search for human slaves on worlds beyond the Commonwealth and punish those holding them are growing. I don't doubt that if the Senate were still in session, the Out World faction would put forward a motion repealing regulations forbidding military action beyond our sphere. Outer system politicians are already publicly calling on Grand Admiral Larsson to act no matter what the government says."

"Why do I suddenly feel as if we're sitting on an antimatter fuel reservoir and its magnetic containment field is failing?"

"Because we are. And we cannot afford a third Migration War. There are too many species watching our internal troubles with covetous eyes."

Decker gave his partner a searching look.

"You HQ wizards are working on a secret plan. Otherwise we wouldn't be having this conversation."

"We — the Armed Services — will topple the Commonwealth, hoping we can avoid a hot civil war by doing so."

Decker snorted. "And replace it with what? The United Nations of the Stars never worked. The first Commonwealth ended in disaster, and the second

Commonwealth is teetering on the edge of an abyss which will swallow billions of lives."

"An empire. A true empire where the center takes care of defense, diplomacy, and a few common functions while the sovereign star systems freely govern themselves without interference, so long as they respect their citizens' basic freedoms. It need not be an empire with a crowned head of state either."

A low whistle escaped Decker's lips.

"No half-measures in that plan. I can't wait to hear how we'll make this happen."

"We're still short on details, but Ghost Squadron will play a big role in creating the necessary conditions over the next few years."

"Which is why Admiral Kruczek wants to speak with me."

"He wants to sound you out."

"And this idea comes from where?"

"The very top. Grand Admiral Larsson. He knows he won't see it through, but he'll start the ball rolling and make sure the right officer succeeds him once his time is over."

"Well, if you wanted to render me speechless, you almost succeeded. You and I spent years fighting to preserve the Commonwealth from Centralists who wanted an empire of sorts. And now we'll kill the Commonwealth so we can create our own version of an empire." He shook his head. "Astonishing, but now that I think about it, your scheme is probably the best way to avoid another destructive war. I'm in."

"I never doubted it. Just make sure you don't speak of this with anyone. Not even Josh. The only reason I told you is so you're ready for missions aimed at shaping the political landscape."

"Understood. Now, if you'll excuse me, I need to make my manners with Colonel Martinson and let him know I brought everyone back alive and unhurt. Want to come with me?"

She shook her head. "I already said hi. Did you know he's leaving at the end of the year?"

"I knew his time in command was ending. What's next?"

"He'll become Brigadier General James Martinson and shift over to SOCOM HQ where he'll stand up the 2nd and 3rd Special Forces Regiments under a Special Forces division umbrella. Once he's formed them, Jimmy takes over as divisional commander."

"Excellent news. He's a fine officer and a good man. Who will my new boss be?"

"Colonel Kal Ryent."

Decker's eyebrows shot up.

"Our Kal Ryent?"

She nodded, smiling.

"The very same. Your pal Gus is tickled pink at the idea of serving as his old CO's sergeant major for another stretch."

Ryent and Regimental Sergeant Major Augustus Vanleith were not only old friends but had worked with Decker and Talyn twice to support undercover missions when Ryent commanded the 251st Pathfinder Squadron with Vanleith as his top kick.

"Why do I think you're somehow responsible, as in getting folks you know and trust where you need them?"

"Because you're a perceptive man. And since we're on the subject, do you know who's slated to take over from Kal when Jimmy Martinson puts up his second star as the divisional commander and takes Kal as his deputy?"

"No."

Talyn poked him in the chest with her index finger.

"You. That's who. Unless you screw up between now and then or, the Almighty forbid, you catch a bullet."

"Be still my beating heart. Give me thirty minutes with Jimmy, then we can see about those post-mission interviews of yours."

— Thirty-Nine —

"Warrant Officer Kine." Decker waved at her when she entered the Pegasus Club with Miko Steiger and Jory Virk. "I want you to meet someone."

Kine broke away from the others and headed to where he and Talyn sat, drinks in hand. She now wore a gray Constabulary garrison uniform with black stripes on the trouser seams and a warrant officer's silver bars on the shoulders.

"This is Captain Hera Talyn from Naval Intelligence at Fleet HQ. She's Ghost Squadron's taskmaster and gives us most of our missions, including the one to find you."

When Talyn stood and held out her hand, Kine came to attention.

"Then, I also owe you my life, sir."

"Relax. We don't stand on ceremony here." After they shook, Talyn gestured at an empty chair. "Please join us for a bit. Can I offer you a drink?"

When Kine didn't immediately reply, Decker chuckled.

"Jump at the chance Aleksa. The captain isn't normally that generous."

"A gin and tonic?"

The Marine's smile broadened. "You just made a friend for life. It's her favorite tipple."

Talyn turned to the bar, held up her glass with one hand, and extended two fingers with the other.

"And as one of the rare naval officers wearing combat stars on her Pathfinder wings," the Marine observed with philosophical resignation, "she also gets personal service from the staff. Unlike us old jumpers."

Two fresh gins and tonic showed up moments later, delivered by a smiling attendant. "Could you put both on my tab, please, Brin?"

"Certainly, Captain."

"Thanks."

"For you, anything."

As Brin walked away, Decker gestured toward Talyn. "See what I mean? When I finish this bottle, I'll have to get up and fetch a fresh one myself."

Talyn pointedly ignored him. Instead, she raised her glass.

"To your health, Aleksa. Welcome back and welcome to your new home."

"Thank you, sir. After spending so long working undercover, finding myself back in uniform, and on a Marine Corps base is a little strange. But Colonel Decker and the rest of Ghost Squadron are amazingly welcoming.

They make me feel as one of them. It's something I've not experienced in a long time."

"When the crazy people who jump out of perfectly good shuttles from low orbit decide to adopt someone into their tribe, they do it right. I assume you'll be going across to the School at some point so you can wear these too." She tapped at the star-flecked golden wings on her tunic's left breast. "They're how we of the tribe recognize each other. And in case you're wondering why the combat stars, I was once a young and naïve Naval Intelligence liaison officer. Your new CO and I earned a few of these together."

"You were never naïve," Decker growled. "I was the bumpkin when we first met."

Talyn winked at him.

"And now you're one of the best-traveled lieutenant colonels in the entire Marine Corps. You'll no doubt hear about his adventures in due course, Aleksa. Zack does enjoy telling what he calls his war stories. Oh, does he ever."

Movement by the main entrance caught Talyn's eye.

"My apologies, but we'll continue this conversation later. My boss just walked in with his boss."

"I thought only the CNI was coming," Decker said before draining his ale bottle.

"So did I, but I guess Admiral Ulrich managed to clear his calendar."

When Decker saw Kine's puzzled look, he said, "Admiral Kruczek is the Chief of Naval Intelligence, and her boss, Rear Admiral Ulrich heads intelligence's Special Operations Division."

They left a curious Kine to stare at their receding backs as they intercepted the two flag officers, then led them to a private room off the main bar. But she wasn't alone for long. Miko Steiger, in an army green uniform with the black stripes and crossed swords of an army command sergeant on the sleeves, dropped into Decker's chair.

"I see you met the dragon lady. A piece of advice — don't ever cross her. She's what you might call a professional assassin. Or at least she was, once."

A frown creased Kine's forehead.

"But Captain Talyn seemed nice, and she's a close friend of the colonel's."

"Did you gaze into her eyes?"

"No."

"Next time you sit across from her, take a gander, then tell me what you saw."

**

Once Brin left the private room after bringing a fresh round of drinks, Admiral Kruczek raised his glass.

"Congratulations, Colonel Decker. Your actions probably triggered the biggest political storm in living memory, bigger than Grand Admiral Kowalski's reforms late last century. On Grand Admiral Larsson's behalf, and mine, well done. A Marine can't go wrong if he saves innocent lives."

"Oorah, sir."

"I trust Captain, soon to be Commodore Talyn brought you up to speed on our plans?"

"She did."

"And?"

"We'll do whatever needs doing so we can avoid billions of senseless deaths, sir."

"I expected no less of you, Colonel."

"Mind you, I can't even begin to figure out how."

"We're not quite there yet either, but the simple decision to act is already a huge step in the right direction. Whatever form that action takes will depend on opportunities clearly seen and swiftly seized. And on the political leadership in the outer star systems. Ultimately, they must forge a new arrangement, albeit with our support. But we will very much influence its shape and make sure humanity remains united without oppression from Earth or the Core Worlds."

Decker nodded sagely.

"And Ghost Squadron's job will be more of what we just did, to help push the outer star systems in the direction we want."

"Pretty much. Your unit at first, then, as the Marine Corps' Special Forces capacity expands, more of its kind." Kruczek took a sip of his drink. "When we're ready, the first big job will be taking out the SecGen's *Sécurité Spéciale* in the same way Grand Admiral Kowalski terminated the Special Security Bureau last century. We can't tolerate a politicized security intelligence organization working against us. And now, Admiral Ulrich and I would appreciate it if you could run us through the recently completed mission from start to finish.   I think it's important we understand why you acted as you did so we can better plan future operations in support of our goals."

"Certainly, sir.   The operation started as usual, with Captain Talyn visiting Fort Arnhem…"

— Forty —

Secretary-General of the Commonwealth of Sovereign Star Systems Brodrick Brüggemann stood in front of his office window, cognac snifter in hand, staring out at *Lac Léman*. Lost in thought, his eyes didn't see Geneva's nighttime lights dancing on the lake's dark surface like countless fireflies, or perhaps pixies from an ancient European legend.

Firmin, his faithful secretary, was long gone, as were most government officials working in the Palace of the Stars. Many no doubt sat around tables in various restaurants on the lake's southern shore, discussing the current crisis in low tones, while glancing at the palace, whose sole lit window at this hour belonged to him. Others were at home, drink in hand, trying to decide whether a career in government remained a good idea.

The senators who normally met in the palace's Great Assembly Hall had left weeks earlier, many returning to their home star systems. Whether to hide, take a vacation or consult with the governments of the worlds they represented, Brüggemann couldn't tell.

But with the Out Worlders gone, the Senate no longer enjoyed a quorum and was thus prorogued for an indeterminate period. In effect, the Commonwealth was without one of its three branches of government. Brüggemann didn't yet know whether their absence was helpful or a hindrance.

Without legislators, the courts might decide theirs was the duty to make law rather than interpret it. Or not. And if Out World governments decided they would no longer obey the edicts coming from Earth under the doctrine of no taxation without representation, what would it do for human unity in a hostile universe?

Brüggemann looked up at the star-flecked sky, silently cursing Grand Admiral Larsson and his Fleet for putting him in such an untenable situation. Yet he was unable to make out the constellations first traced by the ancients and visible from Geneva at this time of the year, let alone find the star around which Caledonia, the only Commonwealth colony enjoying absolute self-determination, orbited.

Brüggemann took a sip of his cognac and exhaled with feeling. He was no fool and knew of several senators, Core Worlders, all of them, whose families were engaged in questionable practices, though none as patently despicable as the Hogues. Perhaps they were merely venal instead of evil, or maybe they hid it better for now. If Graciela Hogue was connected to the slave trade, even at a remove, then who knew what her colleagues or their families were doing.

Out World presidents and prime ministers were already pelting him with subspace messages seeking answers and demanding decisive action, especially on the matter of humans enslaved beyond the Commonwealth. And many colonial governors, especially those with things to hide, were making fearful queries about their future after the New Oberon affair.

Was the Commonwealth in chaos? Not yet. But it was heading there. Brüggemann drained the snifter and glanced at the bottle standing in isolated splendor on his desk. Normally, he allowed himself one glass before crossing the palace's expansive grounds to the Secretary-General's residence. That single glass had become two, then three in recent weeks.

Things needed to change. But how? Entrenched interests would hold on until their last gasp. They'd done well under the current system. Yet the further away from Earth, the less entrenched they were, and already Centralist allies on the Out Worlds faced pressure to recant or leave. Even the Honorable Commonwealth Corporation — ComCorp for short — one of the biggest and most influential mercantile conglomerates faced investigation by a half a dozen Out World law enforcement agencies. And there were calls for the Constabulary to join them.

Brüggemann gave in and refilled the cognac snifter before returning to the window. He looked up at the stars again and wondered why he, the Secretary-General of the Commonwealth, humanity's top government executive, was so helpless. No, helpless was the wrong word —

powerless in the face of what he sensed would be an upheaval greater than anything in living memory.

Was power passing from Earth to one of her daughters? And if so, which one?

Ghost Squadron will return in 'Deadly Intent.'

About the Author

Eric Thomson is the pen name of a retired Canadian soldier with thirty-one years of service, both in the Regular Army and the Army Reserve. He spent his Regular Army career in the Infantry and his Reserve service in the Armoured Corps.

Eric has been a voracious reader of science fiction, military fiction, and history all his life. Several years ago, he put fingers to keyboard and started writing his own military sci-fi, with a definite space opera slant, using many of his own experiences as a soldier for inspiration.

When he's not writing fiction, Eric indulges in his other passions: photography, hiking, and scuba diving, all of which he shares with his wife.

Join Eric Thomson at http://www.thomsonfiction.ca/ Where you'll find news about upcoming books and more information about the universe in which his heroes fight for humanity's survival.

Read his blog at
https://ericthomsonblog.wordpress.com

If you enjoyed this book, please consider leaving a review with your favorite online retailer to help others discover it.

Also by Eric Thomson

Siobhan Dunmoore

No Honor in Death (Siobhan Dunmoore Book 1)
The Path of Duty (Siobhan Dunmoore Book 2)
Like Stars in Heaven (Siobhan Dunmoore Book 3)
Victory's Bright Dawn (Siobhan Dunmoore Book 4)
Without Mercy (Siobhan Dunmoore Book 5)
When the Guns Roar (Siobhan Dunmoore Book 6)

Decker's War

Death Comes But Once (Decker's War Book 1)
Cold Comfort (Decker's War Book 2)
Fatal Blade (Decker's War Book 3)
Howling Stars (Decker's War Book 4)
Black Sword (Decker's War Book 5)
No Remorse (Decker's War Book 6)
Hard Strike (Decker's War Book 7)

Quis Custodiet

The Warrior's Knife

Ashes of Empire

Imperial Sunset (Ashes of Empire #1)
Imperial Twilight (Ashes of Empire #2)

Ghost Squadron

We Dare – Ghost Squadron No. 1